# Praise for

# PATIENT'S PRIVILEGE

"*Patient's Privilege* is a riveting murder mystery with constant twists and turns. It's a page-turner that will keep you guessing about the story's outcome until the end. Morvillo masterfully weaves aspects of criminal defense and medical privilege into this fascinating novel that's full of surprises."

—**HOWARD LEE KRAMER, author of the novel *Hitching to Bowie***

"In *Patient's Privilege*, Rich Morvillo delivers a story that is both thought-provoking and impossible to put down. His compelling narrative combines riveting suspense with profound ethical insight while exploring the complex boundaries of professional ethics, confidentiality, and betrayal within the world of psychiatry. Incisive and gripping, *Patient's Privilege* is a novel that is sure to linger in the mind long after the final chapter."

—**ANDREW FRANK, chief operating officer at KPR Centers**

"Drawing on his own experience as an accomplished criminal defense lawyer, Rich Morvillo skillfully blends the tension of a criminal investigation with the complexities of the doctor–patient privilege to create a gripping story in *Patient's Privilege*. Morvillo weaves together the ethical dilemmas of privilege with the suspense of uncovering the truth, creating a push-pull between justice and secrecy. Each of the characters is flawed in his own way, adding depth to the tangled web of lies and motives. The ending completely caught me off guard and left me thinking of the novel long after I finished it. Excellent read!"

—**ELLEN MURPHY, partner at Seyfarth Shaw LLP**

"Morvillo delivers a masterful psychological crime thriller that grabs you from the first page and never lets go. With clinical precision and a shocking twist that upends everything you thought you knew about ethics, law, and privacy, *Patient's Privilege* is a novel that lingers long after the final page."

—**STEVEN FERRI, managing editor, digital and social media at Voice of America**

"Rich Morvillo's *Patient's Privilege* is a stunning debut novel that masterfully combines the pulse-pounding tension of a psychological thriller with the suspense of courtroom drama. Centered on a shocking murder and its aftermath, the story dives deep into the tangled intersections of doctor–patient privilege, criminal law, and the moral dilemmas that test both the justice system and the human psyche. Morvillo's background knowledge shines through, bringing authenticity to every legal and psychological twist, while his storytelling ensures you'll be hooked from the first page to the last. For fans of tightly woven suspense who crave both riveting drama and thought-provoking insight, this first novel is an absolute must-read—you won't want to put it down."

—**JEFFREY F. ROBERTSON, special counsel at McDermott Will & Schulte LLP**

# PATIENT'S PRIVILEGE

RICH MORVILLO

www.mascotbooks.com

*Patient's Privilege*



**For more information, please contact:**
Subplot Publishing, an imprint of Amplify Publishing Group
620 Herndon Parkway, Suite 220
Herndon, VA 20170
info@mascotbooks.com

Library of Congress Control Number: 2025924361
CPSIA Code: PRV1025A
ISBN-13: 979-8-89138-857-4

Printed in the United States

TO STACEY FOR HER LOVE AND SUPPORT.

"The armour of falsehood is subtly wrought out of darkness, and hides a man not only from others, but from his own soul."

E. M. FORSTER

# 1

The only reason I remember anything about the first time I met Abner Reeves is because he has reminded me of it often. We supposedly met when I was in my mid-twenties. I was away at school when I got word that both my parents had been killed in an automobile accident. I was working on my thesis when my sister, Eve, called to tell me that a drunk driver lost control of his car and crossed the median into my parents' lane, killing them instantly.

I drove my car down to Westchester the next morning and met Eve at my parents' home. The next several days were a blur. Eve and her husband, who lived on Long Island, stayed in Westchester for a few days to grieve with me. When they left, I was in no shape to drive upstate and remained in Westchester for a few more days.

While not ready to return to school so soon, I was restless and bored. A couple of days after the funeral, I ventured into town to clear my head. I went to the local bar and grill and sat on a stool at the far end of the massive bar. The place was noisy and crowded and smelled like stale beer mixed with cigarette smoke. I remember feeling terribly alone among strangers who had no idea what I was going through. Evidently, that is when I met Abner.

According to what he told me years later, he came into the bar and, recognizing me, took the stool next to mine. Perhaps because of his story, I now vaguely remember a man introducing himself at the bar and saying that he knew my parents. He got me drunk and then drove me home. I was too inebriated to tell him how to get to my house, but he found it nonetheless, claiming that he had been there before.

We did not meet again for another fifteen years. I completed my PhD in clinical psychology and moved to Manhattan to work at the Sommers Clinic, a private mental health facility. Abner was the only psychiatrist in residency; the rest of us were all psychologists. Abner essentially ran the place, even though he had no official position in its administration. As I would later learn, he was the one who hired me.

He was a highly regarded psychiatrist and founded the clinic years ago. In addition, he had a burgeoning practice on the side with which he had difficulty keeping up. He worked from eight to five in the clinic and then from six to nine at his home office. He specialized in treating young adults, and suicide prevention was a primary focus of his practice. It was my interest as well.

He did not initially tell me that we had previously met. It came up out of the blue during a consultation about a suicidal teenage boy. Abner had referred the eighteen-year-old high school student named John Rankin to me. The boy was struggling with depression and anxiety. Abner and I discussed the case at some length. During one of our discussions, I mentioned that I had struggled with the loss of my parents when I was a little older than John. He said that empathy was a hallmark of our profession and that we learned it from our own experiences.

"You apparently don't remember, Tim, but I met you shortly after your parents died," Abner said. "I knew your father reasonably well and saw you at the funeral. A short time later, we had a chance meeting at a bar near your home where you were drinking to forget your sorrows."

"Wait. That was you at the bar that night?"

"Yes. I saw you sitting there alone and tried to console you. There was no stopping your drinking, so I stayed with you to make sure you would not drive home."

I was surprised by his story, especially the fact that he'd known my father. I thought I knew all my parents' friends. I presumed that, since my father was also a doctor, he had met Abner in some professional capacity. When I asked

Abner about that, he smiled and said no, that he and my father dated back to their college days together. I wondered how close they had been since my father had not mentioned Abner, to my recollection.

I soon learned the benefits of practicing with Abner. His knowledge of the field was encyclopedic, and he was a natural teacher. He was always available for a consultation, offering friendly and sage advice. He took therapists under his wing and trained them in his own school of thought. He was the lifeblood of the Sommers Clinic, which was known among the profession as "Abner's Clinic." We had our own townhouse building on East Thirty-Sixth Street.

Abner was a young, vibrant sixty-three-year-old who never seemed to slow down. He was married to Julie, a good-looking forty-two-year-old, and she kept him hopping. *The New York Times* did an article on him about a year before I joined the clinic. It featured a picture of the plain-faced man with empty gray-green eyes and longish hair that extended over the collar of his white gown. It spoke glowingly of his all-around service to the community. He was successful in drawing many patients to the clinic, and its reputation rose with his.

An excellent diagnostician, he picked up on visceral reactions like an animal sensing fear, knowing exactly when to probe and when to lay off. He was incisive and nonjudgmental, always projecting the image of the most normal person you ever met, a man who was comfortable in his own skin and could make you feel the same way.

His self-confidence rubbed off on those around him. Learning at the side of one of the best fed my own ego. I was proud of my education and tended to think that I was the smartest person in the room—except around Abner. My strong points were my compassion and my ability to listen, but I sometimes struggled with being affable and approachable, which could make me seem stiff.

My own self-assuredness was undermined from time to time by bouts of anxiety. I had experienced them as a child, but they were exacerbated by my parents' death and made occasional appearances through my adult life. I thought that it was the stress of the job and largely ignored the symptoms until they got progressively worse. I had my first real panic attack in years and could not breathe, let alone function. It passed after a few minutes, but I knew I could no longer pretend that nothing was going on.

Since a leading expert on anxiety was my friend and mentor, I told Abner about the panic attack the next day. He prescribed some Valium and told me to make an appointment to see him if I had any more attacks. I took the Valium at the first sign of anxiety, and the pills seemed to work. A couple of weeks went by without incident, and I thought the problem had been resolved.

On a Saturday afternoon, I was driving with my little girl, Samantha, in the back seat. I was going too fast, considering the rainy weather. As the traffic light ahead turned from yellow to red, I had to swerve into oncoming traffic to avoid plowing into the pickup truck in front of me. I immediately veered back into my lane, just missing the car headed right at us. When I pulled over to the curb to catch my breath, a panic attack hit me. My twelve-year-old watched helplessly as I writhed, sweating and trying to regain my composure. By the time my anxiety eased enough for me to check on her, she was crying so hard that I thought she might have a panic attack of her own. We sat frozen on the side of the road for a good fifteen minutes. On Monday, I made an appointment to see Abner.

As the appointment got closer, I started to feel inadequate because I could not decipher the cause of my own anxiety. I was embarrassed to reach out for help, something I had told countless patients not to be. Although I trusted Abner to be discreet, I felt that word would somehow get out that one of the clinic's own psychologists had a mental health issue. I thought about canceling the appointment. However, the warning signs were there that my condition was getting worse, and I needed to deal with it now.

My appointment was Thursday at eight p.m. I stayed at the clinic late, doing some work before catching a cab uptown to Abner's place. I arrived at the East Seventy-Second Street address at a couple of minutes before eight. I climbed the steps to the front door of the townhome and rang the buzzer. There was a basement entrance to his office, so I pushed that buzzer as well. I stood on the stoop for a good ten minutes and then called Abner's cell phone. The call went straight to voicemail. I looked at my watch again and saw that another five minutes had elapsed.

I went down the narrow steps and tapped on the casement window of his basement office but got no response. I went around to the back of the house and saw that the back door was boarded up for some construction project in the adjacent kitchen. Then, I went back around to the front and knocked on the townhouse door, thinking that I would at least rouse his wife, Julie. As I pounded the door, it opened slightly. I inched it open a little more with one hand and called out to Abner. There was no response, though I could hear music playing upstairs. I moved inside the house to the stairwell and yelled Julie's name. Again, no answer.

I did not know Abner or Julie well enough to barge into their house. Though I considered Abner a friend, I knew Julie mostly from social events, including her charitable activities on behalf of the needy. She was a celebrity in her own right in such circles, often captured in the society pages of city newspapers for her role in this function or that. It would have been exceedingly brash of me to enter their home uninvited. If she were home, I would risk scaring the hell out of her.

So I retreated to the stoop outside and locked the door from the inside before closing it. They must have inadvertently left it open, and I did not want them to find a stranger in their house when they returned. I tried calling Abner one more time and left when I got no answer. Something important must have come up for the both of them. I stood there, sweating from rushing over to his house and going up and down the stairs several times. I was slightly pissed at Abner for letting me come all that way without giving me the courtesy of a heads-up that he wouldn't be here.

I took a cab home to my place in Chelsea. My wife, Beth, had chased the kids, Samantha and Evan, upstairs so we could have a quiet late dinner in our cozy kitchen. We had our usual evening glass of wine first, and I told her the story of my wasteful trip uptown.

"Why didn't you go in the house to check on them?" she asked.

"It felt creepy and weird being in their home by myself. They probably got caught up at some late-running charitable event."

"Abner would likely have called you if that were the case."

"You're probably right, but sometimes he gets caught up in his own little world. I'll call him again later. How are the kids?"

"I don't know what they're doing with themselves all day now that summer is here. I think Evan spends the day playing those video games with his friends. Even at twelve, Samantha likes to talk on her phone with her friends when she's not at her summer program," she said, chuckling. "Are you feeling any better?"

"Since the attack? Yes, thanks. Has Samantha said anything?"

"She was scared by the incident and your reaction."

"I'm sure. It wasn't my fault, you know. I am going to call Abner to check on him."

There was still no answer. Was Beth right that I should have gone in and checked on the couple? It was strange that the door was open and music was on. Could it be that they were on the third floor and did not hear me? Why had Abner not answered his phone? I thought about getting back into a cab and returning to the house, then realized I had locked the door. Since it was getting too late for Abner to call me back, I crawled into bed and took a Valium to help me relax. I fell asleep quickly.

When I got to the clinic Friday morning, I went to Abner's office to talk to him. It was empty, so I visited my first patient. During our session, the receptionist called to say that there was a mandatory all-hands meeting in five minutes in the lunchroom.

I left my patient behind and joined the gathering crowd in the lunchroom a few minutes later. The head of the clinic, Sue Harnish, presided. Her eyes were red and puffy, like she had been crying. She leaned against a table for support and spoke softly.

"If I could have your attention, please," she said in a gravelly voice. "I have some sad news to report. I am sorry to say that the police discovered Julie Reeves's body in her bedroom this morning. She apparently died sometime last night from stab wounds. They also found Abner unconscious in his basement office. He is alive and doing well. We don't know more than that at this juncture. This is a terrible tragedy, and our hearts go out to Abner and his family. I will let you know about funeral services just as soon as I have that information."

# 2

I am sure the shock showed on my face. Julie had been stabbed to death last night. Judging from the open door at her house, I likely got there during or after the murder. Was Abner lying unconscious in the basement the whole time? I could not see into his office from where I'd been standing, only the reception area. I'd banged on the office door hard, but that would not have woken him if he were unconscious. It sounded like he had gotten lucky that the killer only knocked him out. Had the murderer intended to kill Abner too?

What reason did anyone have to kill Julie and attack Abner? Maybe someone was trying to rob them, and Julie had walked in on the thief. While that might explain Julie's death, it did not explain the separate attack on Abner. It was hard to imagine that anyone would want to hurt either of them, as well loved as they were throughout the city.

I telephoned Beth from my office and told her what had happened.

"Are you kidding?" she said in a shaky voice.

While she did not know either of the Reeves well, she had met them both on several occasions. She was roughly the same age as Julie, and they had gotten along well.

"No. It's surreal."

"Oh my God. You could have walked in on a murder and been killed yourself."

"I know. I did not see or hear anything, but I think I need to go to the police. I have to tell them that I was there at eight. I don't want them finding out some other way."

I identified the precinct that covered East Seventy-Second Street and dialed the number. I was referred to Detective Rita DeCarlo of the homicide division. I told her that my name was Timothy Shea and explained why I was calling. After listening to me for a few minutes, she said she would need a statement from me.

The next morning, on a cloudy day, I arrived at the precinct well before nine. It was a hubbub of activity, with people streaming in and out of a dingy bullpen area. DeCarlo, a stocky woman with black hair and an attractive face with big, dark eyes, escorted me to an interview room. Her partner, Detective Len Hayes, a young man with light eyes and neatly trimmed brown hair, was already seated in one of the metal chairs. The room was cold and dank and had no windows.

After getting some background information, DeCarlo asked me about my relationship with Abner and Julie Reeves.

"I am a friend and coworker of Abner's. I saw his wife, Julie, on rare occasions over the years. I had a professional appointment with Abner the evening of the murder, which is what brought me there."

"Do you mind if I show you a photo of the victim to confirm that it's her?" DeCarlo asked while placing the photo on the table in front of me.

They had already identified her, so I didn't see the point in showing me the photo other than to gauge my reaction to it. I looked at the picture of her body. Her throat was slashed, and there was a pool of blood surrounding her head. I gagged at the sight, turned away, and motioned for them to remove the photo.

I sighed and said, "That's Julie."

"So you had an eight p.m. appointment with Dr. Reeves?" DeCarlo asked.

"Yes, it should be in his appointment calendar."

"And when you arrived, you first went to his front door and rang the bell?"

"Yes."

"And after getting no answer, you rang the bell to his office as well?" DeCarlo continued.

"Yes, and I knocked on both doors too. I went back and forth between the office and the house a couple of times."

"And you say that when you knocked on the house door, it swung open?"

"Not swung. I'd say it opened a couple of inches," I said defensively.

"And then you pushed your way in through the door?" asked Hayes.

"Yes. I entered the front hall of the house. That's when I heard the music coming from upstairs."

"And you called out?"

"Yes, both to Julie and Abner, but there was no reply."

Hayes leaned forward in his chair. "Did you go farther into the house?"

"No."

"Why didn't you go past the hallway?" DeCarlo asked. "You were already inside."

"I felt that I would be intruding if I did. I had called on the cell phone and there was no answer, so I assumed no one was home."

"Did you see or hear Mrs. Reeves?" DeCarlo asked, jotting down notes.

"No, the only thing I heard was classical music coming from upstairs. I could not tell if it was from the second or third floor, but it was faint."

"But you didn't go up and investigate. You didn't consider that maybe someone was hurt and needed help?" Hayes asked, pointing his index finger at me.

"No, I guess not. I thought they weren't home and had left the door open by mistake. That's why I locked it."

DeCarlo's eyes narrowed as she asked, "So you locked the door? And from the inside, right?"

"Yes."

"Did you go into the kitchen?"

I was perplexed and bothered by the question. Where had that come from? "What? No. I left from the hallway and went to knock on the basement office."

"You did not go in the basement office either?"

"No. It was locked. I couldn't see beyond the reception area, and there was no one there that I could see."

"So you don't know how Dr. Reeves was rendered unconscious?"

"I didn't see him, so I didn't know if he was even there, let alone unconscious.

He didn't answer my calls or my knocking."

"Don't you think it's a bit of a coincidence that you happened to show up around the time of the murder? The coroner estimates the time of death to be between seven thirty and nine p.m. And you admit you were there *in the house* at eight p.m. Did you have any kind of beef with either of the Reeves that led you to attack them?" DeCarlo asked.

I had said too much already. I had not envisioned that they would consider me a suspect if I came in and told them why I'd been there. I thought I would be helping with the investigation by telling them I found the door open. Instead, they turned the questioning on me. I was not prepared for that. I decided I needed a lawyer and told them that. Hayes stared at me and closed his notepad. Before he let me go, he fingerprinted me and took a DNA sample.

I was too upset to go to the clinic, so I jumped on the subway and headed home. Beth was surprised to see me. She had just come home from taking the kids to the movies and was sitting on the sectional in our family room with her lesson book in front of her. Her petite frame was lost in the big sofa, and her dark hair contrasted with the beige fabric.

"What are you doing home so early?" she asked with a twinkle in her brown eyes.

I didn't want to tell her the truth. "I'm feeling the shock of everything that has happened. I am having trouble concentrating at the office. Since I had a slow day, I thought I'd take advantage of the fact that you're home. I'm going to spend the day here and be ready for work tomorrow. Are you working on your plans for next semester?"

"Too early for that. One of the benefits of teaching is having some real time off. Have you heard anything about Abner?"

"I have not even called him yet," I said, shaking my head at my forgetfulness. "Sometimes, I don't know where my head is at. They took him to Lenox Hill Hospital when they found him unconscious, but I have not heard what his condition is."

I telephoned Sue and told her I would not be coming in today. I then asked her about Abner, and she told me he was doing better and would be discharged from the hospital later that day or the next day. Since he had been hit in the head by a dull object and lost consciousness, they wanted to hold him for observation. I thought about calling him but decided to wait until he got home. He must have been devastated by Julie's sudden death. They had been married for nearly twenty years, so it would take Abner a long time to recover from losing her, particularly under the circumstances.

When Beth went to pick up the kids from the movies, I contacted a friend of mine, Ed Wyeth. He was a middle-aged partner in a boutique law firm that specialized in criminal defense and had worked as a prosecutor earlier in his career. I spoke to him briefly, and he asked me to come to his Midtown offices to walk through everything. I left Beth a note saying that something had come up at the clinic and that I would be home for dinner.

On the way to Ed's office, I felt like everybody on the subway was staring at me. I started to sweat, and my heart was pounding in my chest. The air in the subway car suddenly got very heavy, and I was having trouble taking it in. Feeling a panic attack coming on, I got off at Penn Station and went to Starbucks. I knew better than to have coffee in my state and ordered tea instead. I sat at a table and popped a Valium to help the anxiety pass, then phoned Ed to tell him I was running late.

There was a *New York Post* left on the table by the previous customer, and I flipped through it. On page five, there was a picture of Julie Reeves and a story about her death. Much of the article was about her charity work, while the final couple of paragraphs recapped the events of the other night. She'd been stabbed three times in the throat and chest and found the next morning in her bedroom by her housekeeper. The knife had been left behind by the killer. The front door had been tampered with. The police found her husband unconscious that morning in his basement office, but there were no signs of forced entry.

When the panic attack subsided enough, I traveled the rest of the way to Ed's office. I didn't know if I was in shape to talk about the case, but the police were pressing for a meeting, so I felt that we needed to accommodate them. His secretary escorted me into a medium-sized conference room with an oblong marble table. A few minutes later, Ed came in with his young associate, Nicole Andrews.

I spent over an hour walking him and Nicole through the events of the other night minute by minute. I explained how I had opened the door and entered the hallway of the house. I noted that I had touched the front door of both the house and the basement office and that my fingerprints would be found on both. I also assumed I had touched some things in the entrance hallway but was adamant that I had not gone any farther than that.

We went back over my actions inside and outside the house. I had to be careful about what I told them because Ed was direct and very precise. He gave me some insights into what the police were likely thinking.

"The police are going to find it curious that you did not enter the main part of a good friend's house under the circumstances. Since you admitted that you were at the Reeves's place for about fifteen minutes, they could conclude that was plenty of time to stab Mrs. Reeves and knock out her husband."

"And how did I supposedly get into his locked office?"

"The newspapers reported that the murderer left the key in the office," Nicole noted. "The police will think the killer got the key from the house when he murdered Mrs. Reeves."

"Dr. Reeves is also going be a person of interest, as spouses usually are," Ed said. "He could have easily knocked himself out after murdering his wife. What do you know about their relationship?"

"Not much. I assumed they were close, given how long they were married."

"Do you know whether Dr. Reeves had a seven p.m. appointment that evening?"

"I don't, but I suspect so because he is always completely booked."

While it was possible that a patient of Abner's was the culprit, that seemed odd because Julie was the one who'd been killed, not Abner. I did not know enough about any of his patients to offer any guesses as to which of them might have an issue with him, let alone Julie.

"The police are going to question one or more of Abner's patients, especially the one whose appointment preceded yours," Ed continued. "Our strategy is simple at this point. You are going to refuse to answer any more of the police's questions."

"Asserting my rights under the Fifth Amendment suggests that I have something to hide. Is that smart?"

"There will be time later to give the police a statement if need be. Since you don't have an alibi, the safest course is to remain quiet for now. I am going to call the detectives and decline their invitation to meet."

I went back to the clinic and tried to concentrate on my patient responsibilities. I sat at my mahogany desk and called Abner to express my condolences, but it went to voicemail. I left a message asking him to call me back when he felt up to it.

Ed called me after he got off the phone with DeCarlo. I could tell from the muted tone that he was upset. I braced for bad news.

"They say your fingerprints are on the handle of the knife used for the murder! What the fuck?"

"Are you shitting me?" I said, gasping for air. "That can't be. Could somebody have lifted my prints?"

"It's possible, but unlikely. Although fingerprints can be transferred from one object to another, the two objects have to come in contact. That would mean someone would have had to have something else you touched and used it to transfer your prints to the knife."

"I didn't touch any knife at Abner's house. There must be some mistake."

"Who said the knife came from Abner's house? Tell me you didn't bring one," Ed said stridently.

"Don't be ridiculous. I was going to a psychiatric appointment. Why would I bring a knife?"

"Beats me. I've got to go see it."

"What kind of knife is it?"

"A chef's knife commonly found in kitchen sets. I don't know the brand, what the handle is made of, or what color it is."

I nervously repeated myself. "It either has to be a mistake or the knife had to have been planted by someone trying to frame me. That would mean that whoever planted it somehow got my fingerprints on it first, and I have no clue how that could have happened."

"The other thing the police said is no surprise," said Ed. "Your fingerprints were all over the door handles and doorbells at the house and Abner's office. That only proves you were telling the truth about going there. Evidently, the fingerprints they found inside the house did not go beyond the front hallway."

"That's good."

"The police also said they had a neighbor who saw you in front of the house that evening, which again corroborates your story."

"So now what?" I asked.

"We need an explanation for the fingerprints on the knife. Think about it."

I was distracted during my afternoon session with a young bipolar woman, Ellen Rosetti, who had been referred by Abner. She could tell I was drifting in and out of our session. Instead of being annoyed, she was understanding, thinking it had something to do with Julie's murder. We ended the session a few minutes early, and I went home.

I had to tell Beth something and prepared myself for that by going into the kitchen to get a beer. We had just had it redone, and I admired the white wooden cabinets and stainless steel appliances she had picked out. As I walked past the butcher block with the kitchen knives, I noticed there were two missing. I opened the dishwasher and looked inside. One was sitting on the top shelf with other kitchen utensils, but the sharp, medium-sized one was not there. I looked in the kitchen drawers where we kept an assortment of kitchen gadgets. Nothing.

Beth walked in and caught me going through the drawers. She looked amused watching my frenetic motion.

"What are you doing?" she asked, munching on an apple.

"I wanted some cheese and was looking for the cheese knife."

She rolled her eyes and pointed to the knife set. "They're all right in front of you, Sherlock."

"One of the knives was missing, and I assumed that it was the cheese knife, so I went hunting for it," I said, shrugging.

"Dummy, the cheese knife is there. It's one of the chef's knives that's missing. It disappeared about two weeks ago, and I have been looking for it ever since. The last time I saw it was in the picnic basket I put together for the clinic's July

Fourth barbecue."

Every year, the clinic threw a barbeque on July Fourth at Abner's house. Everyone showed up and brought something homemade to supplement the hamburgers and hot dogs Abner supplied. All told, there were about thirty people at this year's event.

"You took the knife with you in the picnic basket?" I asked.

"I don't really remember, but it's been missing since around that time, and I can't think of anything else I would have done with it," said Beth. "I know I brought several pieces of dry salami, and I usually use that knife to cut it."

"I vaguely remember the salami. I probably cut some myself. Maybe I left it there? Anyway, time for my cheese. I'll be in my office."

I phoned Ed and told him about my conversation with Beth.

"I think she may be able to explain how one of our knives got there. That will help, won't it?"

"Maybe. What make are the knives?"

"They are Williams-Sonoma and the handles are made of heavy black stone."

"I just sent you a photo. Does it look like one of yours?"

"Yes."

"That's a photo of the murder weapon. How sure is Beth that she had packed the knife?"

"I will be sure to ask her tonight."

We had a pleasant family dinner. I did the dishes while Beth relaxed over a glass of wine. Once the kids were both in their rooms, I felt it was safe to talk. I explained everything to her. She looked at me strangely when I finished the story.

"Your fingerprints are on the murder weapon? How could that be?" She raised her eyebrows.

"I've been asking myself the same question. Maybe from the barbecue?"

"But that was two weeks ago."

"Fingerprints don't just disappear. They are still on the knife."

She looked at me as if she were trying to evaluate whether what I said was even remotely possible.

"This is surreal. I can't believe the police think you might have killed Julie. You hardly even knew her, right?"

"Correct. We spoke at parties at her house, and I saw her occasionally at charitable events, but that's about it."

She scratched her head and looked at me. "You want to know about the knife? I'm sure I packed it in that picnic basket. We must have taken it out there, used it, and left it by mistake. Do you think people will remember seeing it or using it at the barbecue?"

"A plain kitchen knife is not very memorable, I'm afraid."

"Am I going to have to give a statement to the police?" she said. "Of course, I'll do what I can, but it makes me nervous."

"I think so. Is that okay?"

"Yes. I just need a little time to get my nerves under control. And to give everything more thought, so it will be clearer in my mind."

I went to bed thinking about the pressure I was putting on Beth. The police would be skeptical of her story and question her aggressively. I did not know how she would hold up under grueling cross-examination. She had to be certain about things to be an effective witness, yet she was tentative by nature. I was worried for her and for me, but I had to keep the faith that the police would ultimately believe her and recognize that there was an innocent explanation for my fingerprints showing up.

We were scheduled to bring Beth to the police station to give her statement the next day. I was nervous about that, especially because I wouldn't be allowed in the room to give her moral support. To my surprise, she came downstairs the next morning defiant and self-confident. She kissed me on the lips and told me that, having thought about the knife some more, she was absolutely sure she had taken it with her to the Reeves's home. She even remembered cutting dry salami and cheese with it. She was sure I had handled the knife too.

I waited with her in the lobby of the police station until Ed showed up. The bustle in the entranceway seemed to intimidate her. DeCarlo came out, nodded to me, and took Ed and Beth into the interior rooms. I sat there like an expectant father in a maternity ward, waiting for news. I hoped the unexpected self-assurance I'd seen earlier in the morning would not abandon Beth.

This was the third day in a row that I had taken off. I called Sue to tell her I would be in tomorrow and for the rest of the week.

"Between what's happened to Abner and some personal issues, I needed a couple of days off. How is he doing?"

"He's back at work. He's remarkably strong. Though he is laden with grief and sorrow, he had a full schedule today."

"Back so soon?"

"He is a dedicated professional," she harrumphed. "I think the distraction helps him. He's confining himself to the clinic. I'm not sure he will ever see patients at home again, poor thing."

As I finished my conversation with Sue, Beth and Ed emerged from the bowels of the police station. Ed suggested that we go down the street for a chat. He took us to a café, bought three large coffees, and sat down at an outside table across from Beth and me.

"We had a good interview," he said. "Beth did a great job explaining about the knife and was able to identify the one they had as yours. DeCarlo and Hayes were incredulous at first, but Beth was able to describe for them where the table and knife had been in the Reeves' backyard. She even remembered you using it to cut some fruit. She came across as entirely believable."

"That's great! Does that mean they no longer believe I killed Julie?" I asked, feeling the tension drain out of me.

"Not exactly." Ed frowned as he leaned forward, putting his elbows on his knees. "They pulled me into the corner of the interview room out of Beth's earshot and told me the knife was washed after the barbecue and the fingerprints were wiped off. They pointed out that they found no fingerprints on the knife other than yours despite there being plenty of people at the barbecue. They claim they can prove that your fingerprints got on the knife after the barbecue. They say you just grabbed a sharp knife from the Reeves' kitchen and used it to murder Julie."

"That's crazy. I never went into the kitchen that night or any time after the barbecue," I protested.

"I don't know how to explain the lack of other fingerprints," Ed said. "How did somebody wipe them all off except yours? I don't even know if that's possible, but if it is, we need a theory."

Beth just looked at me. It was curious that mine were the only prints left on the knife, and I could tell she was troubled by that. The two people who should have been most convinced of my innocence did not know what to think. I felt their support waning.

"So what happens now?" I asked, fidgeting in my chair.

"I'm not sure. I still don't know what they think the motive was here. I also don't know which other leads they're following. If they're coming after you, odds are that they will give you another chance to talk before arresting you."

"Arresting me? Is that a real possibility?" I asked as I heard Beth gasp.

"I don't think they will go there yet, but I can't guarantee it. There is clearly some pressure on the police to find Julie's killer, and they appear to be moving quickly. We just don't know who else is on their radar."

"I have never been a violent man. Anyone who knows me could attest to that. I don't think I'm capable of homicide, much less a brutal, bloody murder with a knife. The police have probably heard that countless times from men who turned out to be guilty. How do we convince them that I don't have it in me?"

"We focus on timing and try to exploit a lack of motive."

Somehow, I'd been hoping for more than that.

# 3

It was too hot to ride the subway the next day, so I took an air-conditioned cab and avoided the mugginess. I dropped my briefcase on one of the wing chairs in my office and greeted my first patient. I saw Abner walking through the halls after my session. He looked beleaguered in a wrinkled shirt with no tie. There were dark rings under his eyes from lack of sleep. After a moment's hesitation, I approached him.

"Hello, Abner. Words never suffice at a time like this, but I want you to know how truly sorry I am to hear about Julie."

Abner stopped in his tracks, his shoulders stiffening. He turned slowly and glared at me.

"Is it true you were at my house that night?" he asked with narrowed eyes.

"Yes. We had an appointment, remember?"

"I'm sorry. I was not available because someone killed my wife and knocked me out," he said, giving me a dirty look. His response stung like a slap across my face.

"That must have happened before I got there, because I kept pounding on your door and you didn't answer. I also telephoned you. You must have been out cold at the time."

"Did you know the door to my house was open?"

"Yes."

"Why didn't you go in and see if Julie was all right? Or did you go in?"

"Abner, I don't think we should be talking about this," I said, relying on Ed's advice to avoid discussing the case with anyone.

"Are you trying to settle scores? Is that why you did it?" His lip quivered as he spoke.

"I don't know what you're talking about. Let's let the police handle this now."

"I'm not done with you," Abner said, pointing a crooked finger at me and walking away.

The police theory, according to what they had told Ed, was that Julie had been killed before the murderer let himself into Abner's office with a key stolen from the house. If he'd entered the office through the front door with a key, wouldn't Abner have seen the man from the reception area while waiting for his next appointment? If so, the police should have a physical description of the murderer, yet they had not even hinted at that. They must believe Abner had been blindsided by his attacker while in his back office.

While the knife made me look guilty, I thought that the police could not have ruled out Abner's current and former patients as suspects at this early stage. I didn't know how the police would narrow down their search. I trusted they would seek some of the clinic's patient files. I went to see Sue to ask which records the police had obtained and whether any of my patients were under review.

"We are trying to work out a compromise with the police about which records will be turned over to them. Naturally, they want all patient files, but we're pushing back because of psychologist-patient privilege and HIPAA. We've tried to get them to identify specific patients they have concerns about."

"Do the patients have a say in this since the privilege is theirs?"

"That's not practical in a murder investigation."

"Who is going to make the final call as to whose files and which parts of them are released?"

"It's likely going to be Abner."

It seemed to me that Abner had a conflict of interest on this issue. On the one hand, he would want to do everything he could to catch his wife's killer. On the other hand, he had a duty to preserve patient confidentiality. He himself was a suspect. Letting him decide arbitrarily which files were to be handed over could compromise a patient's privacy rights. I felt that they needed to hear an independent voice.

Sue later told me the clinic and the police had reached a settlement, which was approved by a state judge. It provided that the supervising psychiatrist or psychologist would identify patients with a violent history or a serious personal problem with Abner and only produce the part of the patient file necessary to demonstrate that. A handful of patients had some portion of their records turned over to the police, though their identities were not revealed to the clinic staff generally. None of my patients were among them except John, whom I shared with Abner.

A week or so after we started turning over files, I got a call from Detective DeCarlo about John. I told her I disagreed with the decision to produce his file because he was not the violent type. She said his file showed he had self-inflicted wounds, which qualified him under their definition. She asked how he got along with Dr. Reeves, and I told her I thought that they worked well together.

"That's not what Dr. Reeves says. He told us John is temperamental and flies off the handle at him," DeCarlo said.

"I've never known John to act like that. He is well behaved with me."

"Do you know of any reason that he had to be angry with Dr. Reeves?"

"No. I don't know of any rift between them. John has never hinted at a problem."

"So Dr. Reeves never told you that John threw a heavy knickknack at him and threatened him?"

"No."

I did not know whether to be more surprised at John's supposed behavior or Abner's failure to inform me about it. John should have told me about it himself, but it was unforgivable for Abner not to do so as soon as it happened. After my call with DeCarlo, I went back over John's files to see if there were other instances of him lashing out and found none. Abner never even recorded the one incident in the clinic's file. I would need his private notes to determine if he made any record at all of what had transpired, but I knew Abner regarded them as sacrosanct and would not share them with me.

I still wanted to get to the bottom of this, considering that John was an active patient of mine. I telephoned him at home.

"John, have the police reached out to you?" I asked after saying hello.

"Yeah. What the hell? I thought our sessions were confidential. How do they know about them? They knew I used to cut myself."

"There was a court-imposed order that required we turn certain records over to the police because of the criminal investigation. Yours were among them, although I objected on your behalf and was overruled."

"It's bullshit, man."

"Tell me something, John. Did you have a fight with Dr. Reeves?"

He hesitated and then said, "That's between him and me. Why do you care?"

"Because it is not like you to get that angry or violent. The police have heard about it. There must be some explanation, and I'm wondering whether you should share it with the police so they will understand what he did to rile you and that you're not a violent person."

His voice became more animated. "For one thing, he threatened to cut off my medications if I didn't do what he said. It was offensive. I got pissed and threw a little statue at him. It didn't even hit him."

"What did he want you to do?"

"I don't want to say."

"Did you tell the police?"

"No. I just told them that I got mad, not why. I'm not going to get into another fight with Dr. Reeves."

"You have to tell the police the whole truth. They are investigating a murder, and if you had an issue with him, they might consider you a suspect. Understand?"

"His wife got killed, not him. I didn't do that. So what if I was angry at him? I didn't even know his wife."

"He was attacked too, remember? And killing his wife is a terrible blow to him. You have to tell the police everything you know, including what he did to provoke you. You need to defend yourself."

"I should talk to my big brother about a lawyer if the police are going to hassle me concerning my feelings about Reeves."

"That's not a bad idea. See you at our next session."

Without understanding the reasons for the fight, I did not know if I was helping or hurting John by suggesting that he explain it. I realized that, to the extent it helped him, I might be acting contrary to my own interest. If the police did not think John did it, there would be more reason to focus on me. Each patient they crossed off the list moved me up in relative importance.

I was eager to steer them toward Abner's private patients, the most serious cases he treated. While I knew nothing about them, Sue would. Abner needed to clear his treatment of outside patients with her. She would know who they were and for what they were being treated, but she would not share that with me.

Early that evening, I went to her office. It was bigger than mine and decorated with antique furniture and lamps. I sat on her striped humpback sofa and waited for her to acknowledge me.

"Hi, Sue. I'm sorry to burst in on you so late, but you should know John Rankin is bitter that we told the police about his treatment."

"I get it. Did you tell him that I didn't want to turn anything over to the police? You know Abner and Mr. Rankin had a falling out, and Rankin was angry with Abner for some reason. The police know, and they are curious about what had happened between them."

While we were conversing, I watched her take the keys out of her desk drawer and lock the file cabinets behind her.

"Do you know which of our patients other than John have been approached by the police for questioning?" I asked.

"I know a few—those who called to complain that we'd released their files. We warned them all that their files were being produced, but it did not seem to make a difference. They were surprised and angry at getting calls from the police, and they let me know about it."

I watched her put the keys back in her top-right drawer. She then turned off her computer and gathered files to take home with her.

"Any of them my patients?"

She looked at me suspiciously. "None, except John," she said. "But that's because you didn't identify anyone as violent."

With that, she grabbed her purse and her files and brushed past me as I stood. I let her go by and closed the door behind me. I walked back toward my office. Liz Schreiber was also working late, as the lights in her office indicated. I popped my head in her door to say hello. She looked up at me from her desk and gave me a warm smile that made her green eyes sparkle.

"Hi, Liz. What are you doing here this late?"

"Working on a challenging case. Do you have any experience with patients with split personalities? I'd be willing to buy you a cup of coffee to compare notes if you do."

I hesitated at first because she was quite beautiful, and I had a crush on her despite her considerably younger age. "I do, and I love coffee."

"Thank you," she said, as she closed the textbook she was studying.

"For what?" I asked.

"For distracting me. I need to take a break and go home."

"I'm sorry. I didn't mean to break your concentration."

She got up, approached me, and touched my wrist gently. "No. I needed to stop. I can always read more at home." She started to pack up, brushing her long brown hair away from her face. "What about you? Shouldn't you be getting home too?"

"I'm way behind on paperwork since the thing with Abner's wife happened. I need to stay and catch up."

"I'm sorry. Were you and Julie close?"

"No. I didn't know Julie well. I can't believe she was murdered in cold blood. Imagine that."

"Kind of freaky. I sure hope it was not one of his patients trying to get at Abner instead."

"I know the police are looking at several patients. I guess that makes sense in these kinds of circumstances, but I'm praying it's none of them."

As she walked by, I got a whiff of her perfume.

"Me too. I'm sort of hoping that it was a robbery gone bad. Anyway, I'm out of here," she said as she sprang toward the door with a briefcase and a gargantuan handbag. "See you tomorrow. And don't forget our coffee date."

An hour or so later, I checked around the clinic. Everyone else had gone home. I walked over to Sue's office door. Once inside, I turned on her lamp. On the desk was a list of the patients whose files had been turned over, and I took a photo of it. I then went to the desk drawer from which Sue had pulled the set of keys. I identified the ones that fit the file cabinet locks.

The filing cabinet had a drawer for each clinician, including several marked with Abner's name. I opened those first. The top two had records related to his clinic patients. The third had a large folder marked "private practice." Abner did not have a secretary at his home office and trusted Sue with files for all his patients, including those he saw on the side. I pulled out the "private practice" folder and sat at Sue's desk. There was a file filled with forms Abner had completed to get clearance to treat each patient and a few patient overviews that I found interesting. I took pictures of five forms with my phone and put them back in the folder. I made sure to put the folder back in the same spot in which I had found it, locked the filing cabinet, and put the keys back in her desk drawer. I turned off the desk lamp and left her office. I grabbed my briefcase from mine and left for home.

When I got home, Beth was already in bed. I stuck my head in the kids' rooms to say good night and headed to my home office, where I sat down at my desk and downloaded the photos I had taken of Abner's files. These five consent forms stood out because of the brief descriptions of their conditions that Abner had included. I did not know any of the patients, but they did appear to have violent tendencies.

I went to Sue the next day with a proposal I thought she would find attractive economically.

"Sue, can I talk to you about an idea I have? I think we should contact each of Abner's private patients and offer to help them transition to a new therapist. We would offer them consultations while we helped them select a psychiatrist or psychologist with whom they're comfortable. I'm hoping this will induce them to use our services instead of going elsewhere."

"I like that idea. I think Abner will go for it too, since he was giving up these patients anyway."

We got the go-ahead from Abner and made the offer. Three of the five patients whose files I had photographed were among the seven who took us up on it. I agreed to provide my services as interim counselor for those three. The first patient I met was Darren Carroll, a seventeen-year-old who had a fascination with guns. He was big, heavyset, and had a bad complexion that was accentuated by his crew cut. It became apparent during our first session that he was paranoid and extremely defensive. He did not want to be in therapy, but he'd been forced to go after he brought a loaded BB gun to school. He told me the police had contacted him about the Reeves investigation. Evidently, he satisfied them that he had been at a political rally with a hundred others at the time of the murder.

Philip Greenberger, the second patient, walked into my office with a chip on his shoulder. He was tall and well built, with large muscles stretching the rolled-up sleeves of his shirt. He was a drinker, though maybe not an alcoholic, who had a proclivity for busting walls and noses. He told me he was a person of interest to the police because he had the seven p.m. appointment with Abner on the day of the murder.

"The fucking cops think I offed Reeves's wife and knocked him out because I was there around the time of the murder, and he and I would sometimes argue about things during our sessions," Philip said. "I admit that I got a temper, but I didn't kill the lady. I got no reason to do that. I didn't even know her. Me and the doc got along okay for the most part."

"I'm sure you'll be cleared if there is no evidence to tie you to the murder."

Things did not go as well with the third patient, Brett Stone, a twenty-eight-year-old stockbroker who lived not far from the clinic. The strapping, golden-haired young man had an issue with women that was probably rooted in his relationship with his mother. Brett had been going through intense counseling before Julie's death. He was generally belligerent and angry at Abner for disclosing information about him to the police.

"I didn't tell that bitch DeCarlo squat. I suspect every patient has an occasional issue with their shrink, but I am not going to give them any information about my relationship with Reeves. I already feel violated by what they know."

"I trust that you got along with Dr. Reeves, at least until the end," I said.

"I don't really want to get into it, but there were a couple of things he said that were completely inappropriate."

This called to mind what John had said, so I inquired further. "Things he asked you to do?"

He looked at me as if I had just shared one of his secrets. I sensed that he was weighing whether it was safe to tell me.

"I don't want to talk about it," he said with an edge.

I now had a conflict of interest, like Abner. I owed undivided loyalty to my patients, new and old. At the same time, as a potential suspect, I had a personal interest in discovering information that might lead me to conclude one of them was likely Julie Reeves's killer. Three of my patients—John, Philip, and Brett—had issues with Abner I could explore. I rationalized that it would not be a problem so long as I did not disclose what I learned to the police. If I did not *use* the information for personal purposes, then there was no harm in me having it.

The clinic would not see it the same way. If Sue had known I was a person of interest in the Reeves investigation, she would never have let me see any of Abner's patients. Was I deceiving my patients by getting them to talk about the murder investigation and their relationships with Abner? I told myself it was important that I understand their penchant for violence as well as their relationship with their previous mental health provider. If I perchance discovered information that would help prove my innocence, so be it. I would then have to figure out a way to tip off the police without disclosing, at least directly, anything that was privileged.

# 4

I was certain the police had already asked Abner about our interactions the night of Julie's murder—or rather, the lack thereof. Since we had not even seen each other, I did not think there was anything he could say that might hurt me. That included the question of motive. They would naturally have inquired about the relationship I had with both Abner and his wife. There was not much of a story to tell in that regard, and what little there was was positive. I had always gotten along well with both, though my contacts with Julie were sporadic. Nothing had occurred between us over the years to create any hostility.

I was taking that on faith because there was an entire chapter to our backstory of which I was ignorant—Abner's relationship with my parents. I did not know of anything in that history that might give Abner reason to think I meant him harm. Yet, he had asked me if I was "settling scores" the other day. It struck me that he been deliberately vague in implying I harbored some ill will toward him. He had not mentioned anything in all the years we had known each other. If there really was something from the distant past lurking in the shadows, I had to find out what it was.

Abner had always maintained that he and my parents had been friends, even though I saw no evidence of that growing up. I had no memory of ever seeing him around during my youth. I had talked to my sister about him, and she had no recollection of ever meeting him or my parents ever mentioning him either.

When I'd asked Abner in the past about his relationship with my parents, he nearly always spoke in generalities. He only mentioned one specific occasion when we were all together: my tenth birthday party, when we brought a pony to the house for my friends to ride. He described the décor in certain rooms in my parents' home, so I knew he had been in our house. If he was a friend of the family, however, there must be some record of it *somewhere*.

I went up to the stuffy attic and pulled out the boxes of photos and memorabilia left by my parents. Sweating, I sat on one of the rafters and looked through them. The first thing I pulled out was my parents' wedding album. Scanning the pictures of the guest tables, I found one where a young Abner sat next to another man. I then dug into the photo albums for pictures of my tenth birthday and discovered a photo of Abner standing behind the pony with the same man. I spent another hour going through the boxes of old photos and found a few more of Abner. All of them were from my preteen years.

The man in the pictures with Abner looked familiar, but I could not place him. He was always nattily dressed. He was taller than Abner and had a thin mustache and wavy dark hair. I guessed that he was a few years younger than Abner. In one photo, the frail-looking young man stood next to my mother, with an arm around her waist. That was the only photo of him where he did not appear next to Abner.

In later albums, I saw less and less of Abner, until he virtually disappeared in my teenage years. I wondered if he and my parents had a disagreement of some kind. I had a vague recollection that Dad had gotten into an acrimonious dispute with someone when I was about fifteen. I knew only that it had something to do with extended family, and it upset both of my parents very much. They seemed intent on preventing my sister and me from knowing the details of this family secret. They never spoke of it in front of us, but I picked up a few words from hearing them talking with my maternal grandparents. I remember them saying something about how embarrassing the whole thing was for the family.

Though I doubted that Eve knew anything more than I did, I telephoned her from my attic to ask.

"Hey, Eve, I just sent you some photos I want you to look at to see if you recognize the men in them and what you recall about them. I remember something about a family squabble. Do you have any recollection of hearing about one?"

"I got the photos," Eve said. "The man with the mustache was a cousin or an uncle on Mom's side of the family. There was talk of a family rift, but Mom and Dad were very careful to avoid discussing it in our presence. I heard them call it a scandal. I remember Mom shushing Grandma when I came into the kitchen one day. They were talking in hushed tones, and Mom was crying. When I asked what the matter was, Grandma told me I was too young to know."

"Yeah, I also recall something about an uncle or a cousin who did something that Mom and Dad wouldn't talk about."

"What are you trying to piece together?"

"Just some family history. I'm sitting in the attic, sweltering, so I am going to go. Talk soon."

My parents were very concerned about family reputation and could have considered any number of things scandalous. We were not a particularly religious family, though we considered ourselves to be "God fearing" and of good moral character. My parents were politically and religiously conservative and out of step with much of the rest of their generation.

While in the attic, I looked through the scrapbooks in the boxes for clues about the scandal. I found a few stray newspaper clippings at the bottom of one of the boxes. What caught my eye was an article from a Midwest paper about charges of sodomy brought against a local young man in New York. The man in the story photo was the same man who appeared in the photo with my mother, and his surname was the same as her maiden name.

Around the time the article was written, more and more people had started coming out as gay, but in some circles, particularly among religious conservatives, homosexuality was not to be tolerated. According to the article, my second cousin Billy had engaged in sexual intercourse with a sixteen-year-old boy. He was ostracized by his community and, evidently, his family. He was also arrested and charged with a variety of sexual assault crimes.

That had to be what my parents had talked about behind my back. I assumed they had had nothing to do with Billy from that point on. Since it appeared that Abner was my cousin's friend, I could see my parents cutting off their ties with him as well.

It hit me that Abner might have been Billy's lover. I had never considered that Abner might be gay or bisexual given his marriage to, and children with, a beautiful woman. But even if he were gay, I was sure Abner, too, would have been shocked by my cousin's actions with an underage boy. I knew Abner to be a protector of children who would not tolerate such behavior.

From all appearances, if Abner felt slighted by my parents, he got over it without retaining any animus toward me. The best evidence of that was the fact that, as Sue related it, he had pushed her to hire me at the clinic. I saw nothing in the past that could have caused friction between us. Certainly, there was no "score" for me to settle against him.

The next morning, Liz came into the office pantry and watched me pour a cup of office rot for myself. She offered to buy me real coffee. I went back to my office and grabbed my jacket. I had a message from Abner, which I decided to return after the coffee break. I met Liz at the elevators, and we went down to the main floor of the clinic. The smell of her perfume in the elevator was intoxicating, and I moved farther away from her. She had to have noticed but said nothing.

We walked down the shady side of the street to a small café and ordered coffees. We sat on wooden chairs at a small round table where our knees almost touched. She looked at me with those green eyes and a pert smile.

"Let's call this a professional consultation. Maddy McGregor is a forty-two-year-old who alternates between Maddy, the carefree, sexually active dancer always looking for work, and Madeline, the religious conservative who berates Maddy for her lifestyle. Have you dealt with anything like that?" she asked as she crossed her long legs.

"Kind of. I had a patient who spent most of his time as a quiet professional and, on rare occasions, became a barroom brawler who hung out at some bad places."

"I am making good progress with Maddy, when I can get her to take her meds, but Madeline tries to stop that. Claims that they are the cause of her deplorable behavior. I've talked to Madeline and can't convince her to ease up on Maddy," she said, flashing her eyes and leaning forward in her chair. "Got any sage advice?" she asked, bouncing her stiletto-clad foot.

"Do you have any control over which of her personalities you talk to?"

"Some. I can trigger the switch to Madeline. It happens when I say something that really annoys her. I don't like doing it, and sometimes I do it unintentionally. She is very difficult to talk to," Liz said.

"And the drugs help, you said?"

"Yes, I don't have a problem getting Maddy to take them, but when Madeline is in charge, she won't take them because, I think, it helps her maintain that dominance. She does not want to cede control to Maddy."

"How do you keep Maddy in control?"

"When she is active, Maddy runs the show. Like at work. She's good with other people. It's when she is alone and down that Madeline takes over. Sometimes traumatic events flip the switch."

"Does she live alone?"

"Yes."

"Do you think that she might benefit from having other people around so Maddy can interact with them? Maybe she should invite a friend to stay with her a couple of days and see if that helps her maintain dominance and take her meds. If so, get her a roommate."

"Don't you think Madeline will get pissed and make life difficult for the visitor?"

"That's entirely possible, so she should probably invite over a close friend who knows the score. You don't want Madeline scaring off a friend and gaining more power that way. Madeline is not violent, is she?"

"Madeline is a lot of things, but she is not violent. I don't know if your idea will help, but I don't see how it could possibly hurt. Thanks, Tim," she said, gently squeezing my arm. "I see you took on a couple of Abner's private patients," she added, pulling her hand back. "How come?"

"To help them find a doc to replace him. They all seem lost. We're helping them with the transition."

"That's a nice thing to do, especially since it means more work for you." She gave me a big smile that showed her glossy white teeth and dimples.

I admit to being a little confused. She was naturally flirtatious, but it seemed to me that the way she was looking at me was slightly suggestive. I was hoping I wasn't wrong.

"What?" I asked.

"Nothing," she said. "Time to get back to work." She rose and I watched her walk out ahead of me, admiring her slim, athletic body.

As soon as I arrived back at my office, I telephoned Abner. He wanted to talk to me about something but would rather do it in person.

"Let's meet at my house tomorrow," he said.

"I don't know how I feel about coming to your place after everything."

"Nonsense."

"What's this about?" I asked, still uneasy. "We should not be talking about the investigation."

"There are other matters we need to address. So just come at five."

I saw John the next day for a routine session. After we talked about him and his father, he said the police investigation was weighing heavily on him. They were giving him a hard time about his fight with Abner and the reasons behind his blowup. He wouldn't talk about it, and this intrigued me. He agreed that it would help the police understand his fit of anger, and yet there was something about what Abner had said to him that John wanted to protect. It must include revealing something about John himself that he did not want people to know. I told John I was seeing Abner in a couple of hours and intended to ask him about it. John begged me not to.

"If he thinks I've gone back on my promise to keep quiet, he could make my life difficult," John said.

"Okay, but at least think about telling me so we can reason our way through this. It's obviously bothering you."

"Believe me, I'd like to, but I don't want anyone else to know."

"The police are going to suspect the worst. If you got mad enough to throw something at him once, they might think you did something more violent after he angered you again."

"I'm not worried about the murder investigation. I didn't murder Dr. Reeves's wife and didn't attack him. Can I ask you a question? What if I told you I did something bad; could you tell the police?"

"As a general rule, no, but there are exceptions," I responded.

"Could you get in trouble for saying something you shouldn't?"

"Professionally, yes. I could lose my license. And I suspect I could get sued for breaching the psychologist-patient privilege if there was damage of some sort."

"What if I were about to commit a crime; could you tell the cops?"

"Generally not, but there are exceptions, as I said. One is if the crime you were about to commit would result in bodily harm."

"So a patient doesn't have to worry about his doctor ratting him out unless he's about to hurt someone?"

"In all but rare cases, that's true. It depends on what you did, but generally the doctor shouldn't be able to divulge what you tell them in a session. They can always breach the privilege if they want to. There may be consequences to them for doing so, as I said, but once they speak, the information is out there."

"Can a court use it?" he asked, leaning forward.

Was that what he was afraid of? He must have done something illegal and was worried that, if Abner improperly revealed his confession to a crime, a court could use it as evidence to convict him.

"I doubt information provided in breach of the privilege is admissible in court," I opined. "You really should talk to a lawyer about this stuff if it's important. I'm no expert."

"So a doctor would have been lying by saying he could lawfully disclose information about my previous actions?"

"Again, it depends. There are exceptions for stuff like child abuse. I think it varies from state to state. Do you have something you want to tell me?"

"No. I just wanted some clarification of the rules."

"All right, that's enough for today."

When John left, I looked at my watch and realized that it was almost time for my appointment with Abner. My Uber rolled up to his place at a few minutes past five, and I went down to his office. He let me in, and we walked past the reception area into his office.

"Abner, how are you holding up? I'm sure it must be very difficult."

"I'm going through the stages of grief and am stuck on the one about anger. I believe the killer went after Julie either as a means of punishing me or because she'd surprised them while they were really looking for me. I have no doubt that the plan to kill me went awry. I consider myself lucky to be alive."

He glared at me as he had the other day and continued. "I want to know the truth. I don't think it was a coincidence that you made an appointment to see me the night of the murder. You had it all planned. How did you get into the house?"

"You already know this, Abner. The front door of the house was unlocked when I came by."

"That's bullshit. I was the last one to leave the house, and I locked up. I always do. Did you pick the lock?"

"No. What are you saying, Abner? I had nothing to do with Julie's murder. Why would I kill her?"

"To get back at me for your father," he said.

I was taken aback. "What are you talking about? What does this have to do with my father?"

"I'm not going to play your little game, Tim," he said, shaking his clenched fists in the air.

He then opened his desk drawer and reached for something. I held my breath. He pulled out an old Dictaphone and placed it on the desk. I had not seen one like it in twenty years.

"I made this tape many years ago when your mother and father thought they were having a private conversation in their own home. We had just finished dining. I had excused myself from the room but did not go far. It was foolish of them not to check if I had actually gone to the restroom, but I don't think they suspected a thing."

He turned the speaker toward me, pushed the play button, and my father's voice filled the office.

"That son of a bitch Abner has it all worked out," my father said, his voice trembling. "I don't know if I can go through with this."

The next voice I heard was my mother's.

"What does he want to do?" she asked solemnly.

"The deal is money for silence. There will be a series of payments not to reveal the truth and especially to keep it out of the papers."

Abner stopped the tape. I am sure I had a puzzled look on my face because I did not understand what I had listened to, though its meaning seemed clear enough.

"I bet you didn't know anything about that in the beginning, did you? What was it like for you when he finally told you? I'm sure he never told you the full story and that you don't know it even today. No, I'm certain he told you just enough for you to hate me. I suspect you've been carrying what little he did tell you around for years, waiting for the opportunity to get revenge."

I stared at him open-mouthed, not knowing what to say. I took my father's angry words to mean that he was paying Abner to keep quiet about something, but I didn't know what.

"So you came after me and took Julie's life," he continued. "Was that part of the plan, knowing what a devastating impact it would have on me, or did she just get in the way? All I have to do is tell the police what happened twenty years ago for them to understand why you had it in for me."

"Abner, you are not making any sense," I said. "I don't know what you are referring to. My father and mother didn't tell me anything."

"Do you expect me to believe that? It made the papers. It was family. You had to know something."

I thought back twenty years and could not remember anything about the family being in the newspapers, except for the article I recently found about my cousin Billy's arrest. Was there something more from that time frame that I had missed?

"I'm telling you—I have no idea what you're saying."

"You don't remember your cousin Billy's suicide?"

Suicide? My cousin?

"No," I said. My breathing was suddenly difficult. I could feel my palms getting wet.

"He killed himself before the trial ever commenced. They found him in your house."

"What? I have no recollection of that. You must be lying. I would have known if what you say is true. Especially if it happened in my house."

"I am sure you knew I blackmailed your father but didn't know the sordid details. He never told you the part about him being gay or having sex with Billy, did he? I heard everything from Billy's lips. It would have destroyed your father in that day and age if his story had leaked. It would even have given rise to suspicion that he had participated in the rape of that boy. Your father never forgave me for taking advantage of the situation. I'm betting he told you just enough for you to want to even things up by killing Julie and trying to kill me. I was the one you were really after. Admit it."

"You're out of your mind. I don't know about any of this and don't believe that it's true. And I did not kill Julie or attack you!" I said as I rose to my feet.

"What I have establishes your motive, and the cops already have proof of opportunity," he said almost gleefully. "I just need to give the police the tape."

"I didn't do it. I swear," I said as calmly as I could. "Why are you telling me all this?"

"Because I am willing to make a deal with you. I can never forgive you for what you did to Julie, but I have a more immediate need than watching you suffer. I will get even with you, I promise that. But in the interim, I have a certain patient who is causing me problems, serious problems. I need to make them go away. I happen to know that he does not have an alibi. If you help me with him, I won't pass on the information about you to the police. Instead, I can say that, after all the confusion has passed, I now remember seeing him outside my office. If you back me up with some information about his hatred of me, he will go down for the murder, and my problem will go away."

"I don't need an out. I didn't commit the crimes!" I said, pounding on his desk. "If you have evidence that he did, you should go to the police."

"I know you did it. Just admit it to me, and it will go no further—at least for now. As I said, I'll figure out that part later. If you don't go along with my plan, I will tell the police about your father and his involvement with Billy. In addition to establishing motive, it will tarnish your family name," he said, standing up behind his desk.

"And admitting to two crimes I did not commit and framing someone else for them won't? You can't be serious," I said flippantly.

"Better than going to prison for murder and attempted murder. What do you say?"

"I can't agree to that. And you know it."

I staggered out of his office and hailed a cab home. I still had not fully absorbed his accusations about my father being gay and blackmailing him. Was Abner making this up to protect himself from being charged with Julie's murder? Why else would he be willing to pin the blame on a patient?

I went home and found Beth waiting in the kitchen. Her head was bent over, but I could see her gnawing on her lip. She pulled out a plain white envelope and handed it to me. It contained a couple of very old newspaper clippings about Billy's suicide while he was out on bail with the criminal sodomy charges pending. It had to have come from Abner.

Beth asked about the articles, and I told her the story that Abner had shared with me. She asked me if I thought going preemptively to the police would be better than waiting for Abner to contact them, and I agreed with her. I telephoned Ed and laid out the story for him. Ed was concerned that I would be giving the police evidence of motive to use against me.

"I swear I only learned about the events involving my cousin a few hours ago," I said.

"That's awfully convenient and hard to swallow. It was in the newspapers, for God's sake. How could you have missed a story about your own cousin?"

"I was young. I didn't read the newspapers regularly."

"And no one mentioned it to you? The police aren't likely to buy that."

"I can't prove it, but it's true. We need to tell the police."

Ed called Detective DeCarlo the following morning. He and I traveled to the station that afternoon to meet with her and Hayes. We sat in the same windowless interview room as before. I brought the newspaper clippings and used them to describe the conversation with Abner from the previous afternoon. I did not get any reaction, except to the part about framing a patient.

"You're saying Dr. Reeves wants to frame a patient of his?" asked DeCarlo, looking at her fingernails before returning her gaze to me. "Now that would avoid charges against you, but what's in it for him? What does he have to gain by blaming a patient for the murder?"

"I don't know. Maybe to deflect attention away from his own guilt. He said something about the patient being a danger to him."

"You sure it wasn't the other way around?" asked Hayes. "You weren't the one to suggest blaming the patient?"

I looked him in the eyes. "It was his idea."

"That's not what he says," Hayes stated. "He says you brought up the whole thing about your father to explain your actions and then asked *him* to frame a patient."

"What? Why would I confess to him? That's crazy. I didn't even know about my cousin until Abner told me yesterday."

"Well, where did you get those old articles if you didn't know anything about the suicide?"

"They came in the mail yesterday. My wife can vouch for that. Obviously, Abner sent them."

"So you admit now that your father paid Dr. Reeves off to conceal the fact that he was gay and may have been involved with the rape of a boy?" DeCarlo asked.

"I don't believe that. Abner told me that, but it doesn't make it true."

"Dr. Reeves claims he has a tape recording in which your father admits to the payoff," Hayes interjected.

I shook my head at the suggestion. "That tape is ambiguous, and who knows if it is even authentic?"

"Oh, so you admit the tape exists?"

Ed interrupted: "Look, we came down here to expose Reeves's plan to frame a witness. I don't know what kind of half-cocked story Reeves has made up, but Tim knows nothing about it other than what he read in the papers and what Reeves told him. It's preposterous to think Tim murdered Mrs. Reeves to get even with her husband twenty years after Mr. Reeves supposedly blackmailed his father. It's utter nonsense."

I could not figure out what Abner was up to. He had beaten me to the police and lied about our conversation. I didn't know how the police would determine when I became aware of the trouble involving my cousin. Even the tape contained nothing indicating that I'd been aware of what was going on. I asked Ed to get in touch with Eve and get an affidavit from her that she, too, had not known anything about our cousin's suicide or any blackmail scheme until I raised it with her this past week.

First the fingerprints. Now the tape and the news stories. I needed a break in the case and had no idea where to look for it. The sessions with my patients had not revealed anything useful in pointing the finger at someone else. At least not yet.

# 5

A storm had blown through during the night, and the air was clean and dry for a midsummer morning. Philip was my earliest appointment. He came from a broken home that his mother left because her husband was abusive. His father, a drinker like Philip, had an on-off switch that, when triggered by booze, turned him into a man looking for a fight. Philip loved his sons but picked on them physically when he consumed alcohol, the way his father had picked on him. He was anxious to explore the causes of his anger, and we agreed to delve into them at our next session.

My ability to keep my mind off the murder investigation vanished quickly after seeing a couple more patients. I did not have a sense of our defensive strategy. We should be in the police's face, pitching our position as the correct one, factually and legally. If that meant going after Abner and his credibility, then that was what we needed to do.

I telephoned Ed that afternoon and voiced my concerns. He convinced me that the real forum for a presentation was the Manhattan District Attorney's Office. He had had some preliminary discussions with ADA Micha Brenner, and she was still evaluating the evidence she had, but Ed said it was too early for a full-blown pitch to the office since we did not have a compelling story about the knife.

He warned me to get things in order at home just in case the DA's office decided to move ahead quickly and things didn't go well for us. I had not told the kids anything about the investigation thus far, so Beth and I sat down that evening in one of our defeatist moods and sketched out what we would tell them when the opportune time arose. We wanted to put that off as long as possible. There was a risk that they'd read something on the internet about the investigation, but since it wasn't public, we calculated that risk as low.

Beth had been supportive in the last several weeks. Naturally, she had her questions, and some of them stung, but she seemed willing to stand by me. We had a candid discussion that night about how she felt.

"You can never truly know another person completely, Tim, so I don't really know what you are capable of. I know you well enough to believe you would never take a life except to save your own, or maybe one of ours. It's absurd to think that you would do so to get retribution for your father. The thing I keep coming back to is the knife. You have to offer a plausible explanation to the DA's office about your fingerprints."

"Don't you think I know that? I have to figure out who is trying to frame me and why. If it isn't Abner, then who? Then maybe I can find out how he or she got my fingerprints on the knife."

"I don't know how important this is, but I was at a charity event this afternoon. There was a lot of drinking and, with it, a lot of loose talk. There was speculation about Julie's murder. People found it odd that Abner survived the attack with only a bump on the head. The most salacious rumors were that he was having an affair and he and Julie were not getting along."

The police had probably heard about Abner's alleged affair and were chasing down that lead. But I still had Beth join me on a call to Ed the next morning with the new intelligence she had picked up at the event. If Abner was having an affair, he and his girlfriend would be lying low at this point and not drawing attention to themselves.

At about eleven a.m. the next morning, I met Liz for another cup of coffee. We went to the same coffee shop and sat at the same table. I had to avoid staring at her because I had never seen her look prettier, in her tailored suit with a short skirt. She was always dressed fashionably.

"Another consultation, okay? This new guy is a referral from Abner. I've only seen him once, but he was incredibly hostile to me. Anyway, I tried to get a sense of why he wants therapy and what he hopes to accomplish. He said he has trouble getting along with other people, especially women. I asked him to elaborate, and he got all defensive, accusing me of being pushy. I asked him how his difficulty getting along with people affects him, and he said he spends a lot of time alone with his widowed mother."

She stopped to sip on her coffee. I could see that some might regard her as forward or direct, though I doubted she was pushy with her patients.

"Did he say anything inappropriate to you?"

"Other than calling me pushy? I guess not, but I know what he meant."

"Sounds a lot like a patient I am currently seeing. His difficult relations with women contribute to his sense of loneliness. Does this happen with male patients often?"

"What? That they are put off by my gender?"

"I guess so."

"You mean, do I intimidate some men because of the way I look?" she said, staring at me with her head tilted slightly, as if fishing for a compliment.

"Whoa. I did not say anything about the way you look," I said, cringing.

Her lips curved up in a coquettish smile. "No, you didn't."

I held up my hands and said, "Liz, most men are going to be fine with a woman therapist, and a few won't be. You won't know with this guy until you give him a chance. You want me to ask him before his next session? I can call him in the name of customer satisfaction and ask him how it's going. Sue doesn't have to know."

"That would be awesome. Thank you!" she said, reaching for my hand.

I let her hand linger on mine for a few seconds before pulling away. I was tingly inside from the touch and my heart was racing. I was acting like an immature high school student who could not distinguish between meaningless flirtation and a come-on.

"Not a problem," I said, nearly stumbling over my words. "I'm always available to help you."

While walking back to the clinic, she hung close to my side. I could smell her perfume again. I was grateful that, when the elevator came, several other people joined us for the ride up so I didn't have to be alone with her in cramped quarters.

Making good on my promise to Liz, I telephoned Nick McCann that afternoon.

"Mr. McCann. My name is Timothy Shea, and I'm on the administrative staff at the Sommers Clinic. After a patient's first session, we like to follow up and determine their reaction to the services we provided and the service provider. Can you tell me how your first session went?"

"It was all right," he said.

"I see you are being treated by Dr. Schreiber. Do you feel that you can establish a rapport with her?"

"I don't see why not. She was a little aggressive with me, but when I pointed that out, she backed off. She seems fine."

"In particular, we wanted to make sure that you don't have any issue with being seen by a woman. Is there any reason you would want to consider a change of therapists?"

"I am just interested in getting help. Don't particularly care who from as long as they're good."

"I'm glad to hear that everything is fine. It looks like you are seeing her again tomorrow. If there is any issue with that, you can reach me at the clinic."

"Thank you, Doctor. I don't think there will be any problem."

"That's great to hear. Goodbye."

While the conversation was fresh in my mind, I went to Liz's office. She came around to the front of her desk, sitting on the corner and showing off her toned legs. I tried not to glance at them, but I think she saw my eyes wander in their direction for a split second. I straightened up and looked in her eyes.

"Your patient did not seem hostile or agitated about having a woman therapist, or you in particular. He says he just wants to ensure that he is getting quality care, and I told him you were great. I think you should continue to see him unless you get any contrary vibes."

"Thanks. I appreciate the advice," she said, touching me on the shoulder.

I was a few minutes late for my appointment with Brett Stone. He was adjusting to the idea that he could actually get along with women in his age group. That discussion led us back to the major heartbreak in his life and the woman he'd been in love with a few years ago.

"I realize she is responsible for the fact that I don't trust women," he said. "It took me several years to start dating again, and my first foray back into the dating game turned out to be a disaster when I got physical with the woman. That was when I sought counseling and connected with Abner."

"Have you started dating again?"

"Yes, but I still have emotional issues, especially with women in positions of authority. I get aggressive around women in charge and am disrespectful. I suppose it's true with men as well, to a lesser extent. Take Dr. Reeves, for example. He shouldn't have taken advantage of his position as my doctor," Brett said, rubbing his temples.

"What do you mean?" I asked.

"I told you. He asked me to do some inappropriate stuff."

"But you wouldn't tell me what," I noted.

"Still won't."

"Why not?"

"Because I don't trust him. He has ways of finding out things, and no offense, but you're a friend or at least a colleague of his, so I don't want to talk to you about this."

I let it drop, and we spent the rest of the session talking about his issues with women, but the fact that two of Abner's patients had said essentially the same thing bothered me. What had Abner done, and how bad was it? If neither patient was willing to tell me, would they tell the police? I doubted it. Since they each mentioned it, I thought that they were looking to get it off their chests. I just had to make them comfortable and convince them I was the right person to tell.

I went into my home office that evening and pulled the door shut. I wanted to see if John's issues with Abner stemmed from the same thing as Brett's. I yanked John's clinic file folder from my briefcase and searched for any information

Abner might have entered about their last few sessions together. The notes were very plain and revealed nothing. I paid particular attention to their last meeting, and the only thing I saw was a reference to John crying during the session. There was no evidence in the file that he had ever cried in any other sessions, and I wondered what brought on such a reaction.

Looking at my watch, I saw that it was getting late. I turned off the light and headed up to bed. As I prepared to retire, I kept on having the same thought: Was it time to let the clinic know about Abner and the possibility that he was making some of his patients do things they were uncomfortable with to secure their secrets? I wanted to have as much information as possible before making that decision.

# 6

The morning sun peeked into our room and woke me early the next day. I left Beth sleeping in the bed and took a shower. I stopped in the kitchen after I got dressed to start the coffee machine and pop some bread in the toaster. I then rushed into my home office to grab my files and put them in my briefcase. The files I had looked at the previous night were not on my desk. I looked in the desk drawers and found nothing.

I went upstairs to rouse Beth. I asked her if she had touched my files, and she said no. I then summoned Samantha and Evan from their rooms and met them in the second-floor hallway.

"Guys, there is some stuff missing from my office. Did either of you go in and touch my files last night?"

"Nope," Samantha said.

"Me neither," Evan said. "What's missing?"

"Some papers I need for work."

"Why would you think we took that?" Samantha said, scrunching her nose.

"I don't. Just checking if you maybe moved them."

I went back to my office and searched again. I felt a slight breeze and checked the door and windows. There was a broken pane of glass in the window next to the rear door. Someone had apparently reached through that hole and unlocked the door. I telephoned the police to report the break-in.

I stayed at home long enough to meet with two officers who came by a few minutes later. They examined the room and concluded, as I had, that someone had broken the window and opened the door from the inside. I told them no valuables had been stolen and only a few files were missing. I explained that we only kept hard copy, paper files and that they were therefore important.

I called Sue to explain why I would be late. She was concerned that this had something to do with the clinic. When I arrived there later, she came by my office and had a lot of questions, especially which files had been stolen. I told her that John's clinic file was one. She rubbed her hands together as if worried.

A few minutes later, I heard a knock at my door and looked up to see Liz leaning on the doorjamb. I invited her in. She told me she had heard about the burglary, and I said I was still trying to make sense of it. She asked if there was anything in the files that anyone could find useful. I said they could embarrass John by releasing the information, but that was all.

She lingered. "I met with that patient, Nick, this morning," Liz said. Her eyes were wide and inviting. She clearly wanted to tell me something about their session. "He was less hostile this time but still had an edge to him. His animosity toward women seems to be based on issues with his mother. She is a pretty tough character, from what I can gather. He is thirty-nine and still lives with her. She controls every aspect of his life. He is anxious to talk about it, but I also think he is embarrassed."

"That's okay. He must be comfortable with you if he's talking."

"I wouldn't go that far. There are times he looks at me with anger in his eyes, like I've gone into forbidden territory. And the way he watches me when I move around the room is creepy."

"But he's opening up to you. That's the important thing."

"Agreed. He even mentioned that he has violent thoughts from time to time. I think they must be directed at his mom."

"Does Abner have him on anything?"

"Yes. Zoloft. That should help."

"Are you worried about him turning violent?"

"He hasn't given me any indication of that yet, and he's very attuned to what he's feeling. I don't think he is prone to violence, especially on his meds, which he is good about taking. Are you worried about me?"

I rubbed the back of my neck, feeling flushed. "Not exactly worried about either of you, though my antennae are up. The violence thing always gets my attention, especially lately."

"Me too. I think I'm going to play this one by ear, one session at a time," she said. "As you said, he is talking about his feelings and receptive to what I say."

At four p.m., John came in for his appointment. I told him what had happened with his file but that I doubted the thief would publish its contents. More likely, the file contained something that was of interest to them, and we should try to figure out what it was.

"I'm concerned," John said. "I think Dr. Reeves put somebody up to it."

Abner was the only one other than us who knew what was in the file. He had written much of the material himself.

John continued, "Things happened during my sessions that Dr. Reeves wouldn't want on any record. He could get in trouble for them."

"You aren't the first of Abner's patients to suggest the same thing. I can't do anything about it, however, since no one is willing to give me any details."

"It was a form of blackmail," John said. "He asked me to do things, or else he would publicly expose some of the things I'd confessed to him in confidence."

"That's a start. Will you tell me more?"

"No, because I don't want anyone to know the things I said to him, not even you. Too much about me has already leaked, and Dr. Reeves knows a lot more."

"You've told him things that you haven't told me?"

"To get the drugs, I'd tell him anything. In retrospect, I shouldn't have, but I didn't think he would use what I said against me," John said almost apologetically. "He's a bastard."

"What about the things he asked you to do? Will you tell me what those are?"

"If I do, he'll find out. He'll make good on his threat, and I'll be screwed. If I don't say anything, he won't say anything. That's the way it works. 'Silence for silence,' to quote him."

That sounded a lot like Abner's "silence for money" comment to my father.

"Is that why you got mad at him?"

"Yes, because he holds the trump card and loves to wave it around to get me to do things I don't want to do. He's still trying. The only thing that will help me is Reeves dying."

"Don't say that."

"I didn't mean it as a threat."

When we had finished talking about Abner, we turned to John's anxiety and depression. His mother's premature death from cancer had been the start of his bouts with mental illness. He was a cutter who used scissors on his arms and legs and then picked at the scabs. He wore long-sleeve shirts and pants as camouflage but also as a deterrent. The drugs Abner had prescribed for him helped, and so did the exercises we talked about in our sessions. He was hurting himself less as grief ran its course, but the anxiety was still there, and I attributed it in part to Abner.

John had admitted that he had a motive to hurt Abner, maybe even kill him or his wife. Still, I did not believe John was the killer. True, I had begun the discussions with him hoping that he would say something incriminating, but much like Brett, it seemed that John was actually Abner's victim, not the other way around. He was obviously tortured by what Abner was doing to him, yet he seemed to accept that there was nothing he could do about it. And what he'd said about Abner dying felt more like a throwaway comment than a threat or a confession.

"John, I can't get to the root cause of your anxiety and depression without fully understanding your history with Abner. You seem to be coming to grips with everything else. Whatever is going on with Abner is too important in the overall scheme of things."

"You know Dr. Reeves is a big contributor to my stress level. The details of what he has done are inconsequential," he said, grabbing the arms of the chair so tightly that I could see the strain in his biceps and wrists.

"You are never going to fully master your illness if you don't confront the most serious threat to your emotional well-being, and that is your subservience to Abner Reeves."

With an exasperated shake of his head, John stood, grabbed his jacket, and headed for the door. "I confront it every day. I just don't want to talk about it."

John's limits on what he would share with me had to be based on fear and uncertainty. Abner held the cards and had been using them to exploit John for his own purposes. I wondered if he had been doing this with other patients aside from John and Brett. I was determined to find out.

That afternoon, I had a message from Abner. I was leery about calling him back. Nevertheless, I sat back in my chair and dialed his cell. He answered on the first ring.

"Abner," I said, "my lawyer says we should not talk about the case. Is there something else you want to talk about?"

"Yes. I want to tell you I have discovered that John Rankin is a pathological liar. I found out a number of the things he said to me during our sessions are utter falsehoods. You need to be careful in relying on what he says."

"You think he is lying to me about his history?"

"I do. I know some things about him that I haven't shared with you. I don't know if you are still treating him, but if you are, be skeptical of what he says."

"And why should I believe you after you've lied to the police about our conversation?" I asked pointedly. "You're not trying to protect me."

"You're right about that. I told you I had a patient who was causing me trouble. It's John. He is waging a campaign of vicious lies about me and will try to use you as the mouthpiece. If you follow him down the rabbit hole, you will force me to take steps that will be disastrous for you."

"What are you afraid of, Abner? That he'll tell the truth about you?"

"Listen to me, Tim. You've already caused me great anguish. I will do what I need to do to stop you from adding to that, and you and your lawyer won't like it. Goodbye."

The timing of Abner's call bothered me. He could easily have checked the schedule and known that I had spoken with John earlier that day. Abner must have been afraid that John would divulge whatever Abner had made him do and wanted me to stay out of it. My legal position was already tenuous enough; I didn't need Abner to interfere more. Though I recognized that John might be lying too, I had no doubt that Abner was trying to erode my confidence in his accuser. The last thing Abner wanted was patients casting aspersions at him that could ruin his reputation or worse.

I went to talk to Sue after finishing up with Abner. I figured she was in league with Abner, but she was still the chief administrator. I had to run this up the flagpole with someone in charge.

"I'm considering giving up John Rankin as a patient because he is not being forthcoming with me about some traumatic events in his life. It's hard to counsel him without knowing the full story."

"I should think you'd be used to that by now. Many of them keep secrets. If you stick with him, he might come around to being more open with time."

As we were talking, I noticed a clinic file on her desk. They all looked pretty much the same except for the scribbling on the front cover. I tried to get a closer look at it, and, noticing my roving eyes, Sue pushed some other papers on top of it, but not before I made out the *Ra* in blue marker pen on the cover. I used blue marker pen to mark clinic files and recognized my scribble. It had to be one of the files that had gone missing from my place, yet I said nothing.

How had Sue gotten that file, and did she have the others? There was no chance that she had broken into my house, so she had to have gotten it from someone else. Had Abner put someone up to it? Had he done it himself? I was willing to bet that John's file had been altered. I was one of the few people familiar enough with it to detect the alterations, but since Sue had not told me John's file had appeared, she clearly wanted to hide it from me. I still had the feeling that Sue had a thing for Abner and would protect him at all costs. I had been getting along without the file for some time. Sneaking into her office a second time would be risky, so I had to figure out another way to see those files.

A couple of days later, the police who had been to my house after the burglary visited the clinic. I saw them enter Sue's office and knew why they were here, since I had given them an anonymous tip that the stolen files had reappeared. The tip evidently caused them to reach out to Sue to see if it was true and whether the files were still intact. About fifteen minutes later, they came to see me in my office with Sue.

Officer Hanson reintroduced himself and his partner to me and said that they had retrieved what looked like the files that had allegedly been stolen from my home office. He dropped them on my desk and wanted me to verify that they were one and the same. He stood there with his arms crossed.

"Dr. Harnish here says they just showed up on her desk a couple of days ago. Very strange," Hanson said.

"Let me look at it and see if there is anything missing from the one file I know well," I said.

I leafed through John's file, keeping in mind what I remembered of it. After a few minutes, I closed the file and handed it back.

"It's been tampered with," I said. "There are pages missing, mostly notes from Dr. Reeves. Someone selectively removed pages."

Officer Hanson asked, "Why would anyone do that?"

"I don't know," I replied. "Maybe there was something sensitive in there that the thief did not want anyone to see."

"But who would see the files other than you, Dr. Reeves, and Dr. Harnish?" the officer asked.

"No one that I know of," I offered.

"Somebody didn't want one of you three to see what was in those files? That doesn't make sense. You already had access to them."

"I don't get it either," I said. "But some papers have disappeared. There is no longer a record of various things that transpired."

"This is all pretty weird. We're going to take these and dust them for fingerprints, but I don't understand why anybody would screw around with the files," Hanson said. "Which one was tampered with? John Rankin's?"

"Yes."

When they left, Sue stared at me with a look suggesting that she knew I had tipped off the police. She did not say anything, but I could tell she was angry. I don't know why she had concealed the fact that the files had shown up unless she knew that they had been altered. I wondered if she knew what the missing entries were and whether we would ever see them again.

# 7

It was now August, and the city was relatively quiet. The heat and humidity were unbearable, driving people to the mountains and the ocean. I desperately wanted to get out to see my sister and her kids and take some time at the shore.

As I was getting ready to call Eve about that, Ed telephoned me and said the police and ADA Micha Brenner wanted to ask me some questions. He had tried to put them off, but they told Ed that this might be the last time I would have the opportunity to respond to their inquiries. They were willing to give me an immunity or "Queen for a Day" letter that forbade them from using what I said against me except to prove that I lied.

We met the next morning with Hayes, DeCarlo, and ADA Brenner. A short time later, a second ADA joined the meeting. After reviewing the proffer letter, we started going over the evening of Julie's murder. We covered my arrival at the house and how I went back and forth between the front door and the basement office, trying to get someone's attention.

"I must have arrived after Abner was knocked out because I made quite a racket, and he didn't come to the door. If he were awake, he would have at least heard me. Anyway, that's when I went back to the front door of the house," I said.

"Is that when you discovered that the front door was open?" Brenner asked.

"I'm pretty sure my pounding on the front door at the end was what jarred it open."

"You didn't push on the door? It just opened?"

"I knocked pretty hard, as I said, and it opened a few inches. I called out and, hearing nothing, pushed the door open."

"And then you went in the house?"

"Into the hallway, yes."

"And from there you went and got the knife?"

"No, I did not go beyond the hallway and never got a knife," I said, raising my voice.

"How do you explain your fingerprints on the knife?"

"Unless they remained there from July Fourth, I can't."

"You're saying that, of all the people at the barbecue, including your wife, the only prints that stuck to the knife were yours, and they were there for two weeks?" Brenner asked.

"I don't know how that could be, but it's the only explanation I have. I did not touch a knife in the Reeves house the night I was there."

"Now, you dislike Dr. Reeves, don't you?" Brenner continued.

"No, I don't dislike him. I no longer trust him. There is a difference."

"Didn't he blackmail your father when you were a child?"

"Wait a minute," Ed said. "We're not talking about events from years ago."

"It goes to motive," Brenner said.

"Abner recently told me that, but I had no idea before he did. And I don't believe it."

"And when did he tell you?" Brenner asked as she pulled out a file.

"Several days after the murder, and he sent me some articles about my cousin that supposedly buttressed his story."

She slid the file back to Hayes and continued after looking at her notes. "There was a tape, too, wasn't there?"

"That tape is ambiguous, and I'd suggest it was doctored," Ed objected.

"Yes, he played me a tape, but it didn't prove anything," I said.

"That's the same day he told you that you should confess to him and that together you'd blame your patient; do I have that right?" asked Brenner.

It sounded preposterous coming out of her mouth, and for the first time, I was really scared. I tried to control my leg from jiggling.

"Yes, that's right. I told him I didn't kill his wife or attack him and that I would not confess."

"What did you know about Dr. and Mrs. Reeves's marriage?"

"I had not heard about the affair or affairs, if that is what you mean."

"What affair?" Hayes asked, tilting forward in his chair.

"It's all over the street that Abner was cheating on his wife and Julie was upset. I had not heard it at the time."

"So as far as you were concerned, he and his wife were close and killing her would devastate him, right?" Hayes continued.

"I had no insight into their marriage. And I did not kill her."

I was getting aggravated and knew that was what they wanted. They were hoping my emotions would get the better of me and that I would say something stupid or against my interests. I had to control my temper.

"You were actually looking for her husband when you went into the house, weren't you?"

"Yes, we had an appointment."

"And you intended to kill him, didn't you? You know what I think?" asked Hayes. "I think you went in, got the knife, and came upon Mrs. Reeves by surprise. When she saw you, she screamed, and you killed her. Then you went to kill her husband."

"That's absurd. Why would I leave the knife if I intended to use it again? I didn't kill or try to kill anybody." My tone did not conceal the umbrage.

"Why didn't you just kill Dr. Reeves too? You knocked him out. Would have been easy enough to do. Or did you try to kill him and just didn't hit him hard enough?" Hayes asked, standing up and gripping the ends of the table.

"I never stepped foot in his office that night. Besides, I had no reason to kill him. I didn't even know about the thing with my father, if that is even true, which I doubt."

"But you're a liar, aren't you, Doctor?" DeCarlo asked. "You lied about the knife, you lied about going in the house, and you lied about the files supposedly stolen from your home office."

"No, I didn't lie about any of those things."

"You faked the disappearance of your files to remove some entries that worried you, didn't you?"

"No."

"What do you say about the neighbor who saw you go into the house?"

"The neighbor would have seen me go in the hall and come back out thirty seconds later. I wasn't there long enough to kill anybody."

"What if she didn't see you come out thirty seconds later?"

"Then she must not have been looking."

The questioning continued for another forty-five minutes, and I was exhausted. After huddling among themselves, the prosecution team came back and said they'd have more questions for me at a later time. They asked me if I had any plans to travel and told me to stay in the metropolitan area.

I asked Ed on the way out if that was a normal proffer session. He said it was not unusual for them to be aggressive in their questioning. Apart from gathering information, they were trying to size up how I would perform on the witness stand. Ed thought that the neighbor's testimony might be important. He was going to send one of his investigators, Tom Ronaldo, to try to find out who the neighbor was and what he or she had said to the police.

Philip was my first appointment for the afternoon, and he came in loaded for bear. After drinking too much the previous evening, he had gotten into it with one of his kids again. He had not touched the boys in months with the help of anger management exercises and the Prozac, and I thought that he'd been making real progress.

"My oldest," he said, "got suspended for getting into a fight, and I slapped him. I felt horrible about it afterward, so I put an ice pack on his cheek to control the swelling before going to the bathroom to cry."

"How did you feel at that moment?"

"I felt like I had taken a step backward. I worry that my son's temper is just like my own. I don't want him growing up to be a fighter like his dad. And yet, after drinking some, I used my fists to discourage him from doing the same."

"Hitting your son is not okay, and I could report you because he's a minor.

There are medications available to help reduce your dependency on alcohol. Ignoring the problem will likely make it worse. You need to see a doctor to get a script."

"That's not my only issue. The cops questioned me again the other day. They claim I didn't leave Dr. Reeves's office until close to eight that night, even though I told them—*again*—that I left immediately after my appointment and went out for the night. Anyway, Dr. Reeves and I had an argument that night about my drinking, and he must have told the police about it. They said I had enough time after my appointment to kill Mrs. Reeves and return to the office to knock Dr. Reeves unconscious."

"Don't tell me anything else, because I don't want to become a witness. I'm no lawyer, and I don't want to get into the nuances of privilege and find that I have to testify against you."

"I don't give a shit about privilege. I did not do it, and I'm happy to have you tell the police I said that."

He then proceeded to tell me about the rest of the police interview. I learned that they had surveillance footage of the nearby street corner that showed Philip and a few others on the Reeves's street. I wondered if I was on the tape and whether it captured anything that transpired at the house itself. That would depend on where the camera was located, but I could get Ed to check that out.

I finished up at the clinic by five thirty and phoned Beth. She suggested an early meal at Verona's on West Fifty-First Street. I arrived at the bar around six fifteen and had a cocktail. Eric Denahy walked into the restaurant right past me and sat down at the bar a couple of seats away. Eric was a psychiatrist at Bellevue Hospital I had known for years. We would sometimes go out drinking together, but things had been too hectic lately to get together.

"I didn't know I was invisible," I said loudly enough for him to hear.

He looked at me and then his eyes widened. "Tim, how are you? Didn't see you sitting there by yourself." He came over at sat down next to me. "You alone tonight?"

"No. Waiting for Beth. You?"

"Same. Waiting for Marianne. So, how are things at the clinic?"

"The usual."

"Oh, I doubt that, with the Julie Reeves thing. Lots of rumors going around the hospital about the murder."

"Come on, what's the latest?" I asked. Eric had always been a rumormonger.

"That Abner himself is a suspect, but there are other persons of interest, including a patient. Constant chatter about this. This is not good for Abner's reputation. The guy built a career on being a stand-up citizen at the top of his field, and now he gets talked about in rumor mills. And all this talk about a young woman in her thirties."

"A young woman? I had not heard that. I heard he was having an affair, though," I said.

"She's the latest, although I don't know if the rumors are true. He and Julie were married a long time, whichever way that cuts. Lots of people have affairs without killing their spouses. Do you think the cops are any closer to making an arrest?"

"Who knows? We'd love to put this behind us at the clinic. It's a distraction, and it does not do our image any good."

"I bet. Oh, here comes your lovely wife," Eric said.

Beth greeted Eric with a gentle kiss and sat at the bar between him and me. We bought Eric a drink while he waited for Marianne. As we were finishing our drinks, his wife came in. They asked us if we wanted to join them for dinner, and we politely refused, citing date night.

Over a quiet dinner, I told Beth about Philip and his interview with the police. Then, I mentioned my conversation with Eric.

"He says the rumors at Bellevue are that Abner has himself a younger woman."

"Julie was a young woman herself," Beth remarked. "I heard that this one is really young from a friend at Lenox Hill. The place is abuzz about Abner and a woman in her early thirties."

"I don't place much stock in this sort of stuff. At the same time, I'd rather him be a suspect than me."

"Now, there is Philip too. And don't forget John," she said.

It was good to have an opportunity to spend some time with Beth. I had been taking her for granted for some time, and it seemed like we didn't really talk about anything other than clinic-related matters.

"Summer is flying by. Are you sure you want to go back this school year?" I asked.

"Yes. The kids are busy, and I wouldn't know what to do with myself at home."

"I don't know. I'm exhausted and could use a break."

"I can tell that you're tense. Sometimes I think you are unhappy."

She looked at me with knowing eyes. I wondered if my interest in another woman was apparent. I was trying to resist, but it was tough sledding.

"I'll be all right. Just some real malaise around the office over everything that's happened."

"You'd tell me if something was up, right?"

"Yes, I promise."

The kids were still up when we got home, and we spent some time with them, talking about the coming school year and what they wanted to do before it started. From upstairs, I heard a knock at the front door and wondered who would come by so late. I peered through the upstairs curtains and did not see anybody at the door. There was no second knock, so I relaxed. I told Beth I would check that the door was locked when I went downstairs for a nightcap. She asked me to bring her one.

After putting on my pajamas, I descended the stairs and got a couple of glasses of cognac. I stopped at the front door on the way back and opened it. There was a large envelope on the front stoop. I put it under my arm and took it upstairs with the two cognacs.

After handing Beth her drink and taking a sip of mine, I opened the envelope. There were about a dozen pieces of paper jammed in it, and I carefully removed them. It only took me a few seconds to realize that these were the missing pages from John's clinic file. Most of them were notes in Abner's handwriting, but there were a few pages in a different scrawl I did not recognize.

Where had they come from? I looked at the envelope for a clue, but it had no writing on it. Had the thief returned the pages, or did someone else find them and send them to me? Sue was the one with the files now. Had she removed these sheets from them at an earlier time, and if so, why?

I examined each sheet for alterations. They looked pristine, and they were sorted chronologically. Abner's notes were cryptic, and I could not always get the gist of them. The notes in the handwriting I did not recognize were more detailed. I had not focused on the different handwriting the last time I had gone through the notes and now realized that Abner had another doctor see John on occasion.

The other doctor's notes went back to the period before I started treating John. Abner had written a couple of entries indicating that John was "aggravated" and "hostile." It did not surprise me that John might have been in a sour mood during a few sessions, but *hostile* was a strong word. More alarming was the other doctor's more recent notation that John was "livid" with Abner. Then, I found an entry in the same handwriting from a few weeks later saying that John "lost it over something Dr. Reeves said."

I needed to find out who the other doctor was. I was not ready to tell John—or anyone else—I had the missing parts of the clinic files. I wanted to understand more about them before I sprung them on John.

"John," I said when I reached him the next morning, "I need some information. The police tell me the files they have on you show that a third doctor saw you before I did. I don't want to call Dr. Reeves and ask about this, but I'm wondering if you can help me out."

"I already told the police about her. Didn't you know?"

"No, neither you nor Dr. Reeves ever mentioned her."

"It's strange that Dr. Reeves didn't tell you. I assumed he had, as he was the one who asked me to see her. It was Dr. Schreiber from the clinic."

I should not have been surprised, but I was. Liz knew I was treating John, yet she had never said anything about having seen him. I wondered how long it had gone on and why they had stopped seeing one another. I hunted her down and told her it was my turn to buy her a cup of coffee. She seemed pleased with the invitation.

At three p.m., we went to our favorite café. We spent a few minutes catching up on things. She was her radiant self, and I liked looking at her.

"Liz," I said after sipping on my coffee. "I just learned that you saw my patient John Rankin a few times."

She looked at me curiously and said, "I thought you knew. Didn't Abner tell you?"

"No, he didn't."

"I'm sorry. I would have told you if I had known that."

"We can consider this a consultation so that you can share things with me. John is in a bad place right now and is thinking of quitting therapy even though he is making progress. Anyway, he seems to have some bad feelings toward Abner, which are coloring his thinking, and I was wondering if you have any information about that."

"That's the reason Abner asked me to see him. They had an odd relationship. John always seemed angry at Abner, but he went to his appointments and did not want to change doctors. I remember a couple of times John was really pissed and said that he got close to punching Abner. And yet, he'd go right back for his next session with Abner after seeing me," Liz said.

"What did Abner supposedly do?"

"I never knew," she said, sipping her coffee. "John would not tell me. I tried to get it out of him, believe me, but no dice. He was very up-front about the fact that this was not an area open to discussion."

Her lips turned down. She looked frustrated and demoralized, as if she had failed her patient.

"So what happened?" I asked curiously.

"I didn't seem to be doing him any good. I talked to him about how he needed to open up. It didn't change anything, and we parted ways about the time you started seeing him."

"Did you ever talk to Abner about their fights?"

"I tried that, too, but Abner said it was up to John to decide what about their relationship he wanted to share. I told John that he should get a new doctor, that he needed to be with someone he was comfortable talking to. I think that's how you got involved."

"I don't get that either. He still has hostility toward Abner that he won't let me in on. I'm afraid I'm going to lose him because I've been pressing him on that. It is clearly an unresolved issue he needs to face."

She shifted in her chair and continued to stare at me, jiggling her right ankle nervously.

"So that's why you wanted to have coffee?" she asked, pouting.

"Uh. Yeah."

She sighed, then uncrossed those shapely legs and stood up. She did not seem angry, but it felt like she was leaving in the middle of a conversation. In some ways, I was relieved to see her go. She was a temptress. After watching her leave, I closed my eyes and refocused on John.

# 8

My cell woke me up the next morning. It was Brett Stone, and he said that he needed to talk. I asked him if I could wake up and have a cup of coffee first. I got out of bed groggy and went downstairs to turn on the coffee machine. I listened to the weatherman predict afternoon thunderstorms as the coffee brewed. After the caffeine from the first cup hit me, I dialed Brett's number.

"What's up?" I asked.

We spent the next thirty-five minutes talking about his feelings of rejection and how they affected his attitude toward women. He told me that while he was still physically attracted to women, he had been experimenting sexually with men for some time, and he found the experience just as enjoyable. He'd begun to embrace his bisexuality despite his family's disapproval. He hinted that he had moved on from an older man to a younger one. Abner had been encouraging him to discover this side of himself.

"It was during this discussion that Abner said some inappropriate things to me," Brett said.

"Will you tell me what those were?"

"I can't."

"Why not?"

"Because I could get in trouble."

His story was too much like John's for me to think they weren't connected, but Brett's insinuation that Abner's directives were sexual in nature was a new piece of the puzzle. I had a hollow feeling that Abner had asked much of Brett and John and that was why they would not divulge it.

I was now in the position I had feared. I had privileged information indicating two of Abner's patients might have been motivated to beat Abner and kill his wife. And I was not able to reveal it to help my own defense. Even if neither had stabbed Julie, Abner's blackmail would be of interest to the police. The irony of the situation wasn't lost on me—both Abner and I were in possession of patient secrets we could exploit for our own good. The difference was that he deployed them in a blackmail scheme, whereas I wanted to find a lawful way to get the police information that might prove exculpatory in my case.

My curiosity about how widespread Abner's practice was got the better of me. I started to wonder about other patients. As I was noodling over that, Liz walked into my office.

"Hi, Tim. Sorry to drop in on you like this, but I need to talk to you. Nick is getting to me, and I've been meaning to see if you want to take him on. I can't stand any more of the leering—at least, not from him."

"Sure, I'm happy to take Nick on. Do you know if he had any problems with Abner?"

"The answer to your question is no. Nick only saw Abner a couple of times, and as far as I know, they got along fine."

"What about any of your other patients? Did any of them complain about how Abner was treating them?"

"Not really. Why do you ask?"

"I'll answer that over coffee—or a drink," I said as she turned to leave.

I had lunch with Sue at her invitation. She never asked me to lunch, so I knew she wanted something. She asked me if I would treat Nick because he was making Liz uncomfortable. She was disappointed that Liz couldn't handle Nick.

"She dresses so provocatively, it's no wonder male patients notice," Sue said.

Though I was loath to do anything for Sue, I agreed to take Nick on because I had promised Liz. After lunch, Sue and I returned to the office to find almost the entire staff in the lunchroom. There was a sea of long faces that prompted

Sue to ask what was going on.

"Haven't you heard?" Sue's assistant, Gloria, said. "Our patient Philip Greenberger was arrested for the murder of Julie Reeves and assault on Dr. Reeves. It just hit the news."

"What?" I exclaimed. "Did the police issue a statement?"

"Yes," Gloria said. "They said that Greenberger and Dr. Reeves argued the night of the murder. When he left his appointment with Dr. Reeves, Greenberger took the keys to the house off the doctor's desk and used them to get inside. Once there, he planned to wait for the doctor and stab him with a knife he got from the kitchen. Mrs. Reeves surprised him, and he panicked and killed her. He then headed back to the office, opened the door, and hit Dr. Reeves over the head, intending to kill him. He's been charged with first-degree murder, attempted murder, and assault."

I felt relieved, though I was sad that it was Philip who had been arrested. He had probably argued with Abner over his drinking, but that was a constant source of irritation between him and me as well. It was not the sort of thing that would cause someone, not even one as volatile as Philip, to go berserk and commit murder.

Two things about the police story did not make sense to me. First, why didn't Philip just kill Abner when he was in his office for the appointment when they were having their argument? That would have been the time that Philip would have been angriest, and Abner was right in front of him for the taking. And second, if Philip returned to the office while Abner was still conscious, wouldn't Abner have seen Philip before he was struck and later reported that to the police?

It was about six p.m. when I left the clinic, and I was mentally drained. When I got home, Beth gave me a warm hug despite my sweatiness and handed me a glass of wine. She had seen the news and thought our ordeal was over. I disappointed her because I did not feel like celebrating. I was tired and just wanted to go to bed.

The next morning was a glorious one, and the fact that Philip had been arrested sunk in. I went to the office and read the statement issued by his lawyer.

He asserted that Philip and Abner had not argued the night of the murder and that Philip had not stepped foot in the house. He claimed that Philip had left the area before the murder occurred, and they were therefore going to fight the case.

Abner telephoned me just after I'd finished reading the statement. I was reluctant to pick up the phone, as no good was coming from these conversations. But there was always the possibility that Abner would make a mistake and say something I could use against him.

"Hello, Abner. Why should I talk to you?" I asked. "You are just interested in building your own narrative. You're not concerned with the truth."

"I'm calling about the latest travesty. I don't believe Philip did it. I've told the police that. He didn't know Julie, and he had no problems with me that I know about. I mean, I saw him for treatment at seven o'clock, for God's sake, and he was fine. We had a little argument, but it was normal for me to bug him about his drinking. Not likely that he suddenly lost his mind and waited for an hour to attack."

"I've got my doubts too," I said, but left it at that.

"Of course you do. An innocent man is sitting in prison for something you did. That's just screwed up."

"Do you really think I killed Julie?"

"I do, and I think the knife proves it. You still don't have an explanation for the fingerprints on it, do you?"

"I'm not going to talk about this any further with you."

"That's what I thought. No explanation. By the way, did I tell you that I'm beginning to have a faint memory of seeing my attacker out the window before he broke in? You know, when he was pounding on the door?"

This was the first time I regretted not taping our calls.

"You've already said you didn't remember seeing me. No one would believe that now. Besides, I've admitted I was there."

"I said it was a faint memory, Tim. You better hope it doesn't improve now that the confusion from your blow to my head is clearing, because it would mean Philip was gone before the murder occurred."

"I don't understand why you are doing this. What do you want from me?"

"I just want my wife's killer to pay. We both know it wasn't Philip. Why don't you just admit to what you've done?"

"Well, you can kiss my ass. I'm not going to do that," I said and hung up.

Afterward, I strolled through the office to get rid of the tension. When I walked past Liz's door, it was just opening, and I was surprised to see John coming out. He had his back turned toward me and did not see me. I ducked into a nearby conference room to hide. I could not believe that Liz would see him behind my back.

While I was in the conference room, Ed telephoned me on my cell. I told him what Abner said. Ed dismissed it as an idle threat, since a change in Abner's story would be assailable on cross-examination after he'd been interviewed several times. He told me that Abner would not dare alter his version of events.

When I left the conference room, I tapped on Liz's door. She opened it and, when she saw it was me, gave me a broad, toothy smile.

"To what do I owe the pleasure?" she asked, standing there with her right hand on her hip.

"Did I just see John leaving your office?" I asked impatiently.

She turned red and fiddled with her necklace before responding. "Yes. I was going to tell you about it. He called the other day and asked to see me. Said he wanted to talk about his therapy."

"And you saw him without telling me?" I said. My tone revealed my annoyance.

She said, "Look, I was doing you a favor. He was not happy. He said you were pressing him about things he didn't want to talk about, and I explained that was part of your job. I encouraged him to stay with you."

"I'm sorry." I put my hands up. "I guess I'm a little sensitive when it comes to my patients."

The tension in her face subsided. "I understand. But you should trust your colleagues, especially me. I would not bad-mouth you, and I most certainly would not try to steal a patient from you."

I rubbed my hand across my mouth and looked at her. "I'm sorry. I feel stupid. Can I make it up to you? Have that drink we talked about?"

She gave me a beguiling smile and agreed—if I promised not to talk about John or any other patients.

"We can do that part now," she said. "I think John feels a little better since Philip was arrested, but he is still mad at Abner. I told him there was no reason to blame you for whatever Abner did or said, and that it was natural for you to want to find out about something that's bothering him. He seemed to accept that and is planning on coming to your next appointment."

"Thank you. Drinks at six?"

"Done," she said.

I knew immediately that I had made a mistake inviting her for a drink. I was hopelessly attracted to her and did not want to act on it, but I just had to. I suggested we go to the bar at Anna's, where I didn't think we'd be seen by anyone we knew. She said she would meet me there because she had an errand to run.

Shortly before six p.m., I walked down Forty-Second Street toward the restaurant. It was a hot August afternoon, and I took my jacket off and draped it over my shoulder. The city was sweltering, and people were walking sluggishly by the park. I crossed Madison Avenue and arrived at the restaurant precisely on time. I walked in past the maître d' and headed toward the bar area. The cool air-conditioned temperature inside was a welcome relief. I checked around the bar for tables, but they were all occupied, so I sat at the back end of the bar and ordered a martini.

Liz walked in a few minutes later. I waved to her, and she came over and sat down next to me. She pulled her stool close to mine.

"It's a scorcher out there," she said. "I must look sweaty."

"Nope," I replied. "You look . . . uh . . . fine."

She giggled and asked me what I was drinking, then ordered the same. The bartender brought us two dirty vodka martinis, and the ice-cold liquor felt good going down. There was no awkwardness coming from her, and I tried to be relaxed and casual too, even though she made me nervous. I wondered if she could tell.

I guess the alcohol helped, because by the time we were on our second drink, we had blown past the office talk and were getting to know each other. I told her about my wife and kids. She told me about her latest breakup. I said I was hoping to have my own practice in the city someday, and she said she wanted the same thing, but only after having a couple of kids.

She swiveled in her stool and placed her hand on my arm. "You've told me that you don't get out much. If you are going to live in New York City, you need to take advantage of what it has to offer. Like this. You have to relax and unwind, especially given our line of work."

"What do you do?" I asked. I was afraid it might sound too much like a pickup line.

"Apart from work? I exercise at the gym. I go out with my girlfriends once or twice a week and try to attend one cultural event every other week."

"You didn't mention dating."

"Still recovering from my last relationship. He was another older guy. It didn't work out. And it's hard to meet anyone worthwhile. There are a lot of jerks around. I'd rather be by myself, to tell you the truth."

"Can't imagine it's a problem for you to meet men," I said, immediately regretting it because it was wistful when I was trying to be cool.

"Thanks, but I'm set in my ways. Only special men need apply." She smiled at me. "Every once in a while, you get this puppy look in your eyes. Like I've said something suggestive."

"Really?" I could feel my face flush.

"You made my point. One minute I think you get it, and the next minute you act like you have no clue. What is it you want?"

"Jeez, Liz. I thought you knew."

"Timothy. I'm not stupid, but I can't read minds," she said, putting on her jacket and gathering her purse.

"Where are you going?"

"To give you the space you need to make up your mind. Thanks for the drink." She smiled and walked off.

I paid the check and took a cab home. The glare from the streetlamps hurt my eyes as we drove down Seventh Avenue. It was on the late side, and Beth could smell the liquor on my breath. She asked what I had been up to. I told her I'd needed a drink because of a conversation I had with Abner and filled her in on that.

"I don't know what you're worried about. The police already arrested Philip for the crime."

"That's true."

"Don't get all stressed. By the way, the reunion with your college friends is coming up."

"I don't feel like going."

"You have to. I thought you were looking forward to it. Is there something else going on? It's not like you to come home smelling of booze. And you missed your daughter's play today. She was crushed. What's up with that?"

"Oh crap, I forgot." My head was pounding from the martinis.

"I don't know what to think with the investigations and the weird behavior."

"I told you why I drank tonight. Can you please just back off?"

She left in a snit.

I went into my home office after a late dinner to relax. I was still awash in thoughts about Liz. I loved Beth and did not want to endanger our relationship, but I felt a growing attraction to Liz. My professional life was devoted to teaching my patients to get in touch with their feelings, but not necessarily act on them. There were consequences to actions that needed to be taken into consideration. Nevertheless, I knew deep inside it would not take much to push me over the edge with her.

My thoughts turned to Abner and how sad I was to know that the mentor I had once regarded as an altruistic genius turned out to be a deplorable man. How easily he confessed to shaking down my father. How simple it was for him to blackmail at least two of his patients. And now, he was prepared to lie about seeing me at this house the night of the murder. What had made him this way? For a psychologist such as myself, that was a burning question.

# 9

Abner, I learned, was born in 1960 in Utica, New York. I wanted to fill in some of the blanks between then and when I first met him, so I did a combination of research on my own and with Ed's investigator, Ronaldo.

His father, Gerald Reeves, was a foreman at the Utica Club Brewery, which made beer popular in upstate New York. He married Sarah Munroe of Schenectady before he went off to fight at the end of World War II. Gerry and Sarah had three children, Abner being the youngest. He had an older sister, Marge, and an older brother, Douglas.

Marge Reeves drowned in a skating accident. Her mother never recovered after that and went into a severe bout of depression. Gerry, who spent much of his afternoons drinking, could not keep up with the house and the kids, and the house was foreclosed on in the early sixties, when Abner was still a child.

The records of what happened after that were scant, but it appeared that Abner and Douglas wound up in a foster home in Utica and then an orphanage. At age fifteen, Abner was arrested for the robbery of a convenience store and sent to a youth detention center until he turned eighteen.

He enlisted in the post-Vietnam Army and was later accepted at a reputable university. There, he majored in psychology. We obtained information indicating that Abner had been threatened with expulsion over a cheating scandal. Another student claimed she'd let Abner copy her biology exam paper in exchange for some marijuana. The girl later retracted her story and left school, while Abner went on to graduate with honors, ace the MCATs, and be accepted at Downstate Medical School. He graduated in 1986 and did his internship and residency at NYU Langone Hospital in downtown New York.

I was particularly interested in his years at the orphanage and the youth detention center. I used Ronaldo to locate Abner's older brother Douglas, who still resided in the Utica area.

"Mr. Reeves," I said when I got him on the phone. "My name is David Sloan, and I'm a newspaper reporter writing a story on how your brother Abner surmounted the problems of his youth to become a leading psychiatrist and philanthropist."

"You want to talk to me? I haven't talked with Abner for almost twenty years. I'm surprised he actually made something of himself. He was always smart, maybe too smart for his own good, but he was also forever in trouble as a kid. He was always exploiting whatever advantage he thought he had. Always lying. He was good at it. Got away with murder. I don't want to speak out of school, but he was lucky not to get caught. Now, he's got everybody fooled, except me. I saved his butt plenty of times, but you think he remembers me now that he is rich and powerful? Shit, no. He couldn't be bothered with his big brother."

"Were you close as a family?"

"Naw, your story should talk about how bad we had it with a mom who went bonkers and an old man who drank himself to death. Abner did what he needed to do. Even as a little kid, he had a knack for having things turn out his way. Didn't matter what got in his path."

"How did he overcome the bad?"

"You know how some young studs use their fists to drive their point home? Well, Abner was the opposite. He wasn't a big kid, and he took quite a few beatings at the orphanage for being a wise guy. He didn't like that and became friends with the bullies, became their leader. They were mostly into pranks, and he was the kid who thought them up. And he almost always had an alibi for when they got caught."

"What can you tell me about Abner's marriage?"

He hesitated for a moment. "I don't know much. We stopped talking a few years after he got married. I think she had something to do with that. She was all refined and regarded me as a hick. He was kind of a ruffian, and I never saw him as the kind of guy who would settle down with a woman like that. But she polished him up and introduced him to the right people. She made him respectable, and I think he was grateful for that. I don't know how much he loved her. It seemed he mostly liked marrying up, but I couldn't tell you how close they were."

"This has been great. Do you mind if I call you with any follow-up questions?"

"Nope, just as long as you don't mention me in the story."

The walk through Abner's past made me think about my upcoming reunion of psych majors from college, which was on Saturday. Beth and I planned to drive to Westchester and back that night. I'd tried to get out of it multiple times, but Beth insisted that we go. I did not want to talk shop with anyone, but there was no way of avoiding it.

August was a weird time for a reunion. To my surprise, many took advantage of the summer to visit home and attend the event, and there was a good turnout. The ballroom was festively decorated and lined with yearbook and other photos of our class. The free bar loosened people up, and old friendships were reborn.

While I was talking to one of my close friends, Bart, a woman came up to us. Her name tag read "Kelly Pressman," and I had trouble placing her. Bart did not and gave her a kiss on the cheek and a hug. She looked at me sideways and smiled.

"Jesus, Tim. It's Kelly. Kelly Stevenson."

"Oh shit, Kelly. Of course. You look so different."

"Lost the glasses and a bunch of weight, but that's all," she said, giving me a peck on the cheek. "I'm still the same Kelly."

"Well, you look fab," Bart said. "I guess you got married too. Tell us about things."

We listened to her recount her life after college, which included med school, marriage, and three children. She was living in Manhattan and working at NYU Langone. I asked her in what field, and she said psychiatry. I told her I was a clinical psychologist working at the Sommers Clinic.

She released a low whistle. "You've had an interesting summer, then."

"Eventful. I don't know that I'd call it interesting."

"They locked up one of the clinic's patients for the murder of Abner Reeves's wife."

I cleared my throat and said, "That would be one of my patients."

"Oh man," Bart said. "I didn't know that. That was the murder on the Upper East Side a few weeks ago, right?"

Beth returned from getting a refill of her wine and joined the conversation, quickly picking up on what we were talking about.

"I thought for sure they were going to charge Reeves himself," Kelly said. "Lots of talk about him having a serious girlfriend. And the story about him getting knocked out but not killed seems kind of iffy."

"I keep hearing these rumors about an affair. Where are they coming from?" I asked.

Kelly shrugged. "Who knows, but they are all over Langone and other area hospitals. And supposedly, this wouldn't be his first."

I sipped my cocktail. "I had not heard that."

"Yes, he supposedly has a history of going after younger women. His wife reportedly knew of his extracurricular activities and put up with them because of the lifestyle he afforded her. He's also turned off a lot of people in the profession, and critics of his are coming out of the woodwork," Kelly said.

Bart jumped in, asking, "What has he done to antagonize people?"

"No one talks about that. Something to do with the way he treats patients. They complain about him to the next doctor they see."

"That's odd. Most of his patients love him," I said.

"Tim is too politically correct," Beth said. "Not all of Abner's former patients like him. He's pissed off a few."

I was stunned that Beth would talk about clinic business in this way with relative strangers. I glared at her. She sighed but clearly got the message and said no more about it.

"Always a couple who prefer a different doctor," I said, smiling.

At the earliest opportunity, I pulled her away and admonished her. She didn't take kindly to it.

"Why are you protecting Abner of all people?" she asked.

"I'm not, but I have to defend the clinic, especially in front of our competition."

"You're more likely to undermine the clinic's reputation by keeping an abusive doctor on board than by dealing with him swiftly and properly. This has already dragged on too long."

There was a certain logic to her position. Good crisis management demands that you find the disease and excise it before it spreads to other parts of the organization. There was evidence that Abner had manipulated or abused at least two of his patients, and the clinic was not remediating the situation because it did not know. I had not been forceful enough in advocating for change, partly because my patients would not divulge the details behind Abner's blackmail.

Beth and I talked about my dilemma on the car ride home. She was less sympathetic than I would have thought.

"You just can't sit on the information any longer," she said.

"But do I have enough to convince the clinic's board to investigate Abner?"

"What more do you need? The board members are honorable, aren't they? You may like controlling the flow of information, but you run the risk that he'll hurt others while you keep his nasty secret. What's stopping you?"

"I don't know who to trust. I'm very much alone in this."

It would have been nice to have an ally on the inside who felt the same way I did rather than go at it alone. If there was any chance of enlisting the support of others, I would have to convince John and Brett to give me a better idea of what Abner had done to them. Vague allegations would not engender the necessary outrage and concern among my peers. I needed specifics that would appeal to their sense of decency and propriety.

On Sunday morning, I got a call from Ed. He had talked to Abner's neighbor, Mrs. Edinger. She had looked out her window a little after eight p.m. the night of the murder and saw a man whom she later identified as me in police photos. I was supposedly loitering, walking back and forth between the house and Abner's office. She saw me pound on the doors before entering and figured the Reeves finally let me in. She closed her curtains at that point and went back to her TV show.

Since she had not stayed at her window long enough to see me leave, her statement did not help me establish that I was only in the house for thirty seconds or so. However, she provided one additional detail: She'd called the Reeves residence as soon as she'd noticed me nosing around and received no answer. That suggested that Julie Reeves was already dead at the time of Mrs. Edinger's call. There was no way the murderer would have gotten by me at the front door if the murder happened between eight and eight twenty, and the back door was closed off. It was more likely that the murder had taken place before I arrived or after I left.

We understood that the police had obtained surveillance footage from the street cameras around Abner's house. We did not know if the camera covered Abner's front door, but perhaps the footage corroborated the fact that I had only been in the house a short while and could not have committed the murder. It may have been the footage that led the police to arrest Philip instead of me.

With Philip's arrest, I focused again on the clinic and what to do about Abner. I googled the clinic's five-person advisory board to get a sense of who would be in Abner's camp. I knew the several board members whom Abner was closest to. I looked for any who were not beholden to him for their positions. There was one, Dr. Melissa Fitzgerald. She had only been appointed to the board three years ago, and not at Abner's urging. She was a psychiatrist also but did not appear to have any deep professional ties to him. Since she worked with young adults, I hoped she would be sensitive to stories about Abner using a young patient's history to blackmail him.

If I was going to the board, I needed to be prepared. I focused on the notes I had taken during patient sessions even though I knew I would not be able to use them directly. I pulled together the snippets from John's file that I thought bolstered the presentation I had to deliver. I spent the rest of my Sunday night dissecting Brett's file.

Brett had said that revealing what Abner knew could get him in trouble, so I automatically assumed he had confessed to Abner to having done something to a girl or young woman. Abner had one entry in his notes from about a year ago with the words *no consent?* That could mean many different things, but given Brett's problem with women, I naturally assumed the worst. If Brett had forced himself on someone, would he have confessed to Abner? Abner clearly had something on Brett, and maybe that was it. Or it could have been perfectly innocent use of the term *no consent.* Since the words themselves did not provide an answer, I resolved to ask Brett about his discussion with Abner.

There was another recent file entry I found interesting: the word *John.* Was this reference to our patient John Rankin or someone else with the same first name? As far as I knew, John and Brett did not know one another, so I assumed it was the latter. Again, I would have to ask Brett.

I was also scheduled to see Nick in the coming week and still did not have a lot of background on him. That would give me an excuse to sit with Liz and have her tell me about their sessions. I looked at the files she'd given me on him and went through them quickly. From what I read, I concurred with Liz's decision to refer Nick to a male psychologist.

I was anxious to talk with her because she would no doubt be able to give me insights I could not glean from the files. However, I had to ask myself if that was the only reason I wanted to meet with her.

# 10

When eleven a.m. Monday rolled around, I strolled down the corridor to Liz's office and tapped on the door. She was expecting me and told me to come in. I did and closed the door behind me. She was seated at her glass desk, and the sunlight from her window cast a reflection off her silken hair.

"I enjoyed the drinks the other night," she said. "We'll have to do that again."

I stood behind her guest chair with both hands on its back. "I need to talk to you about a couple of things, and I want to start by clearing the air. I don't know how to say it without either offending you, which is not my intent, or embarrassing myself or both of us. This is really awkward for me."

She laughed gently. "It's okay, Tim. I know."

"You know what?" I came to a stop and met her gaze, and as I did, I saw a glimmer of recognition in her eyes. I sighed. "Is it that obvious?"

"Sometimes, but it's cute."

"Oh God, that's not the reaction I wanted. I don't know what the fuck I'm doing. Given all the sensitivity training we've done around here, I have been worried you'll think I am harassing you."

"Just relax. Though your looks can be very expressive, I am not offended. To the contrary. But let's let it develop naturally. I admit to being interested, but I haven't made up my mind yet."

"Shit. Paranoid psychologist rejected. That's embarrassing."

"It shouldn't be. I haven't said no. I said I was interested. The surest way to make me decide is for you to become overbearing."

"Okay. I hear you," I said. I relaxed a little at the positive feedback.

We spent the next fifteen minutes talking about Nick and his situation with his mother. He was so totally committed to her that he had no real life of his own—at thirty-nine, he had only lived away from home for a couple of years. She was healthy but bordering on hypochondriac. Nick knew she overplayed that hand, but it made him feel important and useful. Most of the women he dated viewed his living situation as a red flag, and he had not had a serious relationship in years. He mostly stayed home to care for his mother, though he fought with her to gain some independence.

He was growing more aggressive with her, and Liz worried that he was reaching his breaking point. His newfound aggression surfaced in their sessions, where he became reluctant to follow Liz's advice and sometimes even cross. He was flexing his muscles with Liz and probably with his mother, too.

When we finished talking about Nick, I turned the conversation to my concerns about Abner.

"What would you say if I told you I think Abner is blackmailing his patients with information they had shared with him in confidence? That he is suggesting they do—and maybe even forcing them to do—things they find offensive?"

Liz looked at me like I was from Mars. "That's a pretty serious allegation, Tim. You have any proof?"

"Not exactly. I know this is what my patients are mad at Abner for, but so far none of them have been willing to reveal the details. They are afraid of what Abner has on them, but they are also tired of doing what he demands. I think something is going to give."

"I find this hard to believe. Abner cares deeply about his patients."

Had I miscalculated? Was she too loyal to Abner to consider that what his patients were saying might be true?

"The only solution is for the clinic to do an investigation and develop the proof on its own."

"What makes you think the patients will come forward?"

"I don't know if they'll tell all the details, but if I could just get them to admit they are being blackmailed, that might be enough. We need to prevent this sort of thing from happening again. If Abner manipulated his patients, the clinic would probably have to get rid of him to address the problem."

"There is no way this place is going to throw Abner out. He is the institution, and the fact that he may have made a couple of mistakes won't detract from his overall record. The board will never do it."

I threw my hands up. "You can't dismiss these as mistakes. His actions were intentional. Blackmail is a premeditated crime, and he is the beneficiary of whatever actions he is making them take," I insisted.

She came over and placed her hand on my shoulder. "Look," she said, "I care about the institution as much as you do, but you can't go around throwing bombs. The board loves Abner. It is going to take something compelling for them to accept the accounts of a couple of patients over Abner's. They'll want specifics."

"I know. The tricky part here is developing the information without the full cooperation of the patients. I've got to convince them we're trying to protect them and others like them."

She looked at her watch. "I have a session. Be careful this doesn't blow up in your face," she said as I headed for the door.

I was not surprised I'd failed to convince Liz that Abner was a present danger that needed to be dealt with immediately. Abner had a hold over the clinic and its people, including Liz, but that did not seem to be the case for the rest of the world. They did not want to believe anything negative about him, least of all anything that would tarnish his professional reputation. What did people outside the clinic know of Abner that those inside did not? The alleged affairs were one thing, but vague rumblings about his patient care were more distressing. I thought it likely that the rumors about Abner were based on actual instances of misconduct described by former patients. It would not take much negative news to destroy the reputation of the clinic and everyone who worked there.

I was somewhat distracted when I saw Nick later in the day for our first session, but we got on okay. He had sharp, piercing eyes that followed me around the room, and I could tell why that may have made Liz uncomfortable. He was a quiet man until given permission to talk, at which point he would go on, doing much more than answering the question on the table. I told him I had studied his files and talked to Dr. Schreiber, and I had some suggestions for how he could move forward.

"I think part of the problem is that your mother is too attached to you, and we need to wean her off you over time. We need to get back to the way things were before you moved in with her. I know you make great sacrifices to take care of your mother, and while you want to continue being there for her, we need her to become more independent. Does that sound right to you?"

He rubbed his chin and pursed his lips. "I had not thought of it that way. Others have said I'm too dependent on her."

"They are both true. You do get satisfaction out of tending to your mother's needs, but you also get satisfaction out of other things, like work. It is possible to reduce your commitment to her even while you live there and still get the gratification of knowing you are helping her. For example, you could find day care for her and spend less time at the house. How does that sound?"

"I don't think she'd be happy with a stranger taking care of her. She's set in her ways, and I know what they are."

"He or she wouldn't be a stranger for very long and would learn your mother's routine. And a caregiver could be a good companion for your mom. Someone besides you she could talk to. Anyway, you don't have to have someone in every day. Once a week would be a good start. That way you can see if it helps, your mom can get used to it, and you can use that scheduled time to go out with your friends or on a date."

After we'd wrapped up, I stopped Nick on his way out. "Before you go, tell me about your experience with Dr. Reeves."

"I only saw him a couple of times, so I probably shouldn't express an opinion, but he made some remarks I did not appreciate. He kept insinuating that my issues with my mother were sexual. I was ticked and told him so. That's when he got irked and recommended I see another doctor. That's how I got to Dr. Schreiber."

In our brief time together, I saw no sign that Nick had selected his mother as the object of sexual interest. Rather, he seemed to be playing the role of the provider. Even if Abner was correct, it was premature of him to haul out the Oedipus complex after only a couple of sessions with Nick. While it was a theory one might entertain, broaching it at the outset of their relationship seemed to be rushing things based on first impressions. It was clear that Nick was not open to the idea.

"During our third session, he made me feel like a pervert, and I knew I would not go back to him," Nick said. "He really annoyed me talking about my mother that way. I could not listen to anything he had to say after that."

"You say Dr. Reeves made you feel like a pervert. Did he say anything else apart from the things you already mentioned about your mother?"

"He hinted at some other stuff that bothered me, but mostly it was about my mother."

I was regrouping after my session with Nick when Ed telephoned me and said that the police wanted to talk to me again, this time as a potential witness against Philip. I told him I would not reveal anything about my communications with Philip without a court order. He said they wanted to talk about the timing of my visit.

The sky was hazy when we went down to the precinct the next morning to meet with Detectives Hayes and DeCarlo. They read me my Miranda warnings again, and Ed protested since Philip was already in custody. With the investigation apparently still ongoing, we decided not to answer their questions unless it was under the proffer letter. Hayes and DeCarlo called ADA Brenner, and she agreed to our conditions.

DeCarlo started the interrogation by explaining that they were trying to get a handle on when Philip left the scene.

"If I have this right, you arrived a few minutes before eight p.m. for an eight o'clock appointment, right?"

"That's correct. Probably two or three minutes before eight."

"The street surveillance tapes show a car coming around the corner on Seventy-Second Street around that time. Did you go by cab or Uber?"

"I think I took a cab from my office but couldn't swear to it."

"And the first thing you did was go to the house and ring the bell, right?"

"Yes."

"Now, an hour appointment with a psychiatrist like Dr. Reeves is really only fifty minutes, right?" she continued.

"Usually."

"So that would mean the appointment before yours ended at roughly seven fifty?"

"I guess so."

"And it usually takes the patient a couple of minutes to leave the premises, right?"

"It can."

"Sometimes, in fact, one patient will run into another in the waiting area, right?"

"Yes, that happens."

"But you didn't see Philip Greenberger coming out of Dr. Reeves's office?"

"No, I didn't."

"Or out of the house?"

"No."

"If Greenberger left the office at seven fifty and went into Dr. Reeves's house, climbed the stairs, killed Mrs. Reeves, and came back down, you'd agree that that would take a few minutes, right?" DeCarlo asked.

"I don't know how long it would take," I said.

"Well, if he left the office at seven fifty and you arrived at, say, seven fifty-five, he would only have had five minutes to go upstairs, commit the murder, and escape without you seeing him?"

"Yes, that sounds right, but I think I got there a few minutes later."

"Okay, seven minutes. But you didn't see him scurrying down the street making his escape, did you?"

"No."

"The back door was blocked off. Don't you think it's odd that you didn't see him at all if that's the timeline?"

"I don't know if it's odd. All I know is that I didn't see anyone."

"More likely that he left Reeves's office at seven fifty without going into the house and killing Mrs. Reeves, isn't it?"

"What are you driving at?" I asked.

Hayes gave me an exasperated look and responded, "That Greenberger didn't have the time to commit the murder if your story is true. It would have taken at least ten or fifteen minutes to do everything he had to do, which would mean he'd have run right into you on the doorstep. But that didn't happen because he was gone before you showed up. He didn't commit the murder."

"Now, wait a minute," Ed said. "You said this was about him being a witness. The murder could have been before seven fifty, while Greenberger was still there."

"Mrs. Reeves took a call at seven forty-two. She was very much alive."

"Maybe the murder was after Tim left. The TOD gives you until nine to worry about."

"We know it was around eight. Mrs. Reeves had a charity event she was supposed to chair at eight fifteen. She didn't show or even call to let them know she wasn't coming. And all their later calls to her went unanswered."

"But what if the murderer was still in the house holding Mrs. Reeves at knifepoint when Tim arrived?" asked Ed.

"We thought of that. But according to the street cameras, the only ones to come down the street between eight fifteen and nine o'clock were a couple of teenagers and an elderly couple."

"They could have hidden in the house until after nine."

"That wouldn't explain how Dr. Reeves was attacked shortly after eight. Your client locked the front door, so the killer could not have attacked Reeves around that time and gone back into the house."

"There are other possibilities. That's it. We're out of here." Ed stood, pulling at my sleeve.

When we got out on the street, Ed cursed the police for bringing us in the way they did. He said they were trying to lock me down as to the sequence of things and that that was a bad sign. It could mean they were losing faith in their case against Philip. That would put me back on, if not at the top of, the short list of suspects.

Ed suggested we go to his office, which was only a short cab ride away. We sat in the conference room adjacent to his office with his associate Nicole and talked about weaknesses in the case against Philip. Ed was going to call the ADA to note his displeasure with the police's tactics and to get a read on where things stood.

I left his office about a half hour later and, despite the heat, walked back to the clinic. During the entire walk, I obsessed over the investigation and how it appeared to be rising from the dead. The police did not seem ready to give up on me.

An hour or so later, Beth called me. She told me the news had run a story that the DA's office had dropped the charges against Philip Greenberger. Although he had been arrested and arraigned, no indictment had been returned against him in the forty-eight hours after his arrest. The DA's office released a statement saying that Philip was still a person of interest in the case, but they did not have sufficient evidence to warrant an indictment at this stage and were releasing him from custody.

I told Beth that I would talk to Ed and then call her back. He telephoned me before I could reach him. He told me that the ADA was cagey about their reasons for dropping the charges against Philip. Ed thought the timing issues raised doubts about Philip's guilt but that the DA's other problem was lack of motive. The ADA was noncommittal as to my status, characterizing me as a "subject" of the investigation. That was another way of saying I was not out of the woods. I shared the news with Beth.

"I can't believe this is still going on. You have to promise me that you will tell the kids before something breaks publicly."

"It's still too early for that. I'm just a subject, not a target."

"You said we have to be prepared for anything. I don't want the kids surprised if the police show up at our door someday. You've got to warn them."

"And say what? That there is an investigation and I may get arrested for something I didn't do?"

"I don't know. Something like that, I guess. You can't just let this sneak up on them. And you need to tell them you're innocent. You need to give them hope that the nightmare will end and that things will return to normal. They need to hear it from you."

The evening papers reported on Philip's release from custody. One paper claimed that sources implied an arrest of a second suspect was imminent. That was enough for me, and after consulting with Ed, I told my kids about the investigation and the possibility that I would be charged. I explained the best I could why I thought that was unfair and how I expected everything to turn out all right.

"Are you innocent, Dad?" Evan, my fourteen-year-old, asked when I was sitting in his bedroom saying good night.

"Yes, son. I didn't kill Mrs. Reeves or hurt Dr. Reeves."

"Then why are they going to arrest you?"

"I don't know that they are. They might do so because I happened to be in the same area at the time the murder was committed. It was a coincidence. I had a doctor's appointment scheduled, and it looks like I arrived right after the murder."

"I don't understand. If you got there after, why would they arrest you?"

"As I said, they may not. It's hard to prove exactly when I got there, and the police may not believe my story. But they should because it is the truth."

"Are you going to go to jail?"

"I don't think so. I am innocent, so if the police bring charges against me, my lawyer and I will fight them, and I think we will win. You just need to remember that I didn't do it, and we will be able to show that if we have to. You don't have to worry. It will be hard because there will be stories about me that might suggest I am guilty, but don't you believe them. You know the truth."

I left it there. I knew that they would have a lot of questions I needed to answer over the next few days, depending on what the DA's office did. Above all else, I had to keep harping on the fact that I was innocent.

# 11

Things with Beth got worse after Philip's release. She became more accusatory, asking questions that seemed largely rhetorical. It was like I had the burden of proof and had to convince her of my innocence.

"Why did you go to meet Abner in the evening? And why go to the house as opposed to Abner's office? You could have seen Abner during the workday. He's just down the hall from you and sees patients there every day."

"I have a job during the day. He was seeing patients all day long and had no time for me."

"I don't know what to think. If Philip didn't do it, who did? The police will think it was you. The thing that sticks in my craw is your fingerprints on that knife. It makes sense that the Reeves washed the knife after the barbecue. That's what we would have done."

"Not if you were trying to set somebody up."

"Abner planned this weeks in advance and left your fingerprints on the knife the whole time? Is that your defense?"

I stormed out of the kitchen and into my home office. I telephoned Ed in a rage. I caught him off guard.

"Even my wife thinks I killed Julie, Ed. What are we doing to stop this train wreck from happening? It seems like nothing."

"That's not true. I thought you'd get indicted as soon as they let Philip off.

It's good that they're hesitant to pull the trigger. They must have reservations."

"What are they and how do we exploit them? It's way past time for you to make a no-holds-barred presentation."

"We don't have a silver bullet. We have been planting seeds of doubt all along."

"What? By suggesting the killer may have been in the house for hours on end? Can't you just go in there and lay out the timetable in a way that makes it clear I'm innocent?"

"Our timetable has holes in it. I'm telling you we will have the opportunity to state our case."

"When? At trial?"

"We need more time to develop a defense. You have to trust me on this."

"I don't even know what our defense is other than the prosecution not being able to prove their case." I slammed the phone down and spent the rest of the evening alone with a bottle of scotch.

The next morning, I was still in a tailspin and impulsively went to see Liz. She was sitting in her office, waiting for her first appointment to arrive. I must have looked like a man on a mission, because she craned her neck and raised her eyebrows when she saw me.

"What's with you storming in here?" she asked.

"Everything is turning to shit," I said. "The police cut Philip loose in Julie Reeves's murder. Now, apparently, I am one of the suspects."

"What? You?"

"I had an appointment at Abner's the night of the murder, but no one answered the door. The attack must have already happened."

"So why do they think it was you?"

"Because, as I said, I was there around the time she was killed. Evidently, they think I'm lying about the murder. Why would I kill Abner's wife? It's bullshit."

"Why are you telling me all this?" she asked quizzically. "I don't think I want to hear it. I don't think it's smart for you to be talking about your case."

"Why? Because I need a friend. I'm tired of talking to my lawyer, and I can't talk to my wife."

"So now we're friends. I thought you wanted something more," she said, deftly changing the subject.

"I do, but it's hard to ask a woman out if you might get indicted for murder."

"You're serious, aren't you?" she said as the color drained from her face.

"About everything I just told you. I don't know what the DA is going to do." I watched her squirm. "Sorry, I just need to let a little steam off."

"Can't you do that at home?"

"My wife doesn't know what to think. The possibility that I may be arrested has left her catatonic."

"I'm sorry to hear that," she said, placing her hand over her heart.

I ran my hands through my hair and looked into those dazzling eyes.

"Thanks for listening," I said as I turned on my heels and exited her office as quickly as I had come in.

My five minutes with Liz had not calmed me down as I had hoped. I had not told her about the fingerprints, as that would have been the final straw. I had to be careful with what I told anybody, Liz included, to be sure I did not make any admissions that would be usable in court.

John showed up for his appointment on time. I pretended I did not know he had gone to see Liz and started our session as I normally would. We spent a half hour or so talking about how he was feeling and what he was doing to control his anxiety and depression. He seemed fidgety the whole time and I asked him why.

"Reeves has some stuff on me about the past that I'm afraid he will reveal. If what you told me before is true, he is lying to me about the circumstances in which he could disclose my past behavior," John said.

"He's known your secret for some time. Why is this coming up now?"

"Because he is calling me and rattling sabers. Something has him spooked."

"Are you going to tell me what he has on you?"

He looked at me and shook his head. "Sorry, but I'm not going to make the same mistake again."

For the second time, John had let on that he was literally being blackmailed by his own doctor. I could not sit on that any longer. It did not matter that I did not know what he was being blackmailed for or what John was doing for

Abner to maintain his silence. The blackmail itself was unethical, if not illegal.

It was clear he wanted to talk about something other than his issues with Abner. We closed the session by discussing the fact that he hadn't cut himself for weeks now. He said he was counting the days and had recently set a new record. I told him that was quite an accomplishment given the strain he was under and encouraged him to keep it up.

When he left, I locked the door to my office and prepared myself mentally for what I was about to do. There was no way to do this anonymously, so I had to endure the ignominy within the clinic of being the whistleblower. I did not know whether my actions would be protected from retaliation under the law, but I was willing to take that chance.

As a board member, Dr. Melissa Fitzgerald knew immediately who I was when I telephoned her. I told her I had some serious allegations to make about the clinic and asked if I could meet with her. She wanted me to bring my allegations to the full board, and I responded that some of the board members might have conflicts of interest. She agreed to meet with me the next afternoon at her office.

The following day, I left the clinic around four thirty and headed downtown. Melissa maintained an office not far from Langone in a partnership with three other psychiatrists. I arrived on time and waited for her to finish her session with a patient. She greeted me warmly and invited me into her spacious office. I sat on the love seat kitty-corner from her desk. We chatted for a few minutes, but I was nervous and wanted to get right down to business.

"I believe Abner Reeves is using confidential information to blackmail several of his patients into doing things and threatening to tell the police secrets relating to their prior misconduct if they refuse. Although I don't know precisely what Abner is making them do, it appears to be illegal based on what the patients told me."

She looked up from taking notes and scratched her head.

"Why not take the matter up with the full board? They'll want to know."

"I think several members are too close to Abner and would not take an independent look at the allegations."

"Are you calling for an investigation?"

"I think that's the clinic's only viable course of action. If you simply confront Abner with the allegations, he will strenuously deny them."

"This is all very upsetting," she said, shifting in her chair. "You must know that an investigation of this sort will hurt the institution. Are you sure you want to push this?"

"I thought long and hard about this," I said. "He is an agent of the clinic, and it bears responsibility to ensure that none of its doctors are engaging in unethical conduct or something even worse."

She sat back in her chair and put her pen down. "I want to consult with our lawyers about this. I will let you know after I talk to them. In the interim, I don't want you sharing anything about what we discussed with anyone else inside or outside the clinic. Do you understand?"

"I do."

"Do you have any documents you can share that shed any light on what you've said?"

"I don't have much, and whatever I do have is protected by the patient confidentiality privilege."

She rose, as if prepared to say goodbye, and stopped. She came around the desk and stood next to me, leaning against its corner. She looked me straight in the eyes.

"Is there anything about your relationship with Dr. Reeves I should know about? Anything that might affect your objectivity?" she asked.

"He'll think so, but no. This has nothing to do with our personal relationship. I'm happy to answer any questions the investigators have about that."

I went straight home after that. When the kids went upstairs to talk to their friends, I sat Beth down in the kitchen for a serious discussion. I wanted things out in the open.

"I told a member of the advisory board about Abner and called for an independent investigation."

"That's good," she said.

"I am having a difficult time with everything and I need your support. I do not want our marriage to fall apart too. Please search your heart for the strength to stand with me in the face of these accusations. They will find the real killer at some point, and all of this will be like a bad dream. I still love you and know that you still love me."

"I'm scared of losing you, of losing everything. I guess I am lashing out, looking for something or someone to blame. I do not want to believe anything bad about you, but the picture looks bleak. There are too many unexplained coincidences. I need time to sort things out, to regain the trust I had in you. I'm beginning to think we might benefit from some time apart. I'm not sure how else to deal with the doubts."

I wasn't sure how I felt about that. I wasn't altogether surprised nor, with Liz still on my mind, disconsolate. I could use some time on my own. I sat alone in my home office pondering the future. The phone rang. I did not recognize the number, but I answered anyway.

"Hello," I said.

"Tim, it's Melissa Fitzgerald. Sorry to bother you, but I talked to our lawyers, and they agree that the matter should be thoroughly investigated."

"That's great," I said, heaving a sigh of relief. At the same time, I knew this process was going to put me through hell.

"They don't see any real conflicts and think that the investigation should be overseen by the full advisory board. We are going to call a meeting later this week to get things started. Please don't mention anything about this until you are officially notified."

"I'm happy to assist in any way I can."

"Word is likely to get out that you started this. I hope you can take the heat. There won't be any retaliation from the clinic if you raised this issue in good faith. My advice, however, is to stay away from Abner until this is all resolved."

"Once he knows about this, I doubt he'll talk to me anyway. Thanks for taking this on. Goodbye."

Though it would have no direct bearing on the criminal case, the investigation gave me some hope that Abner's improprieties would be uncovered, making him generally less credible. I expected him to lie his way through the investigation and be discredited once the privilege issue was resolved. I expected to be interviewed too. What intrigued me more was whether the lawyers would interview the patients. I did not see how they could uncover the facts without hearing what the patients had to say. At the same time, venturing beyond the four walls of the clinic with word of an investigation meant there could be leaks to the outside world.

Since the lawyers could not force the patients to reveal their confidences, they might not discover the truth. None of the therapists could reveal what they had been told in confidence. The lawyers had to have known that patient confidentiality was an issue that would have to be dealt with up-front if they expected the therapists to talk about what they knew.

I started the next day with a visit with Brett. I did not tell him about the investigation but probed a little regarding his relationship with Abner. I told him I'd had occasion to review portions of his files and noticed that he and Abner had discussed whether he would or would not consent to something. I could tell from the way he closed his eyes that he knew exactly what I was talking about.

"He had this way of getting you to say yes to things you didn't want to do. I hate him for that. Let's talk about something else, please."

"These sessions are for you to tell me what's on your mind. Is there something you'd like to cover that we haven't talked about?"

"Well, I've been seeing someone somewhat younger than I am. That's a positive. It's someone I feel I can talk to and not be judged, which is important given my history."

"You sound happy about it. How long has this been going on?"

"Not too long. But it's been a whirlwind. Things are happening fast."

"Maybe we can talk about it a little more next time."

I saw Liz later that day, and she shook her head at me.

"I see you've been busy. Sue told me that the board is investigating Abner's practices."

"I can't believe she shared that with you. The investigation is supposed to be privileged and confidential."

Liz laughed. "This place is too small to keep any secrets. I expect Abner to tell me too."

"Does everybody know that I was the whistleblower?"

She laughed again. "Don't look at me. I don't tell people what we talk about. Anyway, I hear that Fitzgerald is all fired up about Abner. What the hell did you tell her?"

I couldn't tell whether she was legitimately interested or just prying, possibly on Abner's behalf.

"Very little. Less than I've told you."

"She's concerned about the reputation of the place and is pushing the board to do a full-scale investigation. I don't know if the rest of the board will go along with that."

"Why? Because they're Abner's cronies?"

"There's that. I also think they're reluctant to interfere with a clinician's treatment regimen and pry into a patient's condition," she said before changing subjects with a smirk. "Meanwhile, are you being arrested, or have you got time for a drink tonight?"

"I can break away. You sure you're safe with a murder suspect?"

"At a restaurant at six p.m., I am."

She strutted away toward her office. I was bewildered that she had invited me out for a drink given my status as a suspect. As I watched her go, my phone rang. It was a partner from the clinic's outside law firm who wanted to arrange an interview with me. I told him I wanted my lawyer present and suggested he call Ed to work out the logistics.

Ed called me about an hour later and said he talked to the clinic's lawyers and wanted to meet for drinks to find out what this was all about. I popped into Liz's office and begged off for the evening, making plans for a couple of nights later. I met Ed at the bar at a nearby hotel. I explained my concerns about Abner and how I had urged the board to investigate.

"You did the right thing," Ed said. "Now we've got to prepare for the interview. It's likely that privilege issues are going to get in the way of your ability to answer questions about what your patients told you."

I was sulky and hung my head. "I'm worried that I'm going to be perceived as the bad guy who tried to take Abner down."

"Yeah, so? The way you've got it scoped out, he has nothing to worry about because he controls the board. If they come down on him, it will be because he truly deserves it."

"That's true. Some embarrassing and damaging stuff could come out. What if he committed criminal acts with these patients or made them commit crimes?"

"That's a big what-if. We still have no evidence of that."

"And we may never get it."

"You don't have any confidence in the investigation you instigated?"

"With the full board involved, I suspect that it will be a whitewash."

"I don't know. They have a reputable law firm doing the investigation. Remember, the board members have professional reputations of their own to preserve. The law firm will go where the facts take them. And I think they will push the board to do what is appropriate in view of the facts. If the lawyers develop evidence of wrongdoing, the board is going to have to do something, or they will look like a bunch of pawns."

A couple of days later, Ed and I found ourselves in a massive conference room at the large law firm with two former federal prosecutors, Will Hammersmith and Nancy Khouri, representing the clinic. They said they had been retained by the board to do an investigation into certain allegations related to Abner Reeves and wanted to determine what I knew about the matter. They told me the investigation was privileged, and the privilege belonged to the clinic, not me.

"Let me ask a question to start," Ed said. "Most of what Tim knows comes from his therapy sessions with patients and is therefore privileged, so he cannot discuss any of that with you. How do we deal with that?"

"But he's the one who came forward with the allegations," said Hammersmith. "We're entitled to the details of what he told Dr. Fitzgerald."

"He was careful not to breach the privilege when speaking with Dr. Fitzgerald. You can get the clients' consents, but we can't impart patient information under the privilege or HIPAA."

"Well, let's see how this goes," Hammersmith said, dismissing Ed's concerns. "You have suggested, to put it bluntly, that Dr. Reeves is blackmailing patients to get them to do things against their will under threat of exposing something they did in the past. Is that the sum and substance of it?"

"Yes," I said.

"And you only know that from reviewing patient files and talking to the patients themselves, is that correct?"

"Yes."

"You have already breached the privilege by sharing that information with Dr. Fitzgerald, haven't you?"

"I don't think so. I gave her the general subject matter of my concern but no details. I did not reveal the substance of any communication I had, just my impressions."

"Did you have the patients' permission to share even that much?"

"I did not think that I needed it."

"And you did not get it?"

"Correct."

"Who are the patients?"

"I can't tell you that without breaching the privilege and revealing what they told me."

"But the identity of the patient is not privileged from the institution."

"What they said is, and by disclosing their name, I've essentially told you what they said. That I can't do."

We went back and forth for the better part of an hour debating what I could and could not say. The clinic's lawyers became frustrated and accused me of not cooperating with their investigation. Ed said he did not think the clinic wanted to force its therapists to reveal patient information without the patient's consent.

Khouri snarled. "How are we supposed to conduct the investigation if people like you don't answer our questions?"

"Why don't you talk to the patients themselves?" I asked.

"They won't talk to you about the details, and those conversations are privileged," she said, rolling her eyes. "What makes you think they are going to talk to us when there is no privilege whatsoever? You think they'll confess to their crimes? As I understand it, there are two possible sets of crimes—the ones from their past and the ones you allege Dr. Reeves put them up to. Why would they tell us about either of those?"

"Isn't it enough for them to confirm that Dr. Reeves threatened to reveal privileged information about their past and induced them to do bad things to guarantee his silence?" I asked. "Isn't that the very definition of blackmail? You don't need to know everything to know that you have a problem with what he's been doing."

"You've essentially told us that. We can't do anything based on your statement alone. You have no firsthand knowledge. We need the details from someone with firsthand knowledge," said Hammersmith.

"I don't know what to tell you," I said. "All I know is that Dr. Reeves has been engaging in unprofessional conduct and the clinic has a duty to stop it."

"The board very much wants to get to the bottom of this. You've created an issue where they are now on notice of a potential problem and powerless to do anything about it. What did you have in mind when you came forward?" asked Hammersmith.

"That smart lawyers like you would figure out a work-around."

Khouri flushed. I did not mean to insult them, but I thought they should have an answer at their fingertips. They had had time to research the question.

"Do we know if anyone is in danger?" she asked.

"I suppose it depends on what you mean. I don't know what Dr. Reeves is making these young men do."

The clinic's lawyers called an abrupt end to the meeting. Ed said afterward that, since their review was privileged, they could probably access the patient files, but even that was risky. I told him Abner was too smart to memorialize anything that could get him in trouble. The key was getting the patients to open up, and we both agreed that was unlikely.

"I have an idea," Ed said. "One way to do this is to get the clinic to invoke the crime-fraud exception. When a client and a lawyer communicate 'in furtherance of the crime,' it's not privileged. You can make the same argument about Abner's communications with his patients—that he was furthering a crime with them. I'm going to raise that as a possible avenue for the clinic's lawyers to pursue."

# 12

This time I took Liz to the bar on the first floor of the Libra Hotel. It was another steamy day in Manhattan, and the clouds burst during our walk over to the bar. The rain started slowly, and I took off my jacket and put it around her shoulders. Then, the downpour started in earnest, along with claps of thunder. We ran the last block, which was awkward for her in heels. By the time we made it to the hotel, we were drenched from head to toe.

We both liked the cozy feel of the bar surrounded by books in the tradition of an old library. The bar was crowded. I saw a couple get up from a table in the corner and grabbed Liz by the arm to drag her over before someone else beat us to it. Even with her hair soaked, she looked beautiful. We shook ourselves off and sat down. I ordered a couple of vodka martinis.

"How did the interview with the lawyers go?" she asked, leaning on her elbow.

"Frankly, it was a waste of time. As I expected, privilege issues impeded the questioning and we didn't make much progress. You ready for yours?"

"It's a nonevent. I don't really know anything other than what you told me during our patient consultations, and that's privileged. Are they going to interview you again?"

"That will depend on whether the lawyers can resolve the issues that prevented me from answering their questions last time."

When I looked at Liz, I noticed she was staring at me. She shook her head and said, "I must be crazy. Not only are you married, but you may also be a murderer, and here I am, sipping martinis with you."

"I've wondered about that myself," I admitted. I wanted to make a joke but could see that she was serious.

"Are things any better at home?" she asked.

"Pretty much the same. I'm not going to lie to you. She does not know what to think."

"I don't either. When do you think your situation will become clearer?"

"My situation? That's a nice way of putting it," I said as I leaned toward her. "I wish I knew. Right now, I'm in limbo with everything, including you."

"I'm afraid so. Doesn't mean we can't have an occasional drink, but I'm afraid to go beyond that."

"I understand." I scrunched up my face. "I'm surprised you're even willing to do this."

"I ought to have my head examined. Know any good psychologists?" she joked.

We finished our drinks and had another round, talking about her past, including her most recent relationship. Though she had gone out with some impressive-sounding men, they all turned out to be dirtbags, except the last one. That one was her fault, she admitted. Being on the rebound made her cautious, she said, and her alarm bells were ringing wildly with me.

As she was finishing her second drink, she looked at me and smiled. "I am glad you did not try anything."

"What do you mean?"

"You took me to a bar in a hotel. I wasn't sure of your intentions, not that you would have gotten anywhere. I appreciate you not being a jerk."

I had invited her to a hotel hoping for the best. She had been forward enough with me that I thought she'd drop a hint if she wanted to connect. I was glad I hadn't embarrassed myself by making an aggressive move.

"I'm not experienced at this. I'm happy to let you take the lead."

She smiled again, picked up her purse, gave me a peck on the cheek, and was gone. I asked for the check instead of another martini. The rain had stopped. I walked over to Grand Central to catch the subway for a change and immediately regretted it. The air in the subway tunnel was thick and stale, and it felt as hot as a sauna. I crammed my way into a full car of commuters who, like me, were dripping with perspiration. The air was a little cooler in the car, and I started to relax. It was not a long ride to my subway stop in Chelsea.

After dinner, I helped Beth clean up the kitchen. I made the kids help too so I could hear about their day. Samantha told me about the friend she made at her summer program at school. Evan, a teenager of few words, grunted something about joining a Dungeons & Dragons club that met remotely.

When the kids ran upstairs to play, I sat down with Beth and a glass of wine.

"Do you know that my interview was today?"

"With so much going on, I forgot. I've got bigger issues on my mind than how the clinic deals with Abner."

I ignored her. "It was a missed opportunity. We spent time on a bunch of preliminaries. The therapist–patient privilege got in the way of a real discussion."

"The lawyers should have anticipated that and been ready with a work-around."

"I agree. Ed is offering up a possible solution."

"Fitzgerald won't let this die, will she?"

"I doubt it. I think she understands why it's important to find out what's been happening."

"Can the police do anything?"

"The police? I don't need the police nosing around this too. They're already too close for comfort."

"You need to do something to get them off your back. Maybe they'll look favorably on you if you give them a tip."

"I'll talk to Ed about it, but my instincts are that it's not a good idea. I don't trust Abner, especially if he gets cornered. He'll make shit up," I said, tapping my hands on the kitchen table. "And where are we?"

She drained her glass of wine. "I don't know, Tim. I'm waiting for a little clarity on your status, I guess."

The next morning, I went into the office at the usual time, feeling a little unmotivated. I was not scheduled to see Brett until the afternoon and was surprised when he showed up at my office at ten without calling ahead. My schedule for the day was full, but I knew it must be serious, because Brett never just stopped in. I escorted him into my office, explaining that I only had about ten minutes to give him.

"Some lawyers for the clinic called me and want to talk to me. What did you tell them?" he asked.

"I can't tell you that. It is attorney–client privileged," I said.

"What about my privilege? Have you told them about our sessions together?"

"I haven't told them anything you told me in confidence. I will let them explain what is going on."

"Do they know what I told Dr. Reeves about my past?"

"I don't even know that, so certainly not from me, and I doubt they heard it from Dr. Reeves."

"What about the fact that he's threatened to use that information against me?"

"Brett, if that's true, you should tell the lawyers."

"No. Did you tell the lawyers that?" he asked, glowering at me.

"I already told you I can't share those details, but you haven't told me about any specific threats," I said.

"I don't want to do this. Do I have to talk to them?"

"I don't think they can make you, but if Dr. Reeves threatened to use information you gave him in confidence against you, you should tell the lawyers. He can't divulge what you told him except in very limited circumstances. Worse yet, if he made you do something so he'd keep quiet, that's blackmail. You've basically told me that was the case."

"I don't trust him. He'll find out somehow that I ratted on him."

"Look, you don't have to tell the lawyers about what you did in the past, only that Reeves threatened you with it and made you do things you didn't want to do."

"But if I do, he'll tell them about the past. That's his payback. You can't guarantee that he won't. As I said, I don't trust him."

"I don't think the lawyers will let him intimidate you that way. They aren't interested in whatever you did in your past. Why don't you ask them exactly what they want to know before you decide if you'll answer any questions?"

"I can do that, I suppose. I want to help. I just don't want to get into what I've done. This is all so stressful. My new boyfriend thinks I'm crazy to consider talking to the lawyers, but I want this to stop."

I asked Brett to come back at three for his previously scheduled appointment. He hemmed and hawed for a minute before saying that he would. Still, he seemed more relaxed when he left.

I had a session with Nick and then went to an early lunch with Ed. We ate at an established neighborhood deli. I told him about my brief meeting with Brett, and Ed agreed with the way I handled it. He had not heard back from the clinic's lawyers. It seemed they were getting other interviews out of the way first. I told him Liz was going in late in the day and that her interview would beg the same privilege questions.

Three o'clock came and went, but Brett did not show up. I telephoned him and got no answer. His absence made me anxious, given the state he'd been in that morning, so I left him a voicemail suggesting that he come in at ten the next day. I told him he could confirm that by leaving me a voicemail or sending me an email.

I saw a patient at four and knocked off at five. I grabbed a cab and met Eric for a drink down near Bellevue. Before leaving the bar, I checked my phone. There was no message from Brett, but I had one from Sue. I did not feel like talking to her, so I blew her off. I walked out of the dark basement bar into the late day sunshine and looked for a taxi to take me home.

As I sat sweating in the cab, my phone rang again. I saw Sue's name on the screen and gave some thought to letting it go to voicemail again. I answered reluctantly.

"Hello, Sue," I said. "Just got your message."

"Yeah, right. I've got some bad news for you. Brett Stone was found dead in his apartment today. They found a gun in his hand and a bunch of pills on the night table next to him. Did you have any inkling that he might commit suicide?"

"What? I can't believe this. I just saw him this morning. And he scheduled a three o'clock for this afternoon. When did this happen?"

"Sometime around two, give or take an hour. They have not finalized an exact time of death, but they found him in his apartment around five, and he had been dead for several hours. His neighbors told the police they saw him around noon, and he was very anxious and depressed about something."

"Shit. He was a little agitated this morning, but there was nothing that suggested he was suicidal."

"What was he agitated about?"

"You know I can't tell you that. How did you hear?"

"He had your appointment written in his calendar. The cops contacted us when they looked at his phone, wanting to know what the appointment was about. I'm sure you'll be hearing from them," Sue said and hung up.

I arrived home in a frazzled state over Brett's death. I could feel my hands shaking and my palms starting to sweat, both signs of an imminent attack. I sat in my office and tried to control my breathing. It was no use. I grabbed a Valium and sat out the worst of it, thinking of nothing else.

Would people think I had missed a sign that Brett was a danger to himself? His condition was improving. He was involved in a new relationship. Everything seemed to be moving in a positive direction for him, except his problem with Abner. He had been upset about talking to the clinic's lawyers, but I had been hoping our conversation this morning had relieved some of the tension. It looked like he knew his secret was coming out and chose to kill himself rather than face the consequences.

I walked in on Beth preparing dinner and grabbed myself a beer. I tried to be jovial. I walked over to Samantha and messed up her hair. She told me to stop, laughing. I also tried my hand at one of the games Evan was playing on his iPad. I then asked the kids to go into the family room so I could talk to their mother in private.

"I've got some shocking news," I said, nervously peeling the label off the beer bottle. "My patient Brett apparently killed himself today."

She grabbed at her necklace. "Oh God. Did you see this coming?"

"Maybe I should have, but I didn't."

"I can't believe this. This is the second person associated with the clinic to die in a matter of months. Please tell me you don't know anything about the circumstances."

"Why would I? I just told you it was a suicide." I stormed out of the kitchen and past the kids.

A few minutes later, she came into my home office. She sat down across from me and looked forlorn.

"I'm sorry. I shouldn't have said that. How did he die?"

"A gunshot to the head. They found pills by his bedside too."

"I know you must feel awful, but it was not your fault. Some people just can't be helped."

"I feel so guilty. Was there something I could have done to prevent this?"

I relived my short morning visit with Brett and still thought that he had left in a good state of mind. If anything, he seemed at peace with his decision to talk to the lawyers and see his way through being interviewed. Something had to have happened between the time he left my office and the time he supposedly killed himself.

About an hour after I arrived at the clinic the next morning, I was informed by the receptionist that two police officers were at her desk and had asked to see me. I went out to the reception area and saw Detectives Hayes and DeCarlo sitting there in street clothes. I motioned for them to follow me back to my office. When we arrived, I closed the door.

"What are you doing here?" I asked politely. "You know you're supposed to talk to me through my lawyer."

"This is not about Julie Reeves," Hayes said. "It's about Brett Stone. Are you represented in that case?"

"You're investigating his death? I thought it was a suicide."

"Maybe. Maybe not."

"A murder?" I said, stunned.

"The gun was in his hand, and death was caused by a shot to his head, but there was no gunshot residue on his hands. It looks like the shot was fired from more than an inch or two away and at a downward angle."

"Look, I'd like to help you, but I need to clear this with my lawyer first. Can you wait in the reception area while I talk to him?"

"Sure," Hayes said.

I phoned Ed, who was unhappy that the police had not called him first. He instructed me to stall them until he came over. We waited for him to arrive and then gathered in my office with the door closed. I still thought everyone in the office knew.

Hayes started the discussion. "We're investigating the possibility that Brett Stone was murdered. We know he was scheduled to see you yesterday at three."

"Does your investigation into Stone's death have anything to do with the Reeves investigation?" Ed asked.

"We're treating them as unrelated for the time being."

"How did Stone die?"

"By a bullet to his head at close range. We've pretty much ruled out suicide, as I told your client."

"When did you last see Mr. Stone?" Hayes asked me.

"Yesterday morning at ten o'clock."

Hayes tilted his head and made a note in his pad. "Tell me about the circumstances."

Ed said, "Mr. Stone had been asked for an interview in an investigation the clinic is conducting and had some questions as to whether he needed to give the interview. Some of their conversation touched on privileged areas, and we'll decline to answer questions about those aspects of their conversation on that basis."

"An investigation into what?" Hayes asked eagerly, scribbling in his pad.

Ed said, "I'm afraid that's covered by the clinic's attorney–client privilege. I don't speak for the clinic. I am happy, however, to put you in touch with the clinic's lawyers."

"Can you tell us about Stone's state of mind when you saw him yesterday?" Hayes asked.

"He was nervous and agitated about the lawyer interview. But he calmed down after we talked for a while," I said.

"Did he seem distraught?" Hayes asked.

"Not really. If you are asking me whether I was concerned that he might hurt himself, the answer is no."

"Did he tell you why he was nervous?"

"I'm afraid that is privileged," Ed said.

Hayes thought for a minute and then asked me, "Did you offer him any nonprofessional advice? You know, not as his psychologist."

"At one point, I told him I did not think the clinic could make him submit to the interview or answer questions he didn't want to answer. I also suggested he talk to the clinic's lawyers about his concerns. And I suggested he come back at three to talk some more with me."

"Do you know if he talked to the lawyers?" DeCarlo asked, fiddling with her pen.

"I don't know if he did. He said he was going to call them, so I assume he did."

"Do you have any information indicating that anyone was interested in killing Mr. Stone?"

"Kill him? No."

"Harm him in any way?"

"Sorry," Ed interrupted. "That's privileged."

"Not if he knew of a threat of imminent harm," said Hayes.

"I don't know anything about anybody wanting to physically harm or kill Brett," I said, waving Ed off.

"Where were you between one and three p.m. yesterday?" Hayes asked.

"Here, if I remember correctly. I had lunch with Ed and came back here."

"Can anybody vouch for that?"

"I know I called him when he didn't show up for the three o'clock. That will prove I was in the office then."

"We're more interested in the two-hour window before that."

"I don't know. There were people here who may have seen me. You can ask around."

DeCarlo put her pad away and stood up. “You shouldn’t assume that we are accepting your claims of privilege. We need to check on that with the DA’s office. But before we go, let me ask you this. Do you know of any connection between Mr. Stone’s death and the murder of Mrs. Reeves or the beating of her husband?”

“No, I do not.”

After the police left, I asked Ed what he thought of the interview. He took his time answering.

“I think they’re just beginning to interview people who had contact with Brett. How good is your alibi?”

“I don’t know if anyone saw me that afternoon.”

“Do us a favor and construct a timetable of what you did.”

I knew that the timetable wouldn’t help.

# 13

Later that afternoon, after the police and Ed had left, I was sitting in my office when Sue paid me a visit. Always one with a flair for the dramatic, she came in and closed the door with a loud bang, startling me.

"How dare you tell the police that we're conducting an investigation. That's confidential information."

"That's what Brett came to see me about. It came up in the questions they asked me. What am I supposed to do? Lie?"

"Tell them it's privileged."

"I understand that the existence of the investigation is not privileged. I didn't tell them anything about it."

"Did you tell them it's about Abner? It's bad enough word has gotten around the clinic."

"No, we told them to talk to the clinic's lawyers for more information and gave them the contact details."

"Well, now they want to know all about the investigation. They want to know what role Brett played in it and why he was going to be interviewed. You've put us in a very awkward position. We have to tell them something."

"The truth is a good place to start."

"Sure. Besmirch Abner and the clinic because you have some cockamamie idea that he is mistreating his patients. If word of the investigation gets out, it could be very damaging."

"We're talking about telling the police, not broadcasting a story."

"You know how things leak out. I wish you had just kept your crazy ideas to yourself."

"He admitted to me that he blackmailed them. Just the other day, in fact."

She shook her head. "I don't know why you hate him so much. He is a good and honest man who is still grieving over his wife."

I had not thought that my interest in holding Abner accountable to his patients might be interpreted as animus toward him, but I could see that now. I was creating a motive after the fact by being the one insisting on investigating him. I did not need Sue to tell the police that I hated Abner. They might assume my so-called ill will toward him predated the murder and went all the way back to my boyhood days, when Abner supposedly blackmailed my father.

After Sue left, Liz came into my office, looking as good as ever. She told me about her interview with the lawyers and said it was as much about my relationship with Abner as it was about her interactions with his patients. Because they still had not sorted out the privilege issues, she could not give them any information about John. Instead, the lawyers seemed interested in establishing that Abner and I had a falling out and that was motivating me to question his methods. They were trying to pin down when that occurred. She told them she did not know what caused the rift, but it occurred around the time of Julie's death.

I did not want Liz to think that I was worried about anything, but she must have seen some concern in my eyes.

"Are you okay?" she asked gently.

"This whole thing, plus Brett Stone's death, is getting to me. The police were here about that too. They aren't sure it was a suicide. They're wondering if it's connected to Julie's death."

"Really?"

"That's what they said. It's hard to see a connection." She looked at me funny, and I immediately added, "I didn't do it and have no reason to believe that they suspect me of killing Brett."

"It scares me to think there may be another murder connected to the clinic,"

Liz said. "When do they think he died?"

"Between one and three p.m.," I said.

"Oh," she said. "Right after lunch."

I was about to leave the office for the evening when the phone rang. It was John Rankin. He was breathing heavily into the phone.

"Did you hear about Brett?" he asked.

"Yes, it's a shame. I didn't know that you knew him."

"We met at the clinic a few months ago through Dr. Reeves. We became good friends."

"He never mentioned it."

It made me wonder whether the note in Brett's file about "John" was a reference to Rankin. What had Brett told Abner about him?

"I'm scared now. The police came by and said it might not be suicide. That someone may have killed him. They asked me a lot of questions. I don't think I'm a suspect because I was at school when it happened, but I'm worried these murders are somehow connected through the clinic. The police suggested as much."

"I think they're just pursuing every possible angle, especially after Mrs. Reeves was killed. Do you have any reason to suspect anyone at the clinic other than Abner wanted to harm Brett?"

"I don't know. I only know Brett was supposed to give an interview to the clinic's lawyers, and he was really nervous about it. He had a brief preliminary phone call with the lawyers that morning, after which he told me he was going to see them and tell his full story. Then, suddenly, he is dead."

"Do you know what he was nervous about?"

"He was afraid they would ask him about his past and about what Dr. Reeves was making us do."

"But he didn't have to answer their questions. I told him that. He could have told them to pound sand."

"I think the lawyers convinced him to talk. But he was afraid of what Dr. Reeves would do or say if he found out."

"John, if you know something, you should tell the police. We don't know what we're dealing with."

"I can't, because it will all come back to me! Reeves can fuck me if he thinks I'm going to rat him out. I already told you that."

"Have you talked to him recently?" There was a long silence on the other end of the line. "John?"

"He threatened me the other day about the interview. That's why I'm so scared. He was not specific, but he told me I better not talk to the lawyers. That he would find out if I did, and there would be consequences."

"You've got to tell the police about the threat, even if you don't tell them about anything else."

"No way. He'll find out, just as he said he would. I'm just not going to talk to anyone about anything."

Because he told me enough to indicate that he was in imminent danger, I thought I was permitted to share our discussion with the police under an exception to the patient confidentiality rule. I did not have the time to go to the Ethics Committee of the APA for an opinion. I had to go with my gut and a common-sense interpretation of the law. I consulted with Ed, who agreed with me but argued that Reeves would ultimately find out his threats had been exposed and blame John.

With Brett now dead and John refusing to talk, the clinic's investigation would go nowhere. I had to impart what I knew despite the risks involved. Ed persuaded me to raise the matter with the DA's office, not the police. I let him set up an appointment and invite DeCarlo and Hayes so they would not feel disrespected.

We met with the ADA in charge of the Stone case, Javier Luzon, and the two detectives the next day. I told them I thought I was within my rights to breach the psychologist–patient privilege because my patient had been threatened. Luzon stopped me and said he was going to call in a "taint team" to hear the information and determine if there was a lawful basis to share it with the investigative team. He excused himself and the detectives and sent in a new team of investigators, including a different ADA.

I told the taint team about my latest discussion with John and the not-so-veiled threat Abner had made. The ADA, an attractive Black woman in her thirties, said she would try to protect me as a source. Once I debriefed her, she said that she would pass on what she felt was not privileged to Luzon and the detectives.

I left the DA's office with a deep feeling of regret. I had betrayed John's confidence for his own good, but he would not see it that way. He would view it as a breach of trust. I had also jeopardized my relationship with the clinic by sharing confidential information with the police. Though I was sure I had a legal and ethical right to do so, I assumed I had violated the confidentiality provisions of my contract with the clinic. That would be grounds for dismissal. I was making enough trouble that Sue would be anxious to get rid of me if she could.

As my cab pulled up to my office building, I stepped out and headed toward the front door, when a big stranger pulled me to the side. I had never seen him before. He pushed my back up against the corner of the building and glared at me while holding me by the lapel of my jacket.

"You better learn to keep that big mouth of yours shut," he growled. He was gone an instant later, but I remembered his face.

I was trembling from the confrontation. I sat on my haunches to try to stave off the attack I felt coming on. I was able to calm down, but worried that my visit to the DA's office had already been discovered. The thought crossed my mind that I may have been accosted by Brett's killer. I immediately called Ed and described the incident. He passed the information on to ADA Luzon, who had DeCarlo call me and take my brief statement.

That evening, I suggested to Beth that we take the kids away for the weekend. She said she would not mind intruding on my sister for a few days and letting the cousins play together. I nodded my approval.

"Eve," I said when I got her on the phone, "we were hoping that you and Stan could put up with us for a couple of days next week."

"Of course," she said with a lilt. "The kids would love having their cousins around to go to the beach."

"Great. What have you been up to?"

"I've been looking in a couple of old shoeboxes filled with memorabilia and came across a copy of an old check in the amount of twenty thousand dollars made out to cash. Then I found another and still another. The three checks were signed by Abner Reeves and endorsed by Dad. That was a lot of money in those days. Do you know anything about them?"

"Why Abner was paying Dad money?"

The whole thing made no sense. If Abner's story were true, it should have been the other way around. And why would my father have the checks after cashing them if they were drawn on Abner's account? It was ridiculous to think that my father would have done business with Abner after being blackmailed by him. The dates on the checks were well after the reported suicide of my cousin Billy. I couldn't understand why Abner would have been paying my father money at the same time as my father was supposedly paying him.

I asked Eve to give me a chance to look through the boxes when we visited next week. Maybe there was something else among the relics that would help explain the mystery. In the interim, I went online and looked for news stories that coincided with the dates of the checks. I located a short article, dated the day of the first check, entitled "Pedophile Ring in the City." The storyline was that the NYPD was investigating a possible ring of pedophiles believed to include prominent New Yorkers. The article mentioned that one of the alleged group members had recently committed suicide while awaiting trial.

I assumed this was exactly the kind of story my father would have paid Abner to keep from being named in, yet the money was flowing the other way. I looked up the author of the story and learned he had died a few years ago. I combed later editions of the paper to see if he had written any follow-up stories. As far as I could tell, no members of the alleged ring were ever charged.

Abner must have lied about the blackmail. My heart sank at the thought that my father was the one doing the blackmailing. I remembered from the tape that Abner's idea was "money for silence," but it had not been clear from the comment who would be paying whom. Abner was the one in the photos with my cousin, and perhaps he was the one who wanted to protect himself from being outed, particularly if there was an investigation into Billy's allegiance with alleged sexual deviants.

If my conjecture was correct, I had no reason to exact revenge on Abner.

Rather, he had an axe to grind with me and my family. The current investigation at the clinic I had initiated probably added fuel to the fire that had been burning in him for years. He could avenge himself by setting me up to take the fall for the murder of his wife.

I was sure I was right about the blackmail, though I could not prove it. There was no one left who could testify about the matter, except Abner, and I knew what he would say. I needed to run my deduction by Ed and decide when and how to use the information to undermine any suggestion that I had a motive in the Reeves case.

Every time I closed my eyes that night, I pictured the checks. I knew I would bring shame on our family by revealing the truth, but I had to balance that harm with the impact of letting Abner get away with his lies.

# 14

I pulled myself out of bed at seven the next morning without getting much sleep. I peered outside and squinted at the burst of sunlight. The shower helped wake me, but a stiff cup of coffee was what I needed most. I fixed myself one and then headed for the office via the crowded subway.

Ed called before my first appointment at the clinic, but not to talk about Abner. He said my alibi for Brett's death did not pan out because no one at the clinic remembered seeing me between one and three that afternoon. The police wanted to interview me again about my whereabouts at the time.

I told him what I had discovered about the checks and what I thought it all meant. He said it was an interesting theory that called Abner's description of events into question. It seemed we had finally caught Abner in a lie we could use to impeach him if and when he testified.

We met with the detectives at one p.m. in a cold, dark room at the police station. Detective DeCarlo led the questioning. She seemed dubious at the outset, eyeing me standoffishly.

"Do you know of anyone who can attest to you being in the office from one to three that day? No one we talked to so far remembers seeing you."

"I usually stay put in my office and do work when I'm not seeing patients. I had a couple lined up for the afternoon, including Mr. Stone, so I assume that I was there by myself prepping for the sessions."

"Can you think of anyone you saw or talked to during those hours?"

"I probably called home, but I couldn't swear to it. I may have seen Liz Schreiber. Did you check with her?"

"Yes. She says she does not remember whether she saw you or not. Can we get your credit card receipts? Maybe they'll show you ran out and grabbed a sandwich or something?"

"Sure, but didn't I tell you I had lunch with Ed that day?"

"You did. Is it true you had a disagreement with Mr. Stone when you saw him in the morning?"

"No. Where did you get that idea?"

"From you. You told us he was nervous and anxious. Did you have an argument?"

"No. I can't tell you the details of our conversation, but we did not have an argument or disagreement. As I said last time, I gave him some friendly advice I thought calmed him down."

"Didn't you want him to consent to the lawyer interview? After all, the investigation was your idea."

"Yes, but only if he could get comfortable, so I suggested he talk to the lawyers to see if they could allay his concerns."

"You were angry that he was thinking about blowing off the interview, weren't you?" Hayes asked in an aggressive tone.

"No, because I knew he could go in and not answer any questions that made him uncomfortable. They had no power over him."

"Let's be honest here; it was important for you that Stone back your allegations and at least acknowledge the blackmail?" DeCarlo asked, leaning forward in her chair.

"I think he was going to. He seemed to be heading in that direction. I think he even talked to the lawyers that morning."

"How do you know that?"

"I can't answer that because of privilege."

"Did you go see him that afternoon and have an argument over whether he was going to cooperate with the investigation?"

"Absolutely not. I did not see him in the afternoon at all."

When they left, Ed said, "You've got to focus on the Stone case and work on your alibi. Reconstruct the day and find something we can corroborate with a receipt, a witness, something."

"And the Reeves case? What's going on?"

"It's been quiet since they let Philip go, but that doesn't mean they've gone away. They must be shoring up their proof."

We were interrupted by my secretary telling me that John Rankin had arrived for his session. I told Ed I would talk with him later and escorted him out. John nodded to Ed and followed me back into my office. He took his favorite chair across from my desk. He had mischief in his eyes.

"I think you owe me an apology," he said. "I understand you went to the police when I told you I didn't want to. What the fuck was that?"

"I was concerned for your safety because of the threats."

He sat back and clasped his hands together. "The police tried to cover for you, but I knew it had to be you. I ought to fire you for going behind my back. Seems like something you therapists are good at," he said, looking at me accusingly. "But I'm not going to because I think you are helping me. I don't care what you say. I'm not going to talk to the investigators, the police, or anybody else, especially you, about Dr. Reeves."

"You won't even tell the cops about the threat? That doesn't involve anything else."

"Nope."

"Did you tell the police you knew Brett?"

"They already knew that from his phone. We talked often. I didn't tell them we had talked about the investigation. And I'm not going to. I'm just going to pretend that none of this happened and play along with Reeves's rules. If I behave, he'll behave."

"Do you think he had anything to do with Brett's death?"

He clenched his fists and then relaxed them. "I don't know. And I'm not going to get myself killed trying to find out."

He was plainly afraid, considering what had happened to Brett. He must have believed Abner was responsible for Brett's death and was afraid to say so.

"Did you tell the police anything about me and Brett?" I asked.

"No. Just that he was agitated the day he died. I didn't mention you."

He looked at me, stood up, and walked over to the window. He separated a few of the slats in my semi-closed blinds with a couple of fingers and looked out. He continued in a muted voice.

"I am feeling depressed about what happened to Brett. I've never had a close friend die on me before, and I think I need to talk about it."

"I don't see any reason why we can't talk about Brett or your feelings about his passing. It's normal to be down when you lose a friend, especially one as young as he was. And then there are the suspicious circumstances."

After my session with John, I went back through my calendar for the day Brett died. I saw that I had had an appointment with Nick before my lunch with Ed. I telephoned Ed and asked him to find proof that we ate together. He said he had already checked and had a receipt confirming that we had lunch from twelve to one at the local deli. That still left two hours unaccounted for.

My efforts to rebuild my day took me to Liz's office. I explained the situation and told her I had a two-hour gap in my day to fill. I asked if there was anything in her records that might refresh her recollection about seeing me that day. She opened her calendar and saw that she had been tied up from eleven to one and from three to five. She could have seen me around one or so, she said.

Then she looked at me peculiarly. She seemed to be thinking about what she wanted to say.

"I have a vague recollection of seeing you after lunch, but I can't recall if it was that day or the day after, when we knew Brett was dead. I'm sorry I can't be more helpful. Don't tell me you are a suspect in Brett's case now."

"They haven't said so, but I might be. I am probably the last one to have seen Brett alive. And since, for some reason, they are looking to connect his death to Julie's, I've got to be on their radar, given my status in that case."

"I also hear that the investigation by the clinic's lawyers has gotten bogged down," she remarked. "That patients are unwilling to talk to the lawyers, and the board does not know what to do. Even the lawyers are frustrated."

"Where are you hearing that from?"

"Sue. Who else?"

"What a fucking mess," I said, leaning over her desk. "You know what I think? I think Brett was killed because he decided he would talk to them. I see Abner's hand in this."

"Are you kidding?" she said, raising her eyebrows.

"No, I have reason to believe that Brett was going to submit to the interview, but my source won't talk to anybody, not even the police."

John was going through a down period after Brett's death. I tried to help him through the grieving process. The unexpected death of his virile young friend had given John a glimpse into his own mortality, and I did not want him to dwell on it. I did not know how much of his anxiety was the result of fear at the possibility that Brett's death was somehow connected to the clinic or its internal investigation.

I suspected the decision of whether to grant an interview was weighing on him. Since he had all but decided not to answer any questions, I knew he would be bothered if Abner escaped accountability as a result. Nothing would prevent Abner from repeating whatever he had done to John with another patient. That would trouble John, particularly if his friend Brett had decided to come clean and expose Abner. Had John tried to dissuade Brett from doing so? Brett's testimony might have shed light on what Abner was doing to John too. Maybe they had argued about it, and John was feeling guilty that that had been their last interaction.

I left the clinic telling myself that Abner was behind both murders. I kept coming back to the possibility that he had forced another person to commit the killings. I doubted the inducement was money—no, *fear* was Abner's currency. He had a history of motivating people with threats of ruining their public names and destroying their livelihoods. What was the killer so afraid of that they could be compelled to commit murder?

Beth greeted me with a glass of scotch when I got home. She sat me down in the kitchen without the kids.

"I'm not going to your sister's house with the rest of you for the weekend.

I'm going to visit my parents in New England instead. I think we need some time apart, and this is an easy way to get it. I've already told Eve. She's fine with it just being you and the kids."

"I not happy about this," I said. The fact that she wanted to be without us was not a good sign. "And I know your parents. If you tell them what's going on, they're going to bend your ear mercilessly with warnings about me. They'll urge you to stay away from me until the investigations are over."

Beth didn't say anything else, and as much as I hated leaving the matter unresolved, I knew I wouldn't get her to talk until she was ready. Still, as I left the house with the kids on Friday, I was glad for the time with Evan and Samantha. I had been so distracted by everything that I had not paid them much attention. It would give me a chance to answer some of the questions they must have about the investigations and my innocence.

I decided to be preemptive and talk through everything with them again on the car ride to the beach. We drove in heavy traffic from the city to the south shore of the island in the early evening. We chatted about their cousins fighting with one another a lot and how to deal with that. They gave me chapter and verse about what they planned to do at the boardwalk. But any notion of having a serious discussion with my kids went out the window when, before I could raise the subject, they donned their earbuds for the rest of the ride.

We arrived at Eve's house shortly before nine on Friday night. Eve's kids, Jason, aged eleven, and Mia, fifteen, grabbed my kids, and they all disappeared together in a matter of minutes. While they played some kind of game in the backyard, we adults chatted. I filled Eve and Stan in on what was going on in my life.

Before going off to watch a movie with the family, Eve brought me the boxes and placed them on the dining room table. She told me to have fun and joined Stan and the kids in the family room. I sat under the dining room chandelier and picked through the three shoeboxes. I found a business card in the first for the deceased *Times* reporter who'd written the story about the alleged pedophile ring. The card had his home phone written in ink across the bottom front in my father's hand. I remembered that they had been friends. In the second box,

I found a brief handwritten note from Billy denying "the rumors about me and Abner." It was dated three days before his death. I showed the two items to Eve and Stan. While we were certain that the note was penned by our cousin, we agreed the rumors could be about anything, including the possibility of Billy and Abner being part of a pedophile ring.

We went to the beach on Saturday. It was rewarding to see the kids and their cousins frolicking on the alabaster sand. I had a chance to catch up with Eve as we stood at the shoreline and watched the kids in the water.

"So how are you really doing?" she asked.

"Shitty. I can't get out from under these investigations. They're destroying me. I'm having trouble concentrating on my patients even though they are the ideal distraction."

"How is Beth handling things? She sounded sort of down when I talked to her."

"No, she's a trooper. She knows I didn't kill anyone. I am concerned with what her parents are going to whisper in her ear. They were never fans of mine."

In the early afternoon, I told Eve and Stan I had some work to do at the house, and they agreed to watch the kids. I sat in their dining room with my computer. Changing tack, I did some research on Billy's family. They were originally from Indiana. Billy had a brother who remained in the Hoosier State and a sister who came east and settled in Pennsylvania, near Philadelphia.

I was able to get a phone number for the brother in Terre Haute. I reached out to him and explained that we were distant cousins and I was doing some research on the family. He was happy to talk to me about his parents and sister, but it was a different story when it came to Billy.

"We don't talk about my brother," he said. "He was a disgrace we'd just as soon forget."

"Can you tell me anything at all about him?"

"He was trouble. Not the violent kind, but he was a deviant. Liked men—and boys. That's all I'll say."

He gave me his sister's phone number, saying she was more forgiving. I telephoned her and we talked for a good half hour. She described Billy as a good kid who had struggled with his sexuality.

"He was openly gay by the time he reached twenty, and that was not a popular thing to be in our hometown at the time. He moved east to New York and fell in with the wrong crowd. Next thing I knew, he was accused of raping a sixteen-year-old boy in his apartment. He was fragile and really frightened. It did not surprise me that he committed suicide over the shame he brought to himself and the family and the prospect of years in a state prison."

"Do you know anything about any of the men with whom he was friends?"

"I only know there were a couple of men Billy described as rich who treated him well."

"Did you ever hear him talk of a group of men who liked boys?"

"No."

"How about Billy's relationship with my father? What do you know about that?"

"Nothing really. He was close to your mother, not your father, but that ended when the scandal broke."

As I was about to hang up, she said that she remembered something else.

"When I asked him about the rape charge, he said he was there but did not participate. He claimed one of his friends sodomized the boy, but Billy was the one the boy was able to identify. The other guy never got caught," she said.

I wondered whether Abner was the rapist who got away. Maybe that was why he was paying my father. Were the payments simply to keep my father quiet, or did Dad have an in with the media that could keep Abner's name out of the papers?

When I finally got to the last box of family memorabilia, I found a note to my father from the *Times* reporter, thanking him for the "information." The note indicated that the relationship between them had been a close one. My dad must have had some leverage with his friend and presumably influenced what he wrote in his story about the pedophile ring.

While I was pleased with what I had learned, I still only had informed speculation about Abner's colorful past. There was a reason he'd allowed my father to blackmail him, and it was sordid. I would need to muster proof of what that was if I was going to truly undermine the phony story Abner had told the police.

# 15

We hit the beach on Monday morning for a last hurrah. The drive home that night was long and tedious, as everyone seemed to hit the road at the same time. The kids listened to their music again, so we really didn't have much of a chance to talk. I tuned everything out and plowed ahead, wondering what was in store for me when I got home.

Beth was in the kitchen when we arrived. She was distant and sullen. I showed her the file I had put together, trying to persuade her that it established Abner's motive to set me up for Julie's killing. She looked at it and pushed it aside.

"If Abner killed Julie, why haven't the police arrested him? He's the first one they should suspect, and if jealousy or a fight were the motive, they'd have figured that out by now. But they keep looking in your direction. I can't help but have my doubts. I thought about the investigations a lot over the weekend, and I think maybe you should move out until the dust settles and we know what the future holds. I can't go on the way it's been."

"What? You want me to leave?" I suddenly felt the need to sit down and grabbed a chair.

"I can't get my head round the fact that I may be living with someone about to be accused of a brutal murder. I have tried. I assume you are innocent, but what if I'm wrong? What am I exposing the kids to? I don't want to live to regret my choice. It's just easier if you go for a while and we try to pick things up later if you are cleared."

"I can't believe this. After all this time and you still doubt me?"

"I told you. I'm inclined to believe you, but I want to be smart about this. It shouldn't be for too long. This can't go on forever. I think it's best for me and the kids."

Racing upstairs in a fit of rage, I repacked my overnight bag and threw a bunch of clothes into a suitcase. I sat on the edge of the bed with my phone, looking for a hotel room in the neighborhood for the night. Once I knew where I was going, I told the kids I had to go out of town and was not sure when I'd be back.

I left the house and walked the few blocks to the hotel. I checked in with my two bags and a bottle of scotch I had picked up on the walk over. I sat on the bed and opened the scotch, feeling sorry for myself. After downing a couple of shots, I telephoned Liz.

She must have seen my name on caller ID because she answered by saying, "Well, this is a first. It's after eight o'clock."

"She threw me out, so I'm getting drunk and thought it would be nice to hear your voice."

"Did you deserve it?"

"Only if you believe I killed Julie. She wants to make sure the children are safe from someone who could possibly be the mad killer."

"It's not a completely irrational thought, you know. Though I'd have imagined she'd be more on your side."

"She says she believes me but thinks it's safer this way."

"I'm sorry, Tim. I really am."

"But you aren't sure whether to trust me either. I've come to expect that from my wife. It sucks that, after nearly twenty years together, she isn't standing by me. You, of course, don't know me that well."

"I really want to believe you, and my instincts tell me you are innocent, but I'm wary. I'm just getting to know you. I think you're telling me the truth, but how can I be sure?"

"I am telling everybody the truth, damn it! This is so frustrating. We keep having the same conversation."

We talked for another twenty minutes. We made plans for drinks and dinner for the following evening. She said she would go with me to a restaurant as long as I promised to let her leave early.

I checked out of the hotel at about eight thirty the next morning and, bags in hand, took a taxi to the clinic. I arrived a few minutes before nine. I had a message from Ed waiting for me. When I returned his call, he told me the clinic's lawyers wanted to interview me again, so I found myself back in the same conference room at the law firm later that afternoon. The space was cold, and the glare from the sun through the large windows was distracting. There were three lawyers from the clinic in attendance. Hammersmith made the introductions and established the same ground rules as last time. He sat forward in his chair, making eye contact with me over the rims of his reading glasses.

"Dr. Shea, this has been a very difficult assignment for us with the assertions of privilege and the death of Mr. Stone. In fact, other than Dr. Reeves, we have not had a single witness who is willing to share any information bearing on the allegations you made to Dr. Fitzgerald. The patients won't talk to us, and we can't force them to. The other therapists are all standing on privilege and refusing to answer questions we have about their communications with their patients. Even you won't tell us what you know."

Ed said, "What about the crime–fraud exception to the privilege? Were you able to determine if that applies here?"

"That is not clear-cut, and the clinic is not willing to have its staff answer questions in the absence of clear and unambiguous support for that position."

"Who is the clinic? Dr. Reeves?" Ed asked.

"No, the board. I'm afraid you are our last and best hope. We hope you will answer our questions today."

"Let's take them one at a time," Ed said.

"All right. Did Mr. Stone tell you that he was going to submit to an interview?"

"He said he was going to talk to you about it. He was noncommittal, but my impression was that he was looking for a way to talk to you."

"Did he tell you what he was going to tell us?"

"No."

"Did he ever indicate that Dr. Reeves had threatened him?"

I paused for a second to see if there was a way I could respond. "I can answer that indirectly. As a result of my session with Mr. Stone, I researched the question of whether threats were sufficient to trigger the exception to patient confidentiality."

"Did he tell you that Dr. Reeves had engaged in unprofessional conduct with him?"

"Yes, he did."

"What did he say?"

"He indicated he was being blackmailed. I can't be any more specific based on patient confidentiality concerns."

"You can't have it both ways, Doctor. You can't tell us a little of what he said and then refuse to tell us the rest."

"I can give you the general subject matter of our discussion and decline to provide the details."

"I don't agree with that. Same questions with regard to your patient John Rankin."

"Same answers."

"Did Rankin indicate whether he intends to talk to us?"

"He said he would decline."

"Did he say why?"

"He does not trust Dr. Reeves."

"Did either of them ever indicate that Dr. Reeves said he was going to use confidential information about them to induce them to do something?"

"Yes, but I can't get into the details because of patient confidentiality."

"Did either of them ever admit to harming another person or abusing a child?

"No."

"Did either of them ever specify any acts that Dr. Reeves asked them to perform?"

"No."

"Isn't it true that you encouraged both patients to come forward and allege improper acts on the part of Dr. Reeves?"

"No. I encouraged them to tell the truth about Dr. Reeves, subject to assurance from you about maintaining the confidentiality of what they told you."

Hammersmith took off his glasses and rubbed his eyes. He looked at the outline in front of him.

"Gentlemen, you are putting the board in an untenable position. You insist there has been unprofessional conduct at the clinic but won't specify what it is beyond some general reference to blackmail. You won't be surprised to hear that Dr. Reeves denies the allegations."

"I don't know what you want us to do," I said. "I brought the matter to the board because of its seriousness, and they have to figure out how to deal with it. You know the names of my other patients, including those I inherited from Abner. Have you tried talking to all of them? There's one in particular you might find interesting."

"Who is that? We can't possibly interview all of Abner's current and former patients."

"I'd rather not say, since you can and should talk to all of mine. I know you haven't talked to the one I'm thinking about. I don't know if he'll talk to you. It has not come up."

That afternoon, I gave Nick a heads-up that he would be contacted by the clinic's lawyers, who were doing an investigation into Dr. Reeves. I told him I had not said anything to them about our sessions and that he did not need to talk to them, but I encouraged him to think about it. He did not have a problem sharing his views about Dr. Reeves.

I thought about what more I could do with the information I had. On a hunch, I telephoned Abner's brother Douglas again. I reintroduced myself as the newspaper reporter who had interviewed him a couple of weeks back and told him I was putting the finishing touches on the article, but a question had come up. I found it curious there were no women in Abner's life before he married Julie.

"That's not entirely true," Douglas said. "There was a time when I thought he was gay, but as he got older, he dated a little."

"Ever hear that he had affairs with other men or boys?"

"As I said, I used to wonder about him. Always hanging around with young men, some of whom seemed pretty effeminate to me. I even asked him once if he was gay, and he got all pissed off and hit me, like that would convince me he was a he-man. I didn't know what to think until he and Julie hooked up."

"Did he ever mention a friend named Billy Mack?"

"One of the young men he used to hang out with was named Billy. I don't know his last name. I think he was gay. You're not going to write that my brother is gay, are you? I don't know that."

"No, I'm not writing about any of that. I was interested in whether there was a woman before Julie."

That Abner might be gay fit into the emerging story of the termination of his relationship with my family. It seemed plausible that Abner and his openly gay friend Billy were a couple. If that was the case, it also made sense that, when Billy was charged criminally, Abner sought refuge from the media. It all added up. The story about the pedophile ring. The checks. The note to the newspaper reporter.

I made an early reservation at Pearl at seven and waited for Liz at the bar, sipping a vodka martini. I looked at my watch, expecting her to be fashionably late. She was actually pretty punctual most of the time, which I attributed to living her professional life by the clock.

A few minutes later, she scurried in with beads of sweat on her brow from the heat and took the seat I had saved for her. She saw what I was drinking and signaled to the bartender that she would have the same. She asked about my day, and I gave her a brief report on my interview by the clinic's lawyers, as frustrating as it was. She had gotten an earful from Sue, who complained I did not back off but did not give any details to support my allegations.

"Sue tells me the lawyers are wrapping up the investigation. She hinted that they would not come to any conclusions."

I shrugged. "I expect that, after going through the process, Abner will think twice before pulling the same crap with other patients. Nick is going to talk to the lawyers, though I don't think he has anything earth shattering to say."

"How would he? He only saw Abner a couple of times."

"Don't underestimate Abner's ability to offend."

She placed her hand on mine. I did not stir. We sat like that for a few minutes until the maître d' came by and told me that our table was ready. I followed Liz into the dining room, and we sat across from one another at a nice table. She kept her eye on her watch, as if she had to be someplace else.

"Why do you keep looking at your watch?"

"I have rules for being with you. My curfew is eight thirty. That may sound silly, but it just feels safer to see you early in the evening."

I rubbed the back of my neck at the reminder that this was all illusory. Even though I knew we weren't going anywhere in the short term, I still enjoyed her company. I avoided talking about my family, but she liked talking about hers.

"I moved around a lot as a kid because my father's job took him to different places. I am the oldest of four, and my father treated me like a firstborn son. I adore him for making me strong. My mother and I barely got along, and I moved to New York to attend college and then graduate school. My first marriage was to a college professor, and we split after three years. That is when I took a job at the clinic."

Liz was a little lit. She rubbed her foot on my leg under the table as she stared into my eyes. I promised myself I would not try to take advantage of the fact that her inhibitions were lowered. At eight twenty, I asked for the check, reminding her that it was time to go. She looked confused and a little disappointed at first. Then she gathered herself and thanked me for being a gentleman. I smirked at her and sighed. I helped her into a taxi and walked back to my hotel.

# 16

When I awoke the next morning, I called Ed before going to the office. We had been spending a lot of time on the clinic investigation and none on the Reeves murder case. Weeks had gone by since Philip had been released, and I was curious what the DA's office was doing.

"Is anything new in the Reeves case?" I asked. "It seems strange that it's all still quiet."

"I've been wondering about that too, but you know to let sleeping dogs lie."

"Do you think they are moving in a different direction?"

"I don't know but they are obviously trying to shore up their proof. I heard ADA Brenner was really sick and was out for quite a while. Maybe that has slowed them down. I'm hoping it's something else, like they're still uncertain of the timeline and when the killer left the house."

At about eleven thirty the next morning, Sue swung by my office. Once again, I could tell that she was unhappy just from the way she strutted in. She stood at my desk and accused me of holding back information from the board. I asked her what she was talking about, and she went into a tirade about Nick.

"He was interviewed by the lawyers and told them what Abner said to him. Did you put him up to that?" she demanded.

"No. I told him the lawyers wanted to talk to him and that he should make up his own mind about whether he wanted to answer their questions."

"Did you have any idea what he was going to say?"

"None, other than that Abner pissed him off."

"You didn't know the specifics?"

"Not really."

"Apparently, they're concerned about his allegations. They won't tell me what he said. Only that it casts a new light on the investigation," she said, nostrils flaring.

I could not help but smile, though I tried to hide it. Nick had evidently accused Abner of something unprofessional, and that accredited me. Whatever he told them had gotten the lawyers' attention. It took me a whole five seconds after her departure to telephone Nick and ask him about his interview.

"I told them that at our last session, Dr. Reeves started talking about the 'superego' like Freud. He suggested that mine was 'off' because of my relationship with my mother. He said my sexual desire for her was leading to an internal conflict and driving me toward homosexuality. I told him I was not gay, and he told me I would not know for sure unless I had sex with a man and that he could arrange it through his connections for a small fee. I told him he was crazy and that I was not interested in his help. I left in the middle of the session."

I was flabbergasted. Not only did I question his professional opinions, but I also could not believe Abner was offering his services as a pimp of sorts. The lawyers must have been shocked by Nick's allegations and his willingness to share them. If this is what Abner said to a patient he had seen two or three times, I wondered what he had done with others, like Brett and John. Was the conduct that concerned them also of a sexual nature? With Nick now on the record, the lawyers should be even more intent on getting John and other patients to open up so the board would have the full picture.

The clinic would be desperate to keep Nick's allegations quiet, even as it decided what to do about them. A leak of this nature might destroy the clinic. I had not considered that possibility when I approached Dr. Fitzgerald, since I did not know how serious Abner's conduct was. Now that possibility felt very real. While it was essential that the clinic sanction Abner, it did not have to do so in a public way. The board would also have to decide whether conduct of this kind needed to be reported to state licensing or other authorities.

I called Ed and gave him an update. Liz showed up at my door a few minutes later and asked if I had talked to Sue. I told her I was up to speed and knew more than I could tell her but that the allegations were serious and potentially harmful to Abner and the clinic. She begged me for more information, and I deflected her questions.

"I heard that Abner blew a gasket when he was confronted with the allegations by the lawyers and denied them, saying that the patient was lying. His lawyer has threatened to sue the clinic for defamation if it in any way divulges the accusations," she said.

"There is no way the clinic is going to disclose this. The board will want the problem to go away quietly. The question is what, if any, discipline Abner will accept."

"Do you feel good about this?" she asked in a scolding way, with her hands on her hips. "I don't know what will happen to the clinic if this leaks."

"I never did this to feel good, but I'm glad this problem has been outed internally."

"This is a dangerous game you are playing."

She turned to leave, but I jumped in. "Wait. What are you doing for the long holiday weekend? Maybe we can do dinner again Sunday night?"

"I don't know, Tim. I feel like maybe we're getting a little too close. Let me think about it, okay?"

A few minutes later, there was a knock at my door. Melissa Fitzgerald waltzed into my office, accompanied by one of the clinic's lawyers, Khouri. Melissa had a stern look on her face. She'd just come from a board meeting where counsel had revealed the latest allegations from one of my patients. She asked what I knew, and I told her to assume that I was fully up to speed, having recently talked to the patient. She said that Abner was invited into the meeting to offer up a defense, and he claimed the allegations were false and the entire investigation was a hatchet job.

"The board can't ignore the allegations made by your patient. We are wondering whether you have any contemporaneous notes or other documents to confirm he made these allegations at the time of the alleged misconduct."

"Not from back then. He was not even a patient of mine at the time, just Abner's."

"Can you tell us when he first made an allegation?" the lawyer asked.

"A couple of weeks ago, I think. It was a very general statement at that point."

"Any reason you didn't share that with us?" asked the lawyer.

"Client confidentiality. I didn't have his consent."

"Given what we now know, you need to turn over your notes on your conversations with John Rankin and Brett Stone," Fitzgerald said.

"I can't under the client confidentiality rules, as you have consistently pointed out," I said.

"We think there is an exception in the circumstances," the lawyer said.

I threw up my hands. "You're going to have to talk to my lawyer about that."

"Do you understand that your failure to cooperate is grounds for dismissal?" the lawyer asked.

"You're going to fire me for abiding by my ethical obligations? Really? And I didn't say I won't cooperate. I suggested that you talk to my lawyer."

"We're going around in circles here. If there is evidence that the communications were in furtherance of a crime, like prostitution, they aren't privileged."

"My lawyer raised that approach weeks ago, and you rejected it. Now suddenly you change your mind?" I scoffed.

"Well, we know more now. There are concrete allegations of a crime—solicitation. Blackmail would be a crime also."

"I told you about the blackmail weeks ago. It's what started this. I would love to cooperate, but I don't want to lose my license or get sued. If you can convince my lawyer that I'm protected under an exception to the rule, fine."

I felt like I was on a merry-go-round where everyone kept traveling in the same circle, but there was no gold ring within reaching distance. I had had enough. Someone had to get the ball rolling with patients beyond Nick. I looked up John's address in my records and headed toward Columbus Circle around five p.m. I entered John's apartment building and gave his name to the doorman. Though John was surprised by my visit, he had the doorman let me up. He greeted me at the front door of his apartment with an icy look.

"Why are you here?" John asked.

"Because there's a problem I need your help solving. Another patient has accused Dr. Reeves of a crime, and we need to know if he was guilty of similar misconduct with you or Brett. We don't need to know about whatever you did in the past. All we want to know is that Reeves threatened to expose you and what he was making you and Brett do. We intend to keep all this in-house."

"It's not that simple," John said, standing up and pacing. "There are potential crimes involved. He threatened to go to the police if I didn't troll for young men for him. He did the same with Brett."

"What do you mean, troll for men for him? Be more specific," I said.

He closed his eyes for a moment and let out a deep breath. "He would send me out to pick up young guys for him to have sex with. I'd go to gay bars, clubs, or the street and find someone young for him or his friends to do. If they could get the sex for free, great. If they had to pay for it, that was no problem. Real money. They made me do it every couple of weeks."

"Did he pay you to do this?"

"No, the deal was unless I did it when he asked, he'd cut off my medicine and report me to the police for what I'd done when I was younger. I made the mistake of telling him that in one of our sessions. He has been holding it over my head ever since."

"Was he making Brett do the same thing?"

John hesitated. "Yeah, but in a way, it was worse. The men he met through Brett were mostly underage."

"And the things you and Brett did that he was holding over your head involved crimes too?"

"Yes. So you can see why neither of us wanted to come forward and have our past misconduct aired. We'd get prosecuted because the statute of limitations has not run out. Brett made up his mind that he was going to tell the lawyers about the trolling for underage men part, and I swear to God, they killed him for that."

"Who's 'they'?"

"Reeves and his friends. Some other guys he hangs out with. I don't know who they are, but we trolled for them too."

"Are you willing to tell this to the clinic's lawyers?"

"No fucking way. If Abner's cronies don't kill me, they'll alert the police, and I'll be screwed. The cops will get me for what I've been doing recently and what I did a while back. I'm not going to give them a reason to do either. I got a lawyer who says I don't have to talk, and you *can't* talk. We've got court papers ready to go if you try."

"How are we ever going to stop Abner if you won't come forward?"

"Have him arrested for killing Brett. He arranged it through those same friends."

"Do you know that for a fact?"

"I just know it. Nobody else wanted to hurt Brett. He was executed. Shot in the head, gang style."

I left his apartment feeling conflicted. Since the crimes involved underage boys, there was a colorable argument that I could disclose the communication. But I had not heard the information from Brett—the one who'd solicited the minors—and could not verify it as a result. If I tried telling the clinic's lawyers, John's lawyer would have me enjoined, and I would be looking at a lawsuit and an ethics complaint. Contrast that with the possibility of losing my job if I did not provide the information as instructed by the clinic.

Was John possibly correct that one of Abner's associates had killed Brett to keep him from exposing Abner's and his friends' activities? Sexual assaults on minors were serious felonies. If Abner found out I knew about that, I might be in danger myself. While it was more important than ever that the clinic—and the police—be apprised of Abner's ring of felons, I had to be careful not to become a target.

I called Ed and told him I had a change of heart. I was not prepared to talk regardless of where the clinic stood on the privilege issue. He asked me why, and I simply said that I was committed to maintaining confidentiality as the clients had requested.

"Are you sure there are no other reasons?" Ed asked.

"I'm growing increasingly concerned that Abner is a desperate man willing to take extreme measures to protect himself, and he has surrounded himself with dangerous men. In short, I'm scared."

I did not want Abner to go unpunished. If I could not disclose his patient abuse, maybe I could pursue the strategy John had suggested—have Abner charged with Brett's murder. I doubted anyone would believe that Abner had pulled the trigger himself. I turned my attention to identifying a colleague who might have. I had Ronaldo look into recent newspaper articles and photos of Abner and his social circles. He found about a dozen men with whom Abner appeared to be close personally or professionally.

I started a whiteboard in my hotel room with the pictures of all twelve men and added biographical information to each as we developed it. I learned that one of the twelve had died a few years back, and another was chronically ill. Of the remaining ten, seven still lived in the New York metropolitan area, so I focused on them. I was pretty sure that Harvey Burns, the one with the bulbous nose, was the fellow who had accosted me outside the cab, but I could not be sure.

For a third time, I telephoned Douglas Reeves. I asked him if he got the article I sent him, and he said no. I apologized and asked for his address again, promising to resend it. I told him that I was doing a follow-up article on Abner's friends and asked if he knew any of them. I rattled off a list of names and he recognized three of them: Andrew Townsend, Mark Levine, and Patrick Mulholland. All three had been friends of Abner's since around the time of his medical school days.

I asked Ronaldo to do some research on them. I told him I was looking for evidence that they were involved in Abner's blackmailing. He took a few days and reported back that Townsend was a man of industry, well known in the city for owning and running a cable TV company that did business in upstate New York and parts of New England. He was a widower like Abner. He had two sons, who had moved out of the New York area. He served on the board of one of Julie's charities.

According to Ronaldo, Doctor Mark Levine was a pediatrician with his own practice in Manhattan. He had gone to medical school at Columbia University and done his residency at Lenox Hill Hospital. He was married with two children, and his wife had been a good friend of Julie's.

Ronaldo also let me know that Patrick Mulholland, an investment banker, earned his MBA at Wharton. He had a mixed career. Though he was a successful investment banker, he'd had some trouble with the Securities and Exchange Commission over certain trades he'd placed. He was never formally sued, but he resigned from his large firm because of an investigation and had bounced around ever since. He evidently never married.

The other man who interested me was Major Trent Weston. Ronaldo learned that Weston served in the same Army platoon as Abner, and they had become bosom buddies, the kind of pals who share secrets. He was now stationed at Fort Dix in New Jersey and was married, with a daughter.

I wanted to find out more about each of the five men, so I asked Ronaldo to do background checks and help me narrow down the list of Abner's possible allies in crime. As a retired NYPD detective, Ronaldo still had a lot of contacts and was able to dig up information on each of the men quickly.

He started by looking into the man who had threatened me outside the cab, Harvey Burns. Ronaldo discovered that Burns was an unemployed former security guard who had once been Abner's chauffeur. He had been arrested, but not convicted, for assaulting another driver in a road rage incident, and Abner had let him go. He apparently still did odd jobs for Abner. He lived in Brooklyn with his girlfriend and was a regular at a bar known as Kelly's Tavern.

On the Friday night of Labor Day weekend, I went to Kelly's Tavern hoping to find Burns. I knew he might recognize me from our brief encounter in the cab, but I was not worried about my safety in a public bar. I wanted to ask him some questions and thought I had a way of getting him to answer them.

The tavern was dark, and the air inside was heavy, as the air conditioning was having trouble keeping up with the heat and humidity outside. I saw him sitting at the bar by himself and sidled up to him. I told the bartender that I would have whatever Burns was drinking and to get him another one on me too. Burns looked at me, and his eyes widened in surprise. He had no trouble placing me.

"What the fuck do you want? How did you find me?" he said, turning in his chair to face me.

"I want some answers to my questions," I said.

"And why the hell would I want to do that?" he said, sneering at me.

"Because the police are already looking for you, and I know where they can find you."

"Bullshit. You don't know squat."

"I know where you live and that Abner put you up to killing Brett Stone. That's what the police want you for."

"What? I didn't kill anybody," he said. His ruddy complexion turned pale. He pushed away from the bar with his enormous hands and stared at me with his big brown eyes.

"That's not what the police think. They know you came after me at Abner's request and think it was the same with Stone."

"I don't know any Stone. Abner asked me to scare you. He didn't say anything about killing anybody. I wouldn't do that. The police can't prove anything. Now get out of my face," he said, turning away from me.

Not wanting the conversation to end, I tried to think of how he might be connected to the group of Abner's friends. I took a wild stab.

"Your friends at the gay bar you hang out at have ratted you out. Just a matter of time before the cops find you. I did, and it wasn't hard. I'm happy to help them."

"You're bluffing. I don't go to Fanny's—that's Abner's and his friends' thing. I had nothing to do with Stone's murder. Now get lost before I do something to permanently rearrange your face."

I dropped a twenty on the bar and went out the door. I got on my phone and looked up Fanny's. Then I took an Uber to the Village to visit the underground club.

# 17

The sidewalk area outside the bar was lined with smokers. I walked through the black wood doors and down a dark staircase. The bar was a gray-walled cave with standing room only, except for a small area of tables and chairs on one side. While I saw a few women there, the crowd was overwhelmingly male. The patrons ranged in age from twenties to early sixties.

I sat down at the bar and ordered a beer. The bartender was a pretty, young man in his twenties with short-cropped hair, wearing a Haight-Ashbury T-shirt and jeans. I told him I was just looking for some old buddies who I understood hung out there and showed him photos of Abner's friends. He did not recognize any of them and went back to tending the bar. The fortyish-looking man sitting next to me had obviously overheard my conversation with the bartender, because he turned toward me and asked to see the photos.

"I know that guy," he said, pointing his finger at the picture of Trent Weston. "He comes in here occasionally, looking for some action with the younger crowd. Big, strapping guy in good shape. Looks like military to me."

"How often does he come in?"

"Oh, every few weeks or so. Never alone. Always with some other guy about the same age. They are like a tag team hitting on one, sometimes two guys. They usually don't stay too long."

"That sounds like them. Do you see anybody here tonight who might be able to put me in touch with them?"

"I didn't pay that much attention to who they were leaving with. You might ask that guy over there, Derek, if he knows. He is always here."

"Thanks," I said and meandered across the floor to where Derek was standing with a big bald guy.

He saw me coming and assumed I was a cop. I reassured him I was not and offered to buy him and his friend a drink. I told him I was looking for a couple of guys and showed him the photos. He put on a pair of eyeglasses to look at them before showing one of the photos to his bald friend, who nodded.

"Yeah, I know that guy," Derek said, pointing at Weston. "He took my friend Paulie home to New Jersey. The guy had Army stuff all over his apartment and showed Paulie his guns. That scared the shit out of Paulie, and he bolted from the apartment."

"Is Paulie around tonight?"

"I have not seen him in days. But I saw the guy from the photo in here recently. He was with another man who looked something like this guy," Derek said, pointing to Mulholland. "It was about a week ago. They talked to a good-looking younger man with dirty-blond hair. I remember that because, two days later, I saw photos of the dude in a newspaper article. He committed suicide."

"Does the name Brett Stone ring a bell?"

"No, man. I'm good with faces, not names. You got a picture of him?"

"Sorry. Not on me."

I had accomplished a lot more in one night than I expected and went back to my hotel. My gut told me that Burns was telling the truth. Weston, on the other hand, a big military gay guy who liked guns, sounded like he could be the killer, and I circled his photo on my whiteboard. I circled Mulholland too, since Derek had seen him the night Weston ran into Brett. I crossed out the names of a couple of others who, from what Ronaldo had gathered, were not close to Abner any longer.

After a late night out, I slept in on Saturday. I rallied in the early afternoon and went looking for a less expensive hotel so I could conserve cash. After switching hotels, I telephoned Liz to see if she had made up her mind about dinner Sunday night. She agreed to meet me for drinks at Gordon's in Grand Central Station since she would be coming back by train from a visit with her father. She would ping me when she left her father's place, and we could set a time to meet at the restaurant.

I loafed around on Sunday waiting for Liz's call. I received a text message from her at six suggesting a six-thirty meeting time. I jumped in the shower and threw some fresh clothes on before heading out the door to walk over to Grand Central.

The bar at Gordon's was little more than half full, and I was able to get us a table overlooking the stairs from the ground floor level going down into the station. It looked like people were still away for the weekend, as the main hall was relatively empty and quiet. I did not know which direction Liz was coming from, so I just kept my eyes on the stairs leading to the bar while I sipped on my drink.

A few minutes later, I saw her coming before she got to the stairs. The jeans she wore were low waisted and flattering, as was the T-shirt. She looked relaxed and had a little color from the sun that made her look healthy. She smiled when she saw me and gave me a little kiss on the cheek as she sat down at the table.

We ordered our usual martinis and talked about the weekend. She told me that, after seeing her friends, she went to visit her father for the day since she had not seen him for most of the summer. She reminded me that she was close to him. It was not until our second drink that I hinted at having nosed around about Abner and his friends over the weekend.

"You really think Abner is behind Brett's murder?" she asked.

"I do. I think he wanted to keep Brett from talking about whatever he made him do."

"But why would you think that Abner did not do it himself if that's the case?"

"Not his thing. I think there were others involved with him in the scheme. I've identified a few potential candidates."

I was afraid she would ask me who they were since I was not prepared to share that information with anyone other than Ed and Ronaldo at this point. Fortunately, she did not.

"I think you are going overboard with conspiracy theories. What proof do you have?" she asked, taking the last olive from her martini.

"None, really. Just some interesting connections that make the puzzle pieces fit together."

"I thought maybe we could talk about something else for a change, but you always seem to come back to the same thing. It's getting to be too much, Tim," she said, sounding disheartened. "You just have to let this thing play out. You're not a crime solver. It could be dangerous."

"You're right. It's controlling my whole life. It's hard to think of anything else." I nodded and took another sip of my drink. "I'm famished. You're not going to let me buy you dinner, are you?"

"I don't know." She looked at me softly. "Are you going to talk about this more?"

"If I promise not to?"

"Okay, I'm up for a good steak, but what about letting me pay for a change?"

"Are you sure?" I asked, and she nodded. "I can get the drinks."

I was drunk by the time I crawled back to my hotel room, and it was only eight thirty. As I slowly sobered up, I got bored and started fiddling with the whiteboard. The only thing that stuck out was that Brett was killed between seeing Weston at Fanny's and his scheduled appointment with me. I added a notation that he had decided that morning to talk to the lawyers. Had he communicated that to them? If so, how would his killer have known so quickly?

Monday morning came, and I was not as hungover as I expected. I loaded up on coffee and started my day by telephoning my friend Mickey from Lenox Hill. I apologized for bothering her on Labor Day. I asked if she knew anything about Doctor Mark Levine. She told me that, a few years back, a doctor by that name had been terminated by the hospital for allegedly inappropriately touching a pediatric patient. The allegations were never proven, and he left the hospital to establish his own practice. After getting off the phone, I added this information to the whiteboard and circled Levine's name.

That night I went to a gay bar named Horizons. In contrast to Fanny's, the place was modern and well lit, with a large bar and lots of tables and chairs. It attracted a younger crowd. A man my age tried to pick me up, and I politely told him I was straight. I showed him the photos of Abner's friends, but he did not recognize any of them. I asked him which bar one would go to in Times Square if one were looking for quick action with the younger set, and he suggested Emanuel's on Ninth Avenue.

I walked down Forty-Second Street from Seventh to Ninth amongst the blazing lights of Times Square. Emanuel's was more like Fanny's, though the crowd was less mainstream. I ordered a shot of tequila and showed the bartender my photos. He pointed to one, said, "That's Mark," and went back to tending bar. When I tried to follow up with him, he dismissed me. The other bartender came over and poured me a shot without my asking.

"Mark has a bad rep here, so it's probably better if you don't ask about him," he said.

"What did he do?"

"Hit on a clearly underage kid. I don't even know how the kid got in here. I'm not saying it doesn't happen. Sometimes you can't tell. Anyway, Mark didn't seem to give a shit that he was chasing down a kid. That doesn't go over well here. We told him to find someplace else if that's what he's into."

"Thanks," I said.

"You a cop?"

"No, but I think he's up to no good."

"Him and his Army friend?"

"You know him too?"

"He was in with Mark, but he wasn't any trouble. Seemed like a nice guy, but kind of stiff. Mark was the sleazy one, the one we heard stories about. Supposedly a doctor."

"What kind of stories?" I asked.

"That he likes them young. We got no tolerance for that, as I said."

I had had my limit, so I hopped in a taxi for the ride back to the hotel. Lying on my bed, I called Beth to ask about their weekend. I asked her what she had been telling the children about my absence. She told them I was away on a special project, but it was getting harder to keep putting off the question of my return.

"We should admit we do not know how long I am going to be in limbo and that, until that is over, I am going to live in a hotel and work on my defense," I said. "We should be candid that we don't know what will happen to us as a couple from there. They have a right to know that we have separated on a trial basis."

"You want me to tell them? That we may not get back together again? Don't you think it will be too much for them?" Beth asked.

"We can both tell them. If that's the way you feel, they should know."

As I lay in bed thinking about what was ahead, I realized I might be fired in the morning if I did not answer the lawyers' questions. I left that in Ed's hands, but there was no assurance that he could persuade the board I was not being insubordinate. I decided to tell the board I would go to the press if they terminated me for maintaining client confidences.

My morning began with a call from Ronaldo about his research on Townsend. Ronaldo said the man looked like a boy scout. He had never been in any sort of trouble. He was well loved at his company, partly because he gave so much to charity. He supported youth organizations in poorer parts of the city and got his children involved in altruistic endeavors. He was happily married.

Ed did not call until around eleven, which surprised me, as I was anxious to talk to him. He usurped the conversation by telling me he had good news and bad news. The good news was that the clinic lawyers were not confident enough about their legal position to force me to breach patient confidentiality. They were not going to fire me, at least not yet. The bad news was that my two favorite detectives wanted to talk to me again about Brett, and Ed had arranged an appointment at my office at three p.m.

I had to decide whether I would tell the police what I had found out about Abner's friends. That would probably be meaningless without also telling them what John had said about Abner using him and Brett to troll for gay men and boys. I wanted to develop some additional incriminating information before spinning out my theory.

At three p.m., Ed and the two detectives arrived. Hayes carried an envelope, which he simply placed on my desk unopened.

"Have you been able to come up with any additional information about your whereabouts for the time in question?" Hayes asked.

"Nothing more than what I've already told you."

"And you are sticking with the story that the last time you saw Brett Stone was approximately between ten and eleven a.m. on the date of his death?"

"Yes."

"And that you have never been to his apartment?"

"Correct."

"Do you know where he lived?"

"Not offhand."

"Sir, as we speak, a team of NYPD officers is searching your home, pursuant to a warrant. I am now handing your lawyer one that permits us to search your office."

"Searching my house? With my wife and kids there? For what?"

"What is your probable cause?" Ed asked.

"I'm not going to get into that with you now, counselor. You can take that up with the ADA," said Hayes.

"Do you own a firearm or ammunition, sir?" DeCarlo asked.

"No, I have never touched a gun."

DeCarlo was already up and searching through my office. I went out into the hall and telephoned Beth. She could hardly speak.

"The police are ripping the place apart. It's crazy."

"How are the kids handling it?"

"I took them next door to Jean's when I saw the police arrive. I'm sure they're watching out the window."

"They are searching my office too. I have no idea what they are looking for. Please make sure to take an inventory of anything they take."

They searched my office for more than an hour and found nothing. They looked frustrated. Hayes called someone, presumably his colleague who was running the search at my house, and shook his head at DeCarlo.

I called Beth when they were done, and she told me the police were not quite through there. They had made a mess, but no damage was done, and nothing had been found so far. The kids had a million questions she could not answer. They were embarrassed to go to school, since everyone on the bus tomorrow would know what had happened. I suggested she let them stay home for a day or two.

Hayes was the first one to speak. "Okay, what did you do with it?"

"With what?" I replied.

"The ammo for the gun we found in Mr. Stone's hand. We know you had both."

"You don't know what you are talking about. I've never had a gun or any ammo."

"Did you throw it away recently?"

"I'm telling you I've never had ammo. Whatever gave you that idea?"

"We have our sources. An eyewitness."

"That's not possible. Someone is lying to you," I said.

Ed and I spoke after the police left.

"Do the search warrants mean that the police think I am the killer?"

"Yes. I was worried they were ready to arrest you on the spot. Who might have seen you with a gun and ammunition?" Ed said.

"That story is made up. Is there a way we can force the DA's office to reveal the identity of the witness?"

"No. Witness identification does not occur until after the indictment. What we need to figure out is who would lie to the police about you having ammunition."

"The only person I can think of is Abner."

"No, I don't think so," Ed said. "It would have come out before if Abner said it. I have a feeling that it's somebody else."

I assumed the police had reason to suspect I'd shown the gun to someone shortly before the murder. The only people I would have seen were my patients and my colleagues, plus family and a few friends. The idea that I would show a gun to any one of them was preposterous. And I could not imagine any of them lying about something that serious.

"There must be a way you can flush out the police on this," I said to Ed. "Won't they want to reveal more of what they know to convince me that I am in danger of being charged?"

"They might. I plan on talking to the ADA today and pressing him for more information."

After Ed left, I dialed Ronaldo's number. He said he'd just been about to call me and brought me up to speed on his investigation. He explained that Mulholland and Abner had had a falling out several years back and were no longer on speaking terms. He was still digging for information concerning Weston and Levine. People seemed willing to talk about the doctor but were more reserved when it came to discussing Major Weston. He had an exemplary military record, yet those who served under him were unwilling to say much about him. This made him a bit of an enigma. His wife supposedly had had affairs with a couple of high-ranking officers, but they remained married. They still lived on base, though Weston left Fort Dix often.

I was interested in Mark Levine because he sounded more like a sexual predator. Ronaldo had located Levine's former partner, who'd left their practice a couple of years ago. Ronaldo was planning on touching base with him and would have more to report in the next day or two.

Upon returning to my hotel, I discovered the police had found out where I was staying and searched my room. I assumed, since there was no receipt left behind, that they had taken nothing. Once my room was put back in order, I updated my whiteboard. I added information about Weston and struck Mulholland, Townsend, and two others based on Ronaldo's research.

I then called Beth. She was still upset from this morning's raid, but she confirmed the police had not seized anything. She could not believe I was somehow a suspect in a second murder investigation and said it was a good thing that I had prepared the kids for possible police action. They were both frightened at seeing the police rummaging around the house.

I went to bed thinking about who would have told the police I had a gun. I assumed that whoever was trying to tie me to the gun was working with Abner. The person who jumped to mind was Sue, who I thought was secretly in love with Abner. She seemed jealous of any woman Abner paid attention to, including Liz. While I thought of her as a straight shooter, when it came to Abner, she would do anything.

# 18

I grabbed my briefcase and hustled downstairs into the hotel lobby for a quick breakfast snack. Someone had left a newspaper behind, and I scanned its headlines. A few pages into the paper, I saw a picture of a 9mm pistol under a headline that read, "Murder, Not Suicide." According to the story, the police had confirmed that Brett Stone had been murdered with a gun. This was old news, and I wondered why it was being released only now. The timing of it in relation to the police visit did not escape me—without a doubt, the informant's claims about the gun were the probable cause for the search warrants.

I immediately telephoned Ed, who had just finished reading the article. When I got off with him, my phone rang. It was Beth calling to see if I knew about the story.

"What does this mean?" she asked. "I thought they determined that it was murder some time ago?"

"I don't really know why it's just coming out now."

"Was it your gun? Tell me the truth."

"Damn it, Beth. Someone is trying to frame me for both murders at this stage. I think it's Abner."

"Can you prove that?"

"I'm working on it."

I went to the clinic at about nine. Sue saw me come in and entered my office with a concerned look on her face.

"Is it true the police were here looking for ammunition for that gun?" she asked. "The search warrant did not specify that."

"Relax. They didn't find any."

"This is getting awfully concerning. You don't think the police are going to come here and arrest you, do you? That would be a terrible thing for our image."

There was no empathy in her voice. Her only concern was the institution.

"Sue, I don't know what they are going to do. All I'll say is I am innocent, and arresting me would be a mistake."

I was on pins and needles waiting for Ed's call. The phone rang, and I jumped for it. It was not Ed, but Ronaldo.

"I've got some interesting information about Levine," he said. "Levine's former partner quit the partnership after one of Levine's patient's mothers complained that Levine had groped her eleven-year-old son. Levine quietly paid the boy's family off, but his partner was outraged and left the practice."

"That is interesting."

"Not only that, but the partner came to believe that Levine was part of a small group of gay men who got together periodically 'to look for young meat' at gay bars. The partner met one of them, an officer in the Army, at the office one day."

There was, of course, no issue with men looking to hook up with other men, but the thing that bothered me was that Levine and his group were targeting young ones. In view of Levine's history, I assumed that meant underage men, which was consistent with what Brett had been doing, according to John.

Ed called to tell me he had talked to the ADA, and they were still processing the information they had.

"All Luzon would say is that they had information from a tipster that you had a gun around the time of the murder," Ed continued. "I think they are trying to identify the tipster. That means the limbo continues, at least with respect to the Stone murder."

"Maybe they'll never find him or her."

Ed and I talked about the likelihood of me soon being indicted for Julie's murder. Luzon hadn't said anything definitive, but Ed picked up the vibe that action was imminent.

"It's been too quiet for too long. I think we are living on borrowed time," he said. "Brenner told me things have been delayed because of her illness, but I think it was more than that. After screwing up with Philip, they want to make sure they can get a conviction this time, so they're trying to prepare an ironclad case. With her back a few weeks now, I think they are getting ready to move."

"So what do we do?"

"You need to prepare your family that this could happen any day now. I need to know how much money you can pull together for a bail bondsman. If we get bail, it's likely to be steep."

"Let me talk to Beth. I want to issue a statement to the media denying the allegations. Can you put one together?"

"Sure."

I then called Beth and explained that Ed thought an arrest was coming down the pike soon. I told her what she could expect.

"I just knew it," she said, sobbing into the phone. "What is everyone going to think?"

"When you calm down, we need to talk about money for bail."

"We'll do whatever it takes. I don't want to see you in prison the whole time."

"You know I am going to lose my job. How are you going to pay for the house and feed the family on your salary? If I make bail, I'll set up my own shop with my own patients."

After talking more about finances, I spoke to the children. I told them what I thought was about to happen and tried to help them make sense of the nightmare.

"I thought you said you didn't do it, Dad. Why are they going to arrest you?" asked Samantha.

"Somebody is lying to the police, honey. Don't worry, we'll prove that, and I'll be acquitted."

Ed had read the tea leaves correctly. At six in the morning two days later, there was a knock on the door of my hotel room. When I answered, a group of patrol officers burst into my room and grabbed me, holding me down on the bed. They handcuffed me with my hands behind my back.

"You are under arrest for first-degree murder, attempted murder, and assault with a deadly weapon," one of the officers said as he dragged me into the hallway.

I was gasping for air when they took me outside. A small crowd of people had gathered on the sidewalk outside the hotel. Among them were some press photographers who had obviously been tipped off. A couple of news reporters stuck their microphones in my face, but I kept quiet, knowing we would be issuing a statement later in the day. With a push from an officer, I ducked my head, slid into the police car, and settled in for the ride.

When I got to the station, I was processed and then permitted to make a call to Ed.

"What happened?" I asked.

"Nothing, really. I'm surprised it took them this long," Ed said. "It's the combination of you being there at the wrong time and the knife. In the final analysis, it's all about the fingerprints. I talked to ADA Brenner about bail, and she is opposed to it, so we will have to make an application to the court to release you with the posting of a bond when you are arraigned."

"I thought we'd have another opportunity to pitch them?"

"I have been doing that all along. Every time I talk to them. We just don't have a good answer to their key piece of evidence."

Though I'd seen this coming, I was still shocked and horrified. Nothing had prepared me for what I was feeling. I had always assumed I would be able to post bail and had not thought about the possibility of being incarcerated up through trial. I could hardly afford to defend myself, especially if I had to post a bond. While Ed was willing to take on Julie's murder case for a flat fee, I also needed representation in the Stone case. I dreaded the idea that I might need a public defender to represent me, because they were stretched thin and overworked.

Early that afternoon, I appeared in court with Ed for my arraignment. Beth was in the gallery but, at my request, the kids weren't there. The arraignment took place before Judge Evers in an old wood-paneled courtroom. After I entered a plea of not guilty, the court took up my application for bail. ADA Brenner emphasized the brutal nature of the crime and the concern for public safety. She noted that I was being investigated for a second murder and suggested I was both a danger to the community and a flight risk. Ed focused on weaknesses in the circumstantial evidence, particularly lack of motive. He also talked about my status in the community, noting that I had a family in Manhattan and was not likely to flee. Judge Evers weighed the arguments and, to my surprise, set bail lower than we had anticipated. The court set a trial date for January third, only four months away.

Once I was out, I did not know where to turn. Beth and I had coffee. She looked surprisingly good, dressed in a blue suit with her blonde hair pulled back. She had thought about things and was even more adamant about me not living at home. We could not afford for me to live in a hotel, even a moderately priced one, for months on end. Eve and her husband Stan came through, and the court permitted me to reside with them in their house on Long Island through the date of trial.

The next few weeks proved to be difficult. As I had predicted, the clinic suspended me without pay, so I had to figure out a way to make some money. I rented an office month-to-month in a suite of offices in midtown Manhattan where I could continue seeing the few patients of mine who were not scared off by the murder charges. John, Nick, Ellen, Darren, and Philip all stuck with me.

Most of my friends and colleagues cut me off. The only one from the clinic with whom I stayed in touch was Liz. I did not see her in those first few days after my arrest, but we talked regularly. She didn't seem surprised by the arrest.

"I don't know that this changes anything since you still maintain your innocence," she said. "You've got to reassure me, however, that I'm not being crazy and you're going to prevail."

"I expect to, though you never know with a jury. How are things at the clinic?"

"They've settled down. The board concluded the investigation into Abner's activities. He was given a letter of reprimand for using ambiguous language with a patient that could be misinterpreted as offensive."

I was outraged that the board had not directly taken on the allegations that Abner had blackmailed two of his other patients. Based on the snippet from the memo Liz read to me, the board had found the evidence of such activities to be "inconclusive in view of the patients' unwillingness to share information with the clinic's counsel." I blamed the lawyers for not untangling the privilege issues or finding a way to make the patients like John comfortable talking.

I now had plenty of time to pursue my inquiry into Weston and Levine, the only two names left on my whiteboard. I started to alternate nights between Emanuel's and Fanny's, hoping to run into one of them. There was no sign of either during my first week on the hunt. During my second week at Emanuel's, I put out word that I had a friend who was looking for some action with an older man. It spread quickly in the bar, and a young man approached me to see if my friend might be interested in meeting a couple of older gentlemen. He asked for my friend's picture, and I handed him one of some teenager from the internet. I watched him go show an older man the photo, and a few minutes later, he came back to me.

"I have a couple of older gentlemen who will be here later and might be interested. Where is your friend?" the young man asked.

"He's at his place, waiting for my call," I said. "Are your colleagues businessmen?"

"In every sense of the word. They are successful professionals who understand that paying a fair price is part of business. How old is your friend?"

"I don't really know. Somewhere around eighteen. Does that matter?"

"Not really," he said. Then he looked down the bar and said, "One of them just arrived. Let me see if he is truly interested."

I followed his gaze and saw Weston. I recognized him even without the Army uniform with his short haircut and sharp eyes. A minute later, he was followed by a well-dressed, wiry Levine. They both gathered around the young man to whom I had been speaking. I saw Levine look at the photo and nod. The young man came back and said that one of them was interested and asked how much. We negotiated from there, settling on seven hundred fifty for an hour. I said I would go get my friend.

I left the bar through the back door and took the alley to Ninth Avenue. I turned off my phone's recorder as soon as I got out of the bar. I hustled to Penn

Station to make the train back to Long Island. While on the train, I listened to the recording through my headphones. I finally had something I could use, not with the police but with John. The kid in the photos could not have been more than sixteen, but both Weston and Levine were interested. I thought that the audio and photo together might help John visualize how repulsive it had been for Brett to solicit underage males. If he was angry enough, he might be swayed into telling me what he knew about these men.

I was tired from the late-night activities of the past week or so. I usually did not get to bed much before one in the morning and had to be up by seven to catch the train into the city and then the subway up to my temporary office. I couldn't keep this pace forever, but I was finally making some progress.

# 19

My sister fixed breakfast for me in the morning. I ate with her family instead of rushing out to make the early train. The extra few minutes and the second cup of coffee felt good. When the kids were finished eating, Stan hurried them out the door for the ride to school, while Eve and I lingered over our coffees.

"Tim, where do you go at night? You rarely get home before midnight," Eve said.

"I'm doing some research, trying to expose Abner's evil ways."

I didn't tell her that, while my research focused on the apparent sex scandal, my ultimate objective was to find someone the police could charge with murder. That would have scared her.

"Where? There is nothing open that late at night."

"Now, don't be concerned, but I am helping Ed with stuff related to the cases. I am trying to help him figure out who is framing me."

"It sounds dangerous. What exactly are you doing?"

"It's not dangerous. I just go to restaurants and bars and keep my ear to the ground."

"I don't believe it's as cushy as that. I don't want to see you get hurt. You have a good lawyer; let him do the work."

"I love you for caring, Eve. But this is my life, and I need to help Ed. I promise

I will be careful."

Ed was doing double duty. The Reeves case was proceeding, and he was still working to keep the DA's office from indicting me a second time. There was no evidence tying me to the gun other than a tip from someone who claimed they saw it on me. Even if I had allegedly shown someone the gun, what evidence did the police have that the gun I showed them was a murder weapon? While continuously emphasizing that I did not own a gun, Ed kept trying to raise further doubt in the prosecutor's mind by noting that many 9mm guns looked alike.

With Ed primarily focused on the Reeves case, I did not want to distract him with my attempts to identify Brett's killer. He would have cautioned me to stand down. I was no private eye, and clandestine meetings with strangers in seedy bars could be hazardous, especially if one of them might be a killer. However, I would no longer be satisfied with proving that Weston and Levine, with or without Abner's help, trafficked young men. I also wanted to try to tie Brett's death to the idea that he was going to expose that activity.

I went to my temporary office the next day. John was coming in for a session, and I was going to throw everything I had at him, including the tape. I was willing to take chances with him even if it meant he would drop me as his therapist. We had gotten close to parting ways before, but he was sticking by me. What possible reason could he have for that, aside from knowing I was right about Brett and trying to do something about it?

We sat in my small office in two chairs facing one another. He looked tired and stressed. I wanted him to know at the outset that this was not going to be a normal session.

"How long were you being intimate with Brett?" I asked.

John tilted his head in curiosity. "Hmm. How did you know?"

"Enough signs were there, especially the connection to Abner. Brett told me he was bisexual and in a new relationship, which coincided with you telling me you and he had become friends. Abner played off that relationship, didn't he?"

"He introduced us and got us together. It was my first time with a man, and I realized that, like Brett, I was bisexual. Abner took advantage of the fact that Brett and I fell in love." Tears welled up in his eyes.

"By threatening to out you?"

"No, we didn't care who knew," he said dismissively. "We were in love. He threatened to expose Brett if he didn't pimp for him. Same with me. Both Brett and I have colorful pasts."

"I know you won't tell me about that, but you've got to tell me what Abner had you do. If he is responsible for Brett's death, we need to make him pay."

He closed his eyes and raked his hands through his wavy hair. He wiped the sniffle from his nose with the back of his hand.

I could tell he was weakening, so I continued. "I don't believe you don't know the men in the photos I showed you. Why are you lying about that?"

"They're part of Abner's clique. If I burn them, I burn him, and he makes me pay by revealing my past," John said.

"You suggested that, in Brett's case, the young men were sometimes underage. Was that at the urging of these men?"

"That was in the last six months, and Brett felt awful about it. Like me, he was okay with helping grown men hook up, but helping Abner and his friends with minors disturbed Brett greatly. That's why I think he decided to talk to the lawyers."

"Do you think Abner found out?"

"Someone may have leaked that Brett had accepted the lawyers' invitation."

"So anyone who knew the lawyers' schedules would have known that Brett agreed to an interview, right?"

"At some point they would have, but probably not until the day of the murder. I don't think he made up his mind until a few hours before the appointment."

I again thought immediately of Sue, who was coordinating the schedules with the lawyers, staff, and patients. She could easily have told Abner that Brett was scheduled to come in and meet with the lawyers later in the afternoon. And Abner could have passed the word on to one of his crooked associates.

"I saw two of the men in the photos at a gay bar recently, and they had a young man trolling for them. Is that how it usually works?"

"Yeah, but not always at bars or clubs. Could be anywhere. They have scouts who round up young men for them. That's what Abner called me and Brett. I think there were a handful of us."

"Let me play something for you," I said as I turned on the recording from Emanuel's. "As you will hear, they are still at it."

I watched John as he listened to the tape. What he heard appeared to make him as angry as I hoped. His ears turned red, and his muscles tightened.

"I've heard enough," he said.

"I know the payment you received was his continued silence. Did these other scouts get paid?"

"I imagine so. I don't know any of them aside from Brett."

"Thanks for telling me all this. I think it will go a long way in helping the police investigate Brett's murder."

"Wait. I told you, but I'm not going to tell the cops. All this stuff I did is against the law. And if the police find out what I did some time ago, I could be put away. I loved Brett, but he is gone, and I'm not about to go to prison."

"But what's the point of telling me, then?"

"So you'd know and figure out a way to get the info to the cops without it coming back to bite me. Keep me out of it. My lawyer is ready if we get wind of you telling anyone what I said. He said you'll taint the whole police investigation if you breach the privilege. Plus, as you told me, you'll lose your license."

"How am I supposed to give the police what they need?"

"I don't know. Catch Abner and his cronies in the act, I guess. You said they're still doing it."

"That will only prove they are involved in illegal solicitation and child abuse. It won't pin the murder on them. How do we show the cops that Abner and his gang are behind Brett's murder?"

"I can't prove that, but it seems obvious. The cops will understand that Abner and his friends could not afford to have Brett answer questions about what he'd done for them."

"That's only if they know how bad what Abner asked you to do was. We need to tell them about the involvement of minors. What about trying to get you some form of immunity from prosecution?"

"I've already considered that. I'll still have to plead guilty to something. So

I'd still wind up in prison. That makes it a nonstarter."

We did not make any more progress. He wanted me to find a way to use what I knew to develop evidence against Abner and his buddies. John told me that the group would move from one venue to the next in sort of a rotation. They wouldn't surface at Emanuel's for another couple of weeks, which would give me a chance to catch them at Fanny's in the interim. I would use a stand-in this time.

Through a college friend of mine, I found and hired an unemployed young actor to be my eyes and ears. He was nineteen but looked younger. I paid him a small fee to sit at Fanny's and look and sound "available." I saw him at the end of his first week, and he was nursing cuts and bruises on his face and torso.

"Most nights," the flamboyant redhead said, "I turned down a good bit of action that came my way. The other night, I was approached by a 'scout' for an older gentleman at Fanny's. The scout asked me how old I was, and I said sixteen. He showed back up five minutes later with a proposition. When I insisted on seeing the date, the scout pointed to a man sitting at the end of the bar who looked exactly like Weston."

"Really?"

"Yes." He looked around and then leaned closer to me and whispered, "The scout offered me a healthy 'allowance' to spend the evening with the older man. Since I had been propositioned and knew who made the offer, I figured my work was done and turned the guy away. I left the bar shortly after and got jumped in the alley by two men, one of whom I think was that guy Weston."

"Can you positively identify him?"

"I don't think so. It was dark, and I covered my face and eyes to protect myself from the punches. The only thing I remember is that the older guy wore a red baseball cap."

I apologized for what had happened to him and gave him a little extra cash. He warned me to stay away from the guys who had attacked him. He said Weston was enraged and that the scout had to stop him from continuing the beating.

If Weston was the brawn of the operation, Abner was the brains. He was probably the one who recruited the scouts, and his interactions with Brett and

John confirmed as much. I assumed that his group's activities had been going on for some time and that he had previously enlisted some young men who were now former patients. When I'd broken into Sue's office, I had photographed the names of the patients who had been identified to the police as having violent histories. I googled them and recognized three: Jim Augustine, Corey Shuman, and Alex Fernandez.

Ronaldo found the contact details for Shuman and Fernandez; Augustine had moved out of the area. I started with Fernandez. He lived in a townhouse apartment near the LIRR station in Kew Gardens, Queens. I went to his place on my way back to the island and caught him coming in from work. I introduced myself and said that I used to work at the clinic. I studied his chiseled face and noticed the series of tattoos running up and down his right arm. He was also sizing me up with his penetrating dark eyes.

"We are looking into making reparations for harms Dr. Reeves inflicted on various patients, and your name came up. We have reason to believe that Dr. Reeves was using some of his male patients for improper purposes and, in settling a class action, we are trying to find eligible claimants."

"What do you mean he used patients for improper purposes?" he asked.

"I can't say, but if you are one of them, you'll know."

"He tried to send me out to find boys for him and his friends at bars. Does that count?"

"Yes, that is exactly what we're looking for," I said, pretending to take notes on my pad.

"The old bastard came on to me and said he'd spread word that I was a sexual deviant unless I worked some of the clubs in the area to find him men and boys to have sex with. Him and his friends, that is. They also offered me money to do it."

"You know who they are?"

"I know one of them. A skinny doctor for kids."

"Did you do it?

"Fuck no. I got angry at Reeves and fired him right then and there. Will I really get money if I sign up?"

"Too early to tell. You may have to fill out a claim form summarizing what he did to you. I hope that is all right. I'll make sure you get one in the mail."

I finally had a witness who was willing to talk, though I had induced him to do so under false pretenses. I did not know if I could get in trouble for that. It should not matter to the police that Fernandez did not actually solicit anyone, so long as he was asked to do so. The play, I thought, was simply passing his information along to Hayes and DeCarlo so they could interview Alex on their own.

I got on the train at Kew Gardens and arrived at Eve's house at around seven thirty. After dinner, I called the number I had for Shuman. A gruff voice answered the phone. Using the same line I had with Fernandez, I explained who I was and the purpose of my call. He said that he had not seen Reeves in years and had no information to share.

I then telephoned Detective Hayes. He warned me again about the dangers of talking to him. I told him I had a witness who would testify that Reeves asked him to find young men and boys who would have sex with Reeves and his friends. Hayes asked me if the witness actually solicited any kids, and I said that I did not think so.

"I think Reeves used Brett Stone the same way and had him murdered when Stone decided to blow the whistle," I said.

"So you think Reeves killed Brett Stone to cover up a pedophile ring?"

"Yes. Or he had one of his henchmen do it."

"I need you to come in and fill out a statement about your conversation with the witness."

I went to bed feeling a little bit of relief. All the detective work I was doing on my own was exhilarating, especially because I was finally getting somewhere. Hopefully, Fernandez would corroborate my story and help my credibility with Hayes.

# 20

I was on edge when I got up next morning. I knew it was not a good idea to go to the police station alone. Part of my reason for doing so was financial. I was already feeling the strain of having Ed defend me in the Reeves case. If I could focus the police on Abner and his friends in the Stone case, they might dig something up and save me from having to pay a lawyer for that defense, so I figured it was worth the risk.

On my way to the city, I telephoned Liz and asked her to join me for a cup of coffee. We met at our usual place around nine thirty. She had done something to her hair, and it accentuated her face, making her prettier than ever. She asked about my defense and told me that Abner was crowing about the arrest and looking forward to testifying in the upcoming trial.

"That's odd," I said. "I thought he was unconscious the whole time and didn't see anything."

"Motive. He supposedly thinks he is the key witness on why you did it. Any idea what he'll say?"

"He'll make something up. It will be interesting to see the lies he told the grand jury and the police. We'll be ready to rebut them."

"Anything new with the Stone investigation?"

"Yes, actually. I think I discovered some useful information, and I've turned it over to the police."

"Really? What kind of stuff?"

"Information about Abner and his friends."

"His friends?" she asked, raising her eyebrows.

"Yeah. My conspiracy theory, as you like to call it, includes a couple of his buddies. Let's leave it at that."

"Fascinating. How are you finding things out?"

"From my lawyer, his investigator, and my own detective work. I'm out beating the bushes myself. It's actually kind of fun."

When I left Liz, I went straight to the police station to see Detective Hayes. We walked past his desk and picked up DeCarlo. They escorted me into an interview room, took out some paper to record my statement, and confirmed I was okay proceeding without a lawyer. Hayes then leaned across the table and looked me in the eyes.

"I don't know what kind of crap you are pulling, but it's not helping your case any," he said and then leaned back.

"What do you mean?"

"That Fernandez guy. I sent two cops to see him this morning, and he denied everything. He admitted he'd been a patient of Dr. Reeves for a short time, but he said he knows nothing about looking for men or boys on his behalf. Says you made that up."

"That's not true. He told me the story. I can repeat it to you."

"And he said you lied about who you were. Something about you working for the clinic and reparations."

"That, I admit. I wanted to get him talking."

"So you lied to him, and you expect me to believe the rest of what you say?" he said in a pitched voice, with his palms outstretched to the sky.

"Look. Reeves is running some kind of sex ring, and others are in on it. I'm telling you I know, but I can't reveal what information I have."

"We're back to that again? It's getting a little old," Hayes said, dropping his pad on the table.

"What if I have a recording where you can hear young men soliciting other men and kids on behalf of Reeves and his pals? It doesn't identify the men by name, but I saw them. And what if I sent someone to be a setup for a hustler trying to find boys for Reeves's pal and he got beat up for not going with the guy?"

He furrowed his brow. "Are you running your own sting operation? You're going to get yourself in trouble for that, if not beaten up or worse. Can you identify the men who were there by name?"

"Yeah, but I assume that everyone will deny everything."

"Can you send me the recording? It better be legit."

I forwarded the recording and stood by as Hayes and DeCarlo went off to listen to it. They came back about fifteen minutes later and wanted to know the name of the bar.

"Did you really offer to supply a male prostitute?" Hayes asked as he wrote down the name.

"All I had was a picture of some guy I got online. That's what I showed him."

"Do you know who the guy you negotiated with is?"

"No, but I could probably pick him out in a lineup."

"Who was with him?"

"Their names are Trent Weston and Mark Levine."

I divulged what I knew about them, including their connections to Abner. I added that there was more I could not reveal because of patient confidentiality concerns.

"How many patients are you concerned about?" Hayes asked.

"Two, one of whom is dead. You can figure out the other one."

"Look, I can drag Rankin down to the station, but I can't lean on him to give up the privilege under police protocols."

"He's too scared to talk in any event."

"Scared of what or whom?"

"Of something Reeves knows. I couldn't tell you what it is if I knew, which I don't. I think he's also scared that Reeves is behind Stone's murder."

"He won't even tell you what Reeves has on him?"

"No. I've tried countless ways to drag it out of him."

"This is all highly unusual," Hayes said, scratching his head. "Here I am talking to a man charged with murder about another murder case in which he is also a suspect. And you don't even have a lawyer with you. I don't know if I should be talking to you, let alone believing anything you say."

"The tape speaks for itself," I said. "You heard evidence of a solicitation."

"It's interesting, but it doesn't tell me who spoke and on whose behalf. To get that, I've got to trust you, and quite frankly, I don't, especially after Fernandez denied what you told me. The whole thing could be fake. Now, maybe something you say or do will convince me otherwise, but you're still my number one suspect for Stone's murder. And let's not forget about Julie Reeves."

My credibility as a witness was plainly an issue for them, and I was spouting scenarios that bordered on the fantastic. Had Hayes and DeCarlo put on blinders that prevented them from being open to theories that did not fit with their current thinking? I was counting on the fact that these were seasoned veterans who would follow the evidence wherever it took them.

On the train ride back to Long Island, I spoke to Ed. He told me that we received the witness statements from several people and that he found Abner's neighbor's statement helpful in two different respects. First, she had seen me exactly at eight ten p.m. She knew that because her favorite show, *Wheel of Fortune*, had just gone to commercials when she looked out the window. Second, she had seen two other men near Abner's house in the half hour before that. The first was presumably Philip, as he left his appointment with Abner. But who was the second person she saw minutes later? He could have been a passerby, or he could have been the killer. The police had not told us about this third man.

We also received call logs from the neighbor's phone, as well as mine. The neighbor called Abner's house from her cell at ten minutes past eight and got no answer. My phone showed that I called Abner's cell at seven minutes after eight and again three minutes later and also got no answer. While the call logs weren't definitive proof of anything, neither were they inconsistent with our contention that Abner was out cold and Julie was dead when I arrived.

Then, there were the surveillance tapes from the corner of Third Avenue and East Seventy-Second Street that the DA shared with Ed in discovery because it was potentially exculpatory evidence known as Brady material. They confirmed that two men had walked down the street toward Abner's house between seven thirty and eight o'clock. The tapes also picked up a cab, presumably mine, turning the corner onto Abner's block at seven fifty-six and stopping in front of his house. If, as we believed, one of the two men who came down the street was Philip, the other man was someone the police should naturally have pursued. Why, then, was there nothing about him in the files we had seen?

Had the police neglected to consider that the killer could have been in the house during all or part of Philip's session and simply waited for it to end before he went to attack Abner? If Abner left the house as late as seven p.m. for Philip's appointment, the murder could have taken place between seven forty-two, when Julie answered her phone, and seven minutes after eight, when I called. Thus, the police needed to go back and check the surveillance tapes before seven thirty just in case the murderer got there earlier.

According to Ed, Philip stated that he did not lock the office door when he left after his appointment. That meant the killer did not have to go into the house to get the keys to the office. If hurting Abner was the objective, all the attacker had to do was walk in after Philip departed. Anyone who knew Abner would know that he was in his office from six to nine every night, so there was no reason to go to the house to look for him. The implication from this was that the killer actually went into the house to kill Julie in a premeditated fashion.

Philip's statement also indicated that someone had locked the office door between the time Philip left and I arrived. Since the neighbor had seen me pounding on the locked door, her testimony would support that. Could it have been the third person on the surveillance tapes or someone else who had been hiding in the house?

The next morning, I got a call from John. He sounded frantic. He said the police had contacted him and knew he had information on Dr. Reeves. They asked him to come down to the police station for an interview.

"What did you tell them?" he demanded.

"Nothing. I swear. They know you refused to give an interview to the lawyers and assume you know something. I've been investigating Abner's friends and shared that with the police. They probably want to ask you about those men."

"God damn it. Why can't you just leave this alone? What am I supposed to say?"

"They are going to ask if you know any of his friends, and if so, how? Also, whether you ever trolled for men for them too."

"Shit. I can't answer those questions! Reeves will find out and screw me," he said and hung up.

A few hours later, the clinic and I were each served with a temporary restraining order barring us from discussing any of our communications with John with any third person, except to the extent required by law. Sue telephoned me and asked what this was all about, and I explained John was under the mistaken impression that I was talking to the police about what he had told me in therapy. I assured her he was wrong and that I was continuing to abide by patient confidentiality restrictions.

I phoned John and offered to have the restraining order continue in effect for the duration of the case. I also asked him if he had talked to the police, and he said that his lawyer advised him to take the Fifth Amendment. Upon reflection, I considered this to be a good development for me. Hayes and DeCarlo were going to be more interested than ever in what John was hiding. The fact that John cited his right not to incriminate himself would indicate that he knew of, and was involved in, a crime somehow related to their investigation. One possibility for them to consider would be that John killed Brett. The second was what I had been preaching—that John had information about a sex ring that would not only incriminate him, Abner, and Abner's friends but could also unravel the Stone murder.

Hayes phoned me that afternoon. He again asked me if I was represented in the Stone case, and I said no. He was preparing for his interview with John and pressed me to identify what topics to cover with him. I explained that, because of the recent court order, I could not tell him anything more.

"If the conduct John is a party to involves child abuse, the law recognizes an exception to the psychologist-patient privilege, and you can tell me," Hayes said firmly.

While that was true, we were in a gray area, according to Ed. Since John himself was not involved in soliciting underage boys, the exception did not apply to my conversations with him. I only had indirect information that Brett solicited teenage boys and did not think that I was permitted to speculate about his activities.

"Even so, I am not at liberty to speak," I said. "Sorry. But I stand by what I told you earlier. You should know what to ask based on what I've already told you."

After hanging up with Hayes, I had a session with Nick. It was a pleasure to talk to someone so open after all the others who refused to talk. He had taken some of my advice to heart and hired a woman to take care of his mother from two until five, three days a week. His mother complained about the caregiver but always wanted to know when she was coming back. He still spent most of his evenings with his mother, and she was every bit as demanding as before, but he was able to handle it better, knowing that he would have some time off.

I was caught up in a waiting game with the DA's office and the NYPD. While Hayes and DeCarlo were presumably following up on the information I had provided, I had no visibility into what they were finding and whether it helped me or not. I knew I should sit back and give them their due, but I was not built like that.

Ronaldo had given me Dr. Levine's cell number. I went out and bought a burner phone, then waited until the evening when I was on the island to try him.

"Hello," he said.

"I know your dirty little secret," I said in a raspy voice. "And I'm going to expose you."

"What? Who is this?" the doctor responded.

"You don't know me, but I know what you've done."

"What the hell are you talking about?"

"You and your friends have been bad boys, but the world is about to find out."

"Find out what?"

"Don't pretend you don't know," I said, raising my voice in anger.

"What do you want?"

"For now, just to watch you sweat."

I hung up on that note and imagined what was going through his mind.

He would know what I was talking about. Would his first call be to Abner or Weston? If I was right about the pecking order, he would call Abner. Abner would try to calm Levine down and bring Weston up to speed. Abner must have been aware that I had a basic understanding of his blackmail scheme but was likely in the dark as to how much I knew. He would realize I was the one who had placed the call, though, and that I was aware of the identity of another member of his ring.

I had bet that Levine was the weakest of the three because he had a prior history that was ultimately discoverable. Allegations that he was currently involved with young boys would be viewed as credible once that history came out. He would want to avoid public humiliation at all costs. He would pressure Abner to try to neutralize me, and the three of them would work together to achieve that end. For all I knew, their group was a lot bigger, and they would have help coming after me.

My investigative efforts would be hampered if they decided to lay low for the time being. If I were them, I would avoid sending any scouts out to the usual places, making it impossible for the NYPD to catch them in the act. I did not know how voracious an appetite the group had for underage prey or how long its members would be comfortable sitting on the sidelines. I guessed that, after years of practice, Abner knew all the tricks and would try to figure out a way around the heat of the moment.

My thoughts about Abner were interrupted by my final appointment of the day, Darren Carroll. He suffered from paranoia and adopted unpopular and extreme political beliefs that subjected him to ridicule at school and in his community. He was a gun enthusiast who honestly believed he needed guns for his own protection. He had few friends and recognized that most people considered him to be "a little off."

"Tell me about your affinity for guns," I said.

"I love the feel of them in my hands and the power they give me over other people. You never know when you're going to need to protect yourself from some gangbanger or lunatic."

"What is your favorite model, and what do you like about it?"

"One of my favorites is the 9mm pistol. They're popular because they're light, easy to conceal, have a light recoil, and are accurate in their range."

"Can you tell the difference among styles and brands from a few feet away?"

"A real gun lover might be able to, but the average citizen probably can't."

If Darren was right, the person who said they'd seen me with a gun likely would not be able to say it was a match for the murder weapon—or at least they wouldn't be able to back up that claim. I had to hope the tipster was not an ardent gun lover who might give the jury reason to ponder the similarities between the gun I supposedly had and the murder weapon.

When I finished up with Darren, I packed some files in my briefcase and went to Penn Station to catch a train. I suspected the reason they had not indicted me in the Stone case was that they were having trouble identifying and locating the tipster. I prayed no one would step forward as the witness.

# 21

The next morning, I had a ten o'clock meeting scheduled with Philip. He was on time, and we dove right in. He was struggling with the aftereffects of being arrested. Though the charges had been dropped, people still talked behind his back at work and in the neighborhood. There was speculation in those circles that he was the killer and that the police could not make the charges stick for technical reasons. He did not know how to get rid of the stigma, and I told him time would help.

Following my session with Philip, I called Ed to see if he had been through Abner's statements to the police and the DA. Ed reported there were four of them and he had parsed them all. For the most part, they hung together. Abner stated he had left his house for the office a few minutes before seven, locking the front door of the house. After their session, he showed Philip out at about seven fifty, then returned to his office, from which he could not see the street.

"He gave inconsistent answers about whether the office door was locked after Philip left. In his initial statements, he claimed that he locked it, but then later said he was not sure. He said he didn't hear anybody knocking on his office door after that. He also said he was sitting with his back to the door when he felt a powerful blow to the back of his head and was knocked out immediately. He estimated that the attack took place within a few minutes of Philip's departure, and he did not come to until he was found the next morning. I find that hard to believe. It would mean he was out for a full eleven hours. Doctors tell me that's highly unlikely since he did not suffer any brain injury, as far as they can tell."

"You think he regained consciousness before the police arrived?"

"I do. And if that's the case, I think he would have checked the house and found his dead wife. I don't know why he didn't call the police. Why pretend you were unconscious for hours?"

"You think he killed her?"

"I don't know. I just want to create doubt about whether you did. I'm going to retain a medical expert who will challenge Reeves's assertion."

I telephoned Beth to check on things at home and to update her.

"We've discovered some problems with the witness statements we expect to exploit at trial," I said, trying to share some good news.

"That's good, Tim. This is so hard," she said. I could hear her crying. "The kids and I miss you. I'm having second thoughts about whether I did the right thing by asking you to leave. Maybe I acted too precipitously. You've been telling me you're innocent all along."

"Look, you said yourself that it's best this way until things are clearer. I can imagine it's not easy with the kids, especially without the designated disciplinarian around."

"That's not it. I'm feeling lonely. And guilty for abandoning you."

"Are you suggesting that I come back home?"

Silence, then: "No."

"I didn't think so. Be strong, Beth," I said and hung up.

A few minutes after I got off with Beth, the phone rang. Caller ID showed that it was Liz. I was pleasantly surprised.

"Hi. Good to hear from you," I said in a happy tone.

"You want to buy me dinner?"

"Are you serious? I'd love to."

"Meet you at Cello at six thirty?"

"Perfect," I said.

She beat me to the restaurant this time and was given a choice table. We each had a martini before dinner and chatted. She was effervescent, and her eyes sparkled more than usual. My mood, which was already good, elevated and I became garrulous and goofy.

"If this nightmare ever ends, there are a number of things I'd like to do with you."

"Oh?" she said coyly.

"Don't be a wise guy. I know you like theater and the arts. I'd like to take you out for real."

"This is real, Tim. It's fucked up, but it's real," she said matter-of-factly.

"I'm glad you haven't given up."

"Strangely, I'm actually leaning in the other direction. I decided I don't think you are a killer. I don't know what lead me to that conclusion, and I certainly hope that I'm not wrong."

I sprang forward in my chair and tilted my head, eyes open wide. "What are you saying?"

"I'm not sure. That maybe we can stay out past eight thirty some night," she said, smiling.

My heart was racing. I shifted uncomfortably in my chair. Until that moment, this had largely been a fantasy. A flirtation with a gorgeous and intelligent woman who should have no interest in me. She had kept me at a distance where I felt safe, but now I was in danger of being swept up by her substantial charms.

"Let's slow down a second," I said. "Nothing has changed, including the fact that I'm married and may be headed to jail."

"I know. I'm just talking about a date. You're the one who's married. You have to decide what impact that has. I'm just looking for some fun."

"Jeez, for some reason I'm hesitating. I think I might be a little scared. And I'm not sure of what." I chuckled.

I had dreamed of this, expecting it to go nowhere, but the reality of it was sinking in. Even though I wasn't ready to throw my marriage away just yet, I didn't think I could pass up the "fun" Liz was contemplating.

"I suspect that it's either now or never for us, Tim. Let's enjoy dinner and see if you turn into a pumpkin in an hour or so."

In the middle of our appetizers, I received a call and looked to see who it was. Since it was Beth, I ignored it. A few minutes later, she called again, and I told Liz that I had better take it. I left the table and went outside.

"Hi, Beth, what's up?"

"A man called and gave me instructions to meet him at the entrance to the Port Authority tomorrow at eleven a.m., when he would supposedly deliver proof that you murdered Brett Stone. I'm scared. What should I do?"

"It's bullshit. It must be a trap of some kind. Forget any thought of going. I'll go instead."

I was livid. How dare Abner involve my family in this? I rejoined Liz, feeling demoralized, and she picked up on that right away.

"Is everything all right?" she asked gently.

"Yes. Just some stuff with the kids. Sorry."

"Why don't I believe you?"

"Because you are smart. I don't want to talk about it, and I'll probably regret this, but I have to go. Please don't be mad. The timing is terrible, I know, but I wouldn't be good company right now, anyway."

I did not even give her a chance to respond. I put a hundred-dollar bill on the table and left after giving her a kiss on the cheek. I walked down Fifty-Fourth Street, looking for a cab and thinking about what proof Abner could muster. I was confident that no proof existed that I had ever been in Brett's apartment or touched the actual murder weapon.

This was classic Abner. He would have realized that Beth would call me, all worried. I did not understand why he had inserted her in the middle of this and did not like it. Did he want to meet with me? If so, he would have called me directly, as he had in the past. Not knowing what he wanted and not wanting to fall into some trap, I decided to ignore the meeting. Neither Beth nor I would go. It was my way of saying, *Fuck you.*

Instead, I arranged things so that Ronaldo showed up at the Port Authority at the agreed time and waited on Eighth Avenue. He called me once he was there and said that Harvey Burns was standing by the entrance, looking like he was waiting for somebody. He was carrying a brown envelope. I told Ronaldo to wait with him and call me back if anything happened.

About twenty minutes later, Ronaldo called with his report. He was still at the Port Authority.

"He stayed for about fifteen minutes and then made a phone call. After hanging up, he waited around for about another five minutes before leaving. I followed him to Dr. Reeves's townhome. He went into the basement office, and I waited for a few minutes. When Levine showed up, I cut out of there to avoid being seen."

I had an appointment scheduled with John for later that day, but he skipped it without even letting me know. I assumed that meant he was terminating our relationship but was too afraid to call and tell me. I was down to a few patients and was not contributing much to supporting the family. Fortunately, Beth could keep things going without me. I could not, however, ask her for any more money, and my savings were really starting to dwindle.

I used my downtime to focus on the Reeves case. Ed started to prepare me for taking the witness stand. I did not know whether we would assume the risk of me testifying, but we needed to be prepared just in case. During a dry run of my proposed testimony, I finally got to tell Ed the full story of what I had discovered of Abner's history with my father. He thought it would make for effective cross-examination of Abner, especially as Ed would not have to give the prosecution copies of the exhibits he intended to use in cross. Consequently, Abner would be taken by surprise and unprepared for the questions coming his way.

Ed said there was some risk of alienating the jury by exposing the fact that my father was a blackmailer. Bringing that out would not make the jury sympathetic to our cause, even if it was not strictly evidence and only used to demonstrate that Abner was a liar and a cheat. A typical juror could react the way Beth had and assume the apple had not fallen far from the tree.

Ed also told me the doctor he lined up to testify would impugn Abner's story. In his professional opinion, a patient who was unconscious for more than six hours would show signs of brain injury, and one who was out for as long as Abner said would have serious to severe brain injury. The doctor would offer the opinion, based on his review of Reeves's medical records and his statements at the crime scene, that Reeves was not unconscious for eleven hours as he claimed.

Ed also planned to call the EMTs and ER doctor who had treated Abner to testify as to Abner's mental and physical state after being unconscious. Their reports showed that Abner was cogent and articulate. He did not seem confused about what had happened and gave a comprehensive statement right there and then.

By establishing that Abner was lying about how long he'd been out, we could create doubt about his credibility and whether he'd been unconscious at all. That would undermine his alibi for the time of the murder, as well as the rest of his testimony. If we could also prove that he was having an affair at the time, we might be able to sow further doubt as to his motive to lie to deflect blame from himself.

I left our prep session that day with a bounce in my step. As I entered the office suite, the receptionist handed me a large envelope. I waited until I got to my office room before opening it. It contained a glossy photo of me and Liz in broad daylight, walking down a street. We are all smiles.

There was something familiar about the photo. I had seen something like it before but could not call it to mind. When I got home, I went to my whiteboard and looked at all the articles and photos I had amassed. Among them, I saw it—a photo of Brett's apartment building on West Thirty-Eighth Street. In both photos, the house number *418* stuck out. I checked the news story and confirmed that was where Brett had been killed.

So what if there was a photo of me passing by the building on a "date" with Liz? It was not far from the clinic, and I probably walked by that building many times without realizing it. If this was the envelope Burns had intended to give Beth, it suggested that Abner was now trying to blackmail me for having an affair with Liz. While it would be awkward, I could honestly tell Beth I had not slept with Liz. I regretted the fact that Liz was now tangentially involved, but I did not perceive the photo to represent a serious threat.

Although I assumed I had blown it with her for good, I telephoned Liz and apologized profusely for leaving her at dinner. I explained that one of Abner's associates had threatened Beth the other night, and I needed to deal with it. I did not tell her about the photo I had received but planned to show it to her when we next met. When I finished my explanation, she remained silent. I filled the void by admitting that I thought a lot about what the rest of our night together could have been like. She was intrigued by that and asked me to expound.

"I am definitely not going there. Too embarrassing. And too presumptuous."

"Are you being prudish with me?"

"No, I'm trying not to step on my own . . . er . . . toes."

"Okay. But I was feeling sort of frisky the other night. I'm not sure what next time will bring."

We made a date for Thursday evening. After the call, I looked again at the photo I'd received, searching for anything I missed. I found it on the newspaper Liz was holding in the photo. It was a headline I remembered seeing. A quick google search confirmed I was right—the headline was from the day of Brett's murder.

# 22

Could that be accurate? I had accounted for most of my time that day, leaving open a window of only a couple of hours. The photo had obviously been taken during that time, though I could not tell precisely when. The police would probably be able to tell.

I had lied to the police about my whereabouts on the afternoon of the murder the first time they interviewed me. I said that I was in my office, when in truth, I'd been with Liz. I was pretty sure she had not told the police about our outing either, but the difference was that she had apparently forgotten. The truth was going to come out now. It was just as well, as I had no proof to back up my statement that I had been at the office.

The police would find it incredible that we had both forgotten one day after Brett was killed that we had gone out together the day before. I honestly did not remember where we had gone or what we had done during our time away from the clinic. If the police got their hands on the photo, they would not only be ticked off that I'd lied but would also have questions about exactly when I'd been front of Brett's house and what I'd been doing there.

We were obviously going someplace when the photo was taken. I checked my credit card accounts to see if I had bought coffee or anything else that day and found no record of having charged anything. If I reminded Liz that we'd met up, she might remember where we'd gone. I planned on showing her the photo when I saw her on Thursday. Hopefully, she would say we'd been together the whole time and have a receipt from someplace we went.

In the meantime, I had a patient crisis. Nick was a wreck because his mother fired her caregiver. She also stopped taking care of the house, leaving chores like the laundry and dishes for Nick. She even began to depend on him for medications, forgetting to take them when he was not around. It was all Nick could do to keep up, and he suddenly found himself overwhelmed, with no free time whatsoever.

"I don't know if you are going to get her to stop harassing you as long as you two live together," I said.

"Well, I'm not moving out. She'll just blow up my phone constantly and drive me nuts. It's gotten so bad that I have had dreams of smothering her in her sleep just to get some peace and quiet. I'm sure it does not help that I have not been taking my antidepressant, but I'm always running around, and I forget."

"You've got to get back on those. I'd also suggest you hire another caregiver and make it clear that you are the only one with the power to hire and fire her. It might be a good idea to have your aunt move in for a few days to see if that calms things down. You should resume going out so your mother can get used to the idea. And promise me you will call me if you have any thoughts of hurting your mother."

I took the train back to the island that evening. I ordered pizza for Eve's family, and we all ate together. While I was taking the last bite of my pizza, my phone rang.

"You get the photo?" a man's voice asked.

"Yes." I was not sure, but I thought I recognized Burns's voice.

"There's something that goes with it. But it's a surprise." The line went dead.

"Who was that?" Eve asked. "You turned pale."

"Crank call. Had me going for a second."

I went to bed that night wondering what the surprise was and when I would find out. If they were trying to intimidate me, I did not understand why they would hold back a "surprise." The photo itself was enough to pique the interest of the police and, if there was something else, why not give me a hint and a reason to worry? Perhaps there was something in the background not visible to the naked eye. I resolved to take it to a photo shop tomorrow.

I got up the next morning at the usual time. The morning paper carried a small story of a bust at Fanny's Bar and Grill in Manhattan. The police had arrested five men for carrying out a male prostitution scheme at the bar. They had been processed and released on their own recognizance. I did not recognize any of the men who were arrested. Nor was there any mention of underage men. The police had set up an undercover operation to snare the pimps and prostitutes. I wondered whether any of the individuals arrested had any connection to Abner or his friends. I figured the success of the small operation would give me some credibility in the eyes of the police. Hayes and DeCarlo would have to think twice before simply dismissing what I had to say.

If I wanted their attention, I had to give them something that would help them solve their murder cases. I remembered from my dossier on Levine that he had been fired from Lenox Hill Hospital. I did not know if the police were aware of that, so I called Ronaldo. He said the hospital should have reported the incident since it involved child abuse and agreed to try to find out.

He called me back a few hours later to report that the hospital had settled a dispute with Levine, who had sued them for wrongful termination. Ronaldo found out that, as part of the confidential settlement, the hospital had withdrawn the allegations it made to the Health Department and Social Services about Levine's conduct. His record was expunged, but a confidential settlement agreement still existed that could be obtained by the police.

While not bearing directly on Stone's murder, information suggesting that Levine was a pedophile supported my theory that a ring of perverts was involved. I wanted to keep pounding that message into Hayes's head. I telephoned him and caught him at his desk. As usual, the first thing he did was warn me that he would use anything I said against me in a court of law. I explained what Ronaldo had passed on about Levine. Hayes's questions indicated this was news to him. While I suspected DeCarlo and Hayes were beginning to trust me at least a little, it would take a lot for them to believe the information I was furnishing pointed to my innocence.

I checked in with Nick later that morning. He'd told his mother over dinner that he was bringing back the caregiver, and she threw a fit. They got into a nasty argument, and he started to feel his blood boil. Recognizing that he was losing it, he'd left the house and slept in the car. He said that he snuck in the house the next morning to find his mother sobbing on the sofa. I commended him for walking away. I told him his mother feared losing him more than anything else, and that, while she might put up a fuss, she would go along with his plans for a caregiver if he put his foot down.

Having nothing better to do that afternoon, I walked the distance to Penn Station to take the LIRR to Eve's house. Though she and Stan had not said anything, I felt bad about intruding on their lives for such a prolonged period. We were still months away from trial, and I was sure that they could not wait for me to leave. I decided to start looking for a boarding house or cheap apartment on a month-to-month basis.

When I exited the train, I walked across the street to a local tavern, where I bought myself a beer. The local news was on the TV, and there was a report that one of the men arrested in the raid at Fanny's had been badly beaten outside his home after being released. The victim, identified as Ray Lamond, had fought back and injured his attacker. Given eyewitness accounts at the scene, the police determined that Lamond was defending himself and did not arrest him for the fight. They did arrest his attacker: Harvey Burns.

Though I knew I was being a nuisance, I had to let the police know about Burns and his connection to Abner. I left Hayes a voicemail about Burns threatening me on Abner's behalf. I also stated that Burns was trying to stifle a witness who could talk about Fanny's and the pedophile ring in the case against Abner.

Ed phoned me an hour later and conferenced in Hayes and DeCarlo so we could chat about Burns. I told them about the cab incident, Burns showing up for the meeting with my wife, and him telling me about Fanny's. I also said that someone in Abner's group had likely told Burns to beat Lamond to prevent him from talking.

"Prostitution is obviously a crime," DeCarlo said, "but we have a group of officers in vice who take care of that stuff. Does Burns have anything to do with

Stone's murder, as far as you know?"

"He'll deny knowing anything about the murder, but I suspect he's lying. I think he was there that day, though he isn't the killer. I'm telling you, Abner or one of his friends killed Stone to keep him from exposing this ring and its interest in boys."

Ed called me after we finished our conference call and admonished me again.

"You can't keep playing amateur detective and calling the police with every bit of information you come up with. And you've got to lay off my investigator. I don't want him moonlighting for you. He is not a lawyer, and your communications with him on matters unrelated to my representation of you are not privileged. He really should be working for me if we want to be sure that his work can be protected as attorney work product."

"Okay, I get it," I said. "Where do you think matters stand on the Stone investigation?"

"I don't know, but you heard DeCarlo. They tend to think of this other stuff as just prostitution, which is not their bag."

"We need to highlight the angle of the underaged kids. That makes the case more appealing."

"For some on the force. For these two, it's all about the Stone and Reeves murders."

Since it had not come up in our recent conversation, I was pretty sure Hayes and DeCarlo did not know about the photo of Liz and me. That suggested that Abner was waiting to see whether it was in his interest to reveal the photo and, possibly, the "surprise" to the police. Whether he did so would probably depend on what I did in response to the photo.

I had now gone three days without talking to Beth or the kids. The several calls I placed to her had gone unreturned. I sent her a text asking her to call me. She wrote back that she had nothing to say to me. She was obviously mad as hell about something. The only thing I could think of was the photo of Liz and me. Abner must have sent her a copy. I supposed she thought I was cheating on her. In a way, I was. I did not know how to tell Beth the truth without giving her the impression I was having an all-out affair.

I looked at my watch and realized that Nick was late for his appointment. I tried checking in with him by phone to no avail. I telephoned his home number, and it rang and rang, which was unusual because his mother was always home. I called his work number and was told that Nick had not come in for the day. I waited a while and then repeated the cycle with the same results. It was not like Nick to simply blow off an appointment without letting me know, so I followed my instincts.

Flagging a cab, I went to his townhouse apartment. Nick's mother was seated outside on the stoop in her robe and nightgown, surrounded by two cops and an elderly woman who looked like her. I identified myself to one of the police officers and asked after Nick. The young redheaded officer said Nick was all right but had been taken to the hospital by ambulance with multiple stab wounds. She said his mother had stabbed him when he tried to leave the house, and her sister had restrained her. Apparently, Nick had not fought back. The police were taking his mother in and probably sending her for psychiatric evaluation because she kept claiming her son was trying to kill her despite all the evidence to the contrary.

Saddened that Nick had been on the receiving end of an attack, I hailed a cab to the hospital. He was in the emergency room when I arrived, and I had to wait a couple of hours to see him. When I was finally allowed to visit him in his room, I found him morose and depressed. He blamed himself for the whole fiasco, and I stopped him. I spent several hours talking to him about what had happened and where things would likely go from there.

I left him to catch a train back to the island. On the ride home, I beat myself up for not having the foresight to predict his mother's violent outburst. I had been more worried that he would be the one to attack. I knew his mother was demanding, but he had never let on that she was unstable. I wondered if he was as surprised as I was by the assault.

# 23

On Thursday, I spent most of the day looking for a place to live. Late that afternoon, I found a townhome in Brooklyn Heights that suited me. It had been divided into four one-bedroom apartments and was run by an elderly woman who lived in one of them. The neighborhood of similar brownstones had an old-fashioned charm to it, and there were restaurants and bars within a short walk. It had a different vibe than Manhattan, and I was ready for a change.

As I was in the process of moving in a couple of days later, I met Clare, a pretty graduate student at NYU who lived with her boyfriend in the apartment below mine. She was working on her master's degree in psychology and was excited to meet someone who practiced in her chosen field. She and I sat on the stairs inside the townhome while she peppered me with questions about what it was like to work with patients and the pros and cons of working in a private clinic. I entertained her for a solid hour before her boyfriend came home. It was just as well because I had to shower for my date with Liz.

Once I was dressed and ready, I tried Beth again. She answered this time.

"I shouldn't even talk to you. I'm pissed that you are seeing another woman. How could you?"

"It's not what you think."

"Don't you dare lie to me."

"Okay, but we have not been intimate."

"I don't see how we can get back together now, even if your legal problems go away. We should treat the last month as the beginning of a trial period of separation and see where things go from here."

I was not much in the mood for a date after talking to Beth. Although my life was not going to be any different than it had been the past weeks, there was a certain finality to what we decided, and I was sad that my marriage had all but ended. I had to pull myself together quickly because there was no way I could cancel on Liz or be grumpy when I met her and expect her to see me again.

I got to the Wharf before Liz and was fortunate to get a seat at the long wooden bar. I had nearly finished my martini when I saw her saunter in, wearing a lovely silk blouse and a short pencil skirt. I closed my tab and met her at the hostess desk. We were escorted into the back room and given a lovely table.

She asked about my new place, and I told her about Nick and his mother's attack. I mentioned my conversation with Beth about a separation, and she jumped all over it. She was curious what brought that on, and I told her the photo of her and me played at least a small part.

"What photo of you and me?"

"Oh, I forgot that you have not seen it. Someone, likely Abner, sent a picture of you and me strolling down West Thirty-Eighth Street to me and Beth."

"Gee, I am sorry about that. Thirty-Eighth Street? What were we doing on Thirty-Eighth Street?"

"I have no clue. I thought maybe you'd remember."

"No, I don't. Who do you think took the picture?"

"One of Abner's associates is my guess."

"What a shitty thing to do. What did you tell your wife? We really have not done anything to be ashamed of."

"The truth. That we see each other and that, while nothing has happened between us, I want it to."

"You told her that? No wonder she wanted to separate," she said, looking embarrassed but pleased.

We talked for the next fifteen minutes or so about what this meant going forward. I told her it would just be a continuation of what had been going on for the last month or so. It was somewhat ironic that, at the very moment when we were reaching a new level in our relationship, my marital situation had changed.

"And what level are we now at?" she said demurely.

"Whatever level you want it to be. I don't mean to be presumptuous, but I'm tired of fighting this."

She rubbed her index finger around the lip of her half-empty wine glass, then slanted her head to the side and looked at me with those green eyes.

"I'm not looking for anything serious, you know. I like my life the way it is."

"Neither am I. I can't even think about the long term given everything going on in my life, including my legal problems."

"I just worry about guys on the rebound. I'm up for some fun, but the moment you get clingy, it's over."

I smiled at her. "Let's just go slow and see what happens."

We wound up spending the night at her place, putting the finishing touch on a memorable day. I offered to leave and go back to my place, but she asked me to stay the night. I was glad because I really did not want to schlep back to Brooklyn at almost two in the morning. I fell asleep next to her and slept soundly. She roused me early in the morning and told me I had to leave so she could go to work. We had coffee and toast together in her kitchen, and then I watched her put on her makeup and get dressed.

"You know that photo I mentioned last night? It was taken the day Brett was killed. Does that refresh your recollection about where we went?"

She stopped putting on her eyeliner for a second and glanced at me. She shook her head.

"Not really. I don't remember seeing you, let alone where we might have gone."

"They asked us where we had been within twenty-four hours of the murder. You must have remembered something about it then. I am willing to admit that I lied to the police because I did not want to say I was with you. They are going to know you lied too."

"I am not kidding. I don't remember that we went out. Is it clear what time the picture was taken?"

"Not to me, but I'll bet the police know or will find out—from Abner or his photographer."

"Crap. I only had a couple of free hours, and that was in the afternoon. They can figure it out from looking at my schedule."

"Or mine," I said.

"What do we do now?"

"I intend to tell them the truth—that I lied to protect a secret relationship, and that it was stupid. I'm trying to figure out where I went when I left you."

"I really don't recall anything about that day, including what we did. They are not going to believe us, and they will be pissed we lied."

The following evening, I had drinks with my friend Eric at a place downtown. I was hoping that he had picked up some useful scuttlebutt.

"How is your case going?" Eric asked after our drinks arrived.

I was surprised he asked. The few friends I had left seemed to avoid the topic, but Eric was always very direct with me.

"Honestly, I think it's going pretty well. We need to convince one juror that the prosecution has not made its case, and I'm optimistic about that."

"When is the trial?"

"January third."

"I heard through the grapevine that Reeves is having some legal issues of his own. Something about being mixed up with some two-bit crook who pounded on another guy. I heard that from a friend of a friend who works vice downtown."

"Really? When did you hear this?"

"I don't know. A couple of days ago, maybe."

I wondered if the police had made the connection between Abner, Burns, and Lamond, the one who got arrested for solicitation at Fanny's. Abner would deny any such association because being tied, even indirectly, to a prostitution ring would destroy his reputation. But I had already given Hayes and DeCarlo a statement in which I swore Burns admitted to me that he worked for Abner. Had they followed up on that or, if not, would they now? I wondered if Lamond was cooperating with the cops after Abner had him beaten or whether the intimidation had proved effective in keeping him from talking.

Visiting Kelly's Tavern again was somewhat risky, but it was the only way to see Burns. I had to go there a couple of times before I ran into him at the bar. He still had bruises on his face and his nose was even more swollen than usual. He saw me stride over to him and looked at me disdainfully.

"What the hell do you want?" he uttered.

"Just a minute of your time. I've been asked to identify you in a lineup, and I don't know if I'll remember your face."

"What are you saying?"

"That I'm willing to forget what you look like if you do something for me. All you have to do is give me the name of the guy at Emanuel's who runs interference for Levine and Weston. No police involvement. Just me."

"And I should do that because?"

"Because you're caught up in something far more serious than beating up some guy on the street. The police already think you're involved in Stone's murder. All I have to do is point a finger at you and tell the police what I know of his death."

"I told you before. I had nothing to do with that."

"But I know you were there that day."

"Bullshit. You're bluffing."

"Are you saying someone else took the picture of me and Liz? I doubt it. Let me see your camera roll. I bet you took more than the one photo Abner sent me."

He narrowed his eyes and sighed.

"All right," he said in a muted voice. "Ernesto is the guy from Emanuel's."

"Last name?"

"No clue."

"I also hear your tiff with Lamond has created some legal issues for Abner. Is that true?"

He looked surprised by what I said. I could tell my source was good.

"Nothing he can't handle," Burns said. "A civil suit. Now fuck off. I gave you what you wanted."

I took a cab up to Emanuel's at ten. I struck up a conversation with a young guy at the bar, bought him a couple of beers, and asked about other bars in the area that catered to the same clientele. I told him I was looking for a guy named Ernesto who used to hang out here. He said he had not seen him in weeks, but he'd heard Ernesto was now working private clubs on the Upper East Side. I asked him if he knew the names of any of the clubs, and he suggested I talk to the bartender at the other end of the bar.

I made my way over to meet Rudy, who apparently knew everybody. Forty dollars got me the names of two establishments Ernesto worked at as well as a warning that I was underdressed for both places. I made a mental note of that.

Before going to bed, I added Ernesto's name to my whiteboard under the interconnected circles for Abner, Weston, and Levine. I also added Lamond's and Fernandez's names next to Ernesto's. That was five scouts, including John and Brett. That suggested Abner's clique was not limited to the three men I knew about. The larger it was, the more scouts it would probably employ.

The next morning after breakfast, I took the photo of Liz and me to a camera store. The store owner blew up the photo. He said it had been taken with a zoom lens on a 35 mm camera, and that the photographer was probably across the street from where we were walking. He could not tell what time of day the photo was taken from the angle of the light given the tall buildings in the area, but he guessed, based on the shadows, that it was probably early afternoon.

We examined the blowup together. He pointed out that the enlargement of the door showed the blurry image of a baseball-capped head in one of the windowpanes. Given the height of the glass pane, one could not see below the person's brow. The baseball cap concealed the person's hair, but the eyebrows were dark, probably brown.

Since Burns had not balked when I accused him of taking the photo, I was convinced that he had shot it. I thought he might have been there when the murder took place. My hunch was that he knew someone else was there that day and did not want to identify them. Maybe he knew who the figure in the window was.

Was the baseball-capped person the killer or just a tenant inadvertently captured on film on their way out of the building? I had seen or heard about someone with a cap like that recently but could not recall who. Maybe it would come to me.

# 24

After another uneventful day, I was up for continuing my investigation. I dressed up and took the subway uptown to Eighty-Ninth Street in the evening. I went to a place called the Scammers Club. A large, muscle-bound bouncer stood in front of the door with his arms folded across his chest. After looking me over, he told me this was a private club and I had to be a member or an invited guest to get in. I told him I had been invited to join Ernesto for a drink. He studied me more carefully and eventually let me enter.

The space was beautiful, with a large marble bar below lustrous chandeliers made of cut crystal that sparkled like diamonds. There was a large open area for mingling, surrounded by linen-clothed tables and comfortable dining chairs. Unlike Emanuel's, the men, including the bartenders, looked refined. The majority of the patrons seemed to be older than me, and most were dressed in suits or sports jackets.

I asked one of the waiters to point out Ernesto, and he directed me to a good-looking thirty-something-year-old with styled jet-black hair. He was sitting at the end of the bar with a couple of big men. He wore a black silk shirt, a gray jacket, and tight-fitting black pants. I moseyed over to where he was sitting, trying to look like I belonged. I stopped directly behind him, and sensing my presence, he swung around in his chair to face me. He lowered his glasses halfway down his nose and looked me over from head to toe, rubbing his chin.

He stuck his face in mine and said, "Are you looking for me?"

"If you're Ernesto, I am," I said confidently.

"And who might you be?"

"A friend of a friend."

"The friend have a name?"

"I don't know what you call him. I call him Doc."

"You've got to do better than that. I know several doctors."

"There's actually two of them. They hang out together. One is Abner."

He eyed me suspiciously, raising one eyebrow. "Abner? I haven't heard from him in weeks. You a cop?"

"No."

"What do you want?"

"Just some information about a couple of Abner's friends."

"Motherfucker, do I look like a librarian to you?" He motioned to the big men sitting with him. They pushed back on their stools and stood up with their fists at their sides.

"Wait a minute. I'll pay," I said, reaching for my wallet, which apparently prompted one of the big men to think I was going for a weapon and grab my wrist.

"Yes, you will. You must be working with the cops, if you're not one. They have been asking a lot of questions recently. Get him out of here, boys," he said and turned to face the bar.

With that, the two men picked me up, carried me out to the front entrance, and threw me into the gutter. For good measure, each of them kicked me once in the stomach. I think one of them cracked a rib or two. I would also have a few scratches and bruises from landing hard on my side in the street.

Sitting on the curb, I ordered an Uber to take me home. When I got there, I took some Advil and a hot bath. It was idiotic of me to have tried such a direct approach with a man in the middle of a criminal conspiracy. I was sure Ernesto had already called Abner about the stranger with questions and that Abner knew it was me. I had defied his warnings by continuing to delve into his business, and I worried he would respond in some fashion, perhaps by releasing the photo with or without the "surprise."

The pain from my ribs made it difficult for me to lie down in bed. I spent most of the night sitting in a reclining chair with a bottle of scotch to subdue the aches and throbs on my right side. The over-the-counter pain relievers were not helping much. I would call Eric tomorrow and get a prescription for a painkiller, but there was no use in having X-rays to tell me what I already knew about my ribs.

I had just dozed off when the phone rang the next morning. It was Liz. She asked to see me in the evening, and I had to tell her I was out of commission. I did not give her all the details, but I did say I had been beaten up by people I thought to be friends of Abner. She asked if I had called the police, and I told her that there was no point. She told me I was going to get myself killed if I did not knock off the sleuthing. We made a tentative date for the next evening, and I hung up.

I tried to get some more shut-eye but was interrupted a few minutes later by the phone again. This time it was Ed.

"They have the photo you told me about," he said. "They've already figured out where and when it was taken. They want to talk to you about it."

I told him about the person in the building, and he told me to send him a copy of the photo by messenger. As he was about to hang up, I stopped him. I took a deep breath, which caused a soaring pain in my right side.

"I lied to the police about my alibi," I said.

"You did what?" he shouted into the phone.

"I told them I went back to my office and stayed there after my lunch with you on the day of Brett's murder, but I was out with Liz, the woman in the photo."

"Shit, Tim. Why did you lie about that?"

"To prevent people from speculating about my relationship with Liz."

"That's not good. Did she lie too?"

"She said she doesn't remember. I suspect the picture was taken in the early afternoon around the time of the murder. We were together after lunch."

"Well, at least you were with somebody and that can be verified. How long were you out with her?"

"That, I don't remember. I've been trying to figure out where we went, which would help. I suspect Liz is trying to do the same thing."

In terms of scheduling the interview, I told him that I needed a couple of days to recuperate from a beating I took last night. I explained what had happened, and he gave me another lecture. I told him I learned my lesson this time and I was through doing my own detective work. We talked about him representing me for the next interview and agreed that was the smart way to go. We would discuss what to do about long-term representation in the Stone case after that.

He wanted to call ADA Luzon and tell him about the lie, saying it would be better if we owned up to it and explained what happened. I disagreed because that would make things look bad for Liz. I wanted to let her go first and redeem herself by talking about her refreshed recollection. Ed called me a fool and hung up.

I called Liz to give her a heads-up about the photo. The police had already reached out and were coming to talk to her in the late afternoon. She would let me know how it went at dinner the following night.

I rested the remainder of the day, taking the meds Eric had prescribed. Feeling marginally better, I called Ed back and told him I could make a meeting with the police the next day. I was anxious to get it out of the way, and he said he would try to set it up for three p.m. to give me a chance to rest earlier in the day. We agreed to spend an hour that morning on the phone preparing.

The following afternoon, I took an Uber and met Ed at the station. I was still sore, but I was mobile enough. Hayes, DeCarlo, and ADA Luzon were in a conference room with a large one-way mirror on one side. I gave them the enlargement of the photo. I told them the full story about receiving it and having it enlarged.

"You knew this photo would be of interest to us. Why didn't you turn it over as soon as you received it?" asked ADA Luzon.

"I wanted to see how long it would take for the people who sent it to me to send it to you on their own."

"You sure you weren't just hoping we'd never get our hands on it?" he asked, glaring at me with narrowed eyes.

"I think I know who sent it, and I was sure he was going to send it to you. It's part of his plan."

"You realize this puts you in front of Stone's house the day of the murder, don't you?"

"Yes, but we were just walking by."

"And you still can't tell us where you were between one and three p.m. the day Mr. Stone was murdered?"

"No, I don't know."

"Even after seeing this photo?"

"Let me be clear," I said. "I was not honest with the police when I told them I was in my office the whole time between one and three p.m. I remember going out with Dr. Schreiber after lunch, but I don't know when or for how long. I can't even remember what we did or where we went. This photo may have been taken during that time frame."

They did not seem surprised, which only confirmed that Liz had already told them about the lie. They must have been waiting to see if I would bring it up.

"So you admit you lied to us?" Luzon asked.

"Yes," I muttered.

"Why?"

"Because I didn't want people knowing that Liz and I were seeing each other. Though we were just friends, people might have assumed more."

"You told us you were in your office the whole time. How long were you out?"

"I don't remember."

"Doesn't the day of Mr. Stone's death stick out in your recollection?"

"The day I learned of the killing does, but I don't remember the details of the day before."

"What were you doing on West Thirty-Eighth Street the day the picture was taken?"

I rapped my fingers on the table with impatience. "I don't know. For some reason, I have no recollection of ever being on West Thirty-Eighth Street. I sometimes walk down it when going someplace else, and maybe that's what we were doing. I don't have a recollection of stopping anyplace there."

"The woman in the photograph is Liz Schreiber?"

"Yes."

"And what is your relationship to her?"

"Friend and former colleague. She works at the clinic I used to be at."

"Are you romantically involved?" asked Luzon.

"We became involved recently. Before that, including when this picture was taken, we were just friends."

"How recently?"

"The first time we had dinner was about two weeks ago."

"It was after Mr. Stone was killed?"

"Yes."

"Are you sure?" Luzon asked.

"Yes. We may have had coffee before that."

"Do you think now that you're involved, she would lie to help you?"

"No."

"You talked to her about the photo, didn't you?"

"Yes, after I got it."

"And you asked her some questions about her recollection of that day, right?" Luzon pressed.

"Yes," I admitted.

"If she told us she doesn't remember where she was between one and three the day of the murder, she'd be lying, right?"

"I don't know what she remembered at the time she first talked to you. I'm pretty sure I told her about the picture afterward."

"And did you suggest what she should say to us about the photo?"

"No."

"Did you tell her to lie about being with you the afternoon of the murder outside Stone's house?"

"I did not tell her to lie. I suspect she didn't initially remember the outing."

"Where were you going when the picture was taken?" Luzon continued.

Ed objected. "We covered this already."

"I don't know. I have tried to figure that out, but I can't," I said, throwing my hands up in the air.

"Were you coming or going from Mr. Stone's place?"

"Definitely not. I've never been to his apartment."

"Did you ever acknowledge to anyone that you knew where Mr. Stone lived?"

"I don't remember doing that. I don't think I knew where he lived before he was murdered."

"You don't have his address in your files on him?" Luzon asked, furrowing his brow.

"I'm sure I do. That doesn't mean I know it off the top of my head."

"So we have a picture of you in front of Mr. Stone's apartment on the day he was murdered, and you think it was just coincidence that you were there?"

"We were just passing by. But there were two other people there as well—the photographer and the man in the window," I said pointedly.

"What man in the window?" Luzon asked.

Ed showed Luzon the head through the pane of glass.

"Do you know who that is?" Luzon asked.

"No."

"Do you know who the photographer is?"

"I don't know, but my guess is Harvey Burns, who works for Abner Reeves."

"What makes you think it's him?"

"Because I asked him, and he didn't deny it."

We then went through my conversation with Burns. That led to a whole series of questions about Burns and his alleged relationship with Reeves, Weston, and Levine. In answering this last series of questions, I revealed what I had done the other night and showed them the bruises. Luzon shook his head and warned me against doing anything that might interfere with their investigation.

In our postmortem, Ed said they hadn't been listening to anything I said except the admission that I had lied. I was sure they knew who the photographer was and that the photo was taken during the time window of Stone's death. Ed had me go to his office to review the motions we were about to file in the Julie Reeves murder case. The court had denied our motions to dismiss the indictment, and we were filing discovery motions to make the DA's office turn over exculpatory information, including medical records related to Abner Reeves's head injury and information about any other persons on East Seventy-Second Street during the evening of the murder.

When I got back to the apartment, I had a hard time climbing the stairs to the second story. The pain medication had worn off. I rewrapped myself in the elastic bandage I had bought and sat in the recliner, watching TV. When it was safe to do so, I took another ibuprofen with a glass of white wine.

I went back over the ADA interview in my mind and wondered why he had asked me if I ever told anyone that I knew where Brett lived. It sounded like they had a witness who'd said so. Was it the same witness who supposedly saw me with the gun? Or was someone else willing to lie about me?

It had been a rough day, and I had trouble relaxing even with the booze and the pain pill. I tried to sleep in my bed, but the pressure on my ribs was too great from the tossing and turning, so I sat in my recliner again and turned on the TV to distract me from the aches and pains. Eventually, I dozed off and slept fitfully, dreaming of men in baseball caps.

# 25

I decided to take another day to recuperate. At least that way, I could try to take catnaps in the recliner that would give me a little rest in between periods when the rib pain was intense. I hoped the painkiller would help me relax and make the naps possible. I had my computer with me and I emailed my patients, telling them I was ill and offering to reschedule their appointments.

Abner called me during the morning. I was ready for him this time and turned on the recorder app on my phone. He was angry but calm.

"You have been making a nuisance of yourself, stirring the police up with outlandish tales involving me. Attacking me as relentlessly as you have since Julie's death calls for retribution. That's why I forwarded the police the photo I had sent to you and Beth. I am still sitting on a vital piece of information, but I'm having trouble keeping it leashed up. The others are anxious to see you burn. I want to make sure you don't take us down with you. So I am still willing to make a deal. I will not allow the surprise to get out if you stop pursuing your crusade against me, Weston, and Levine."

"But I'm not doing anything."

"It wasn't you who got beaten up at Scammers the other night?" he said with a laugh. "I don't believe that."

His communications network worked fast. It confirmed that Ernesto worked for him, not that there had been any doubt in my mind.

"You say the surprise will seal my fate in the Stone case? What is it?"

"Let's just say it's icing on the cake. They might still indict you without it."

"I don't understand what you are offering me. Suppose I stand down. What happens in the case of your wife's murder?"

"Nothing. I expect you'll be tried and convicted."

"And what do I get if I agree to back off? Sounds like nothing." I adopted a mocking tone.

"I'm offering you the chance to convince the prosecutors not to indict you in the Stone case."

"Sorry, but I don't see equal value flowing in each direction in this deal. I go to jail either way, and you avoid it altogether if I play ball. That hardly seems fair."

"What would you have me do? You killed Julie, didn't you? You've got to pay for that."

"No, I did not, and I am going to win that trial."

"Not with my testimony against you," Abner said confidently.

"We'll show that you are a liar!" I roared.

"Harsh words from a man I am about to crush. You better think about this. Time is running out," he said and then hung up.

I regretted losing my temper. I would never have agreed to his terms, but I did not have to poke him in the eye. He had made good on his threats before, and I had no reason to doubt he had a "surprise" at the ready. Still, I could tell I was getting to him and his friends. I had to keep the pressure on at least one of them, and I picked the one I thought was the weak link—Levine.

I knew that, in addition to having his own practice, Levine was the school doctor for a well-known private school on the Upper West Side. The school psychologist there, Briana Simpson, was a friend of mine, and I arranged to have coffee with her. She was wary about meeting with an accused murderer at first, but I told her it had to do with one of her students.

"Thanks for meeting with me," I said as she joined me on a bench at Bryant Park. I gave her one of the coffees I'd bought from a vendor. She was fidgety despite the open venue, crossing her stout legs at the ankles just above the hem of her maxi skirt.

"Despite my legal troubles," I continued, "I am still seeing patients, and without getting into confidences, I need to tell you that one of my patients, a student at your school, confided in me that your school doctor—I've forgotten his name—has engaged in inappropriate touching. I thought the school ought to know so you can deal with this quietly."

"Who? Mark Levine? What did he do?"

"I can't get into that as I don't have the client's consent to go beyond what I've just said."

She huffed. "Yes, you can when there is a minor involved."

"Sorry, I'm not going to do it. My patient was explicit."

"This alleged touching. Boy or girl?"

"Boy, but that's as far as I'll go."

"How do I know the kid's telling the truth? Will you let me talk to him?"

"He and his parents don't want that. I think, if the school doesn't do something, the parents are going to raise hell."

"What can we do if we don't even know who the kid is?"

"I'm sorry. That's the way they want it. I can't believe you haven't had anonymous tips before. I'm sure the school will do whatever's appropriate."

"Can you at least tell me when this happened?"

"Which time?"

"Oh shit," Briana said, putting her hand to her forehead and rubbing her hair. "Any indication that this goes beyond one kid?"

"Only that he's apparently been fired for this sort of thing before."

"Are you shitting me?"

"How good was your due diligence?" I asked, making the point that the school could be faulted for not doing enough.

She sighed and got up from the bench. "I suppose I should thank you for this, but you've created a big headache for us without giving us any details. Please let the parents know we will keep it quiet if they come to us." She put her untouched coffee cup on the bench, spun, and left.

I imagined the first thing her school would do was confront Levine, who would deny the allegation. He might even suspect where it came from and claim this was a setup. If the school authorities inquired into his past deeply enough, however, they should be able to discover that he had settled a lawsuit over his departure from Lenox Hill and inquire about the reasons for his termination. While the settlement agreement was confidential, the school could likely force Levine to share the allegations and the settlement terms, unless he was willing to be fired. I could always get Ronaldo to tell the school what Levine's partner had said.

I went from the café to my office for my Zoom appointment with Nick. He was still at home, nursing his wounds. By this time, the thing that was keeping him home was mostly not wanting to explain the bandages. He was, not surprisingly, still depressed. The medications took the edge off, but he was lethargic and still struggling with two conflicting emotions. On the one hand, he was angry at his mother for her savage attack. On the other hand, he missed her and was deflated that she was incarcerated.

He was scared of life without his mother. Too many years of interdependence made it impossible for him to blossom overnight. He felt protected in his mother's home with her around, never mind that she made him angry with her constant demands. Neither of them had to face the world alone so long as they stayed together, and yet suddenly, they were both forced to fend for themselves. She probably had a support group at the hospital to help her. I recommended he join one too.

After my meeting with Nick, I got a delivery from Ed of the DA's oppositions to our discovery motions in the Reeves case. Reading their briefs, I noticed they glossed over the issue of motive. I called Ed to see if that meant they were conceding there was none.

"No. Motive is not an element of the crime of murder but is simply a means of convincing the jury that the defendant did it because they had reason to."

"I thought they had to prove I bore animus toward Julie or at least Abner."

"They will probably try because the jury will want to know why the murderer did it, but they aren't required to."

"So the DA's office may not even have Abner testify about his feud with my father if they think the case is otherwise compelling. That Abner is willing to lie about that goes to his overall credibility, and we need evidence of what really happened to show that he was a habitual liar."

"We are better off holding the evidence in reserve and pulling it out on cross-examination to show that he was lying *if* he testifies about motive."

"No, we should bring it out *whether or not* he testifies about motive to attack his credibility generally. Telling the ADA and the police about it also lends credibility to my theory in the Stone case that Abner is a deviant and is mixed up in a criminal enterprise."

"Under the evidentiary rules, you cannot generally use one bad act to show that a witness has a propensity to engage in illegal conduct, even of the same kind."

"He's apparently engaged in pedophilia before. We've got to bring that out."

He sighed deeply. "What are you talking about? The story you heard from your cousin that Billy did not actually sodomize the boy, but someone else did? And you think that someone must be Abner? You have no proof."

"Okay, but we need to prove he is a liar generally so the jury will believe that Abner is lying about being unconscious during the murder."

"Tim, the fact that Abner might not have been out for eleven hours does not mean he was not unconscious at all. Our own expert would have to concede that it's possible he was out for up to six hours. He could well have been unconscious when the murder was carried out."

"I thought the idea was to use the testimony of the expert to plant doubt. Don't we want them to disregard Abner's testimony altogether?"

"That would be nice, yes. I'm all for shaking the jury's confidence in his veracity but don't lose sight of the fact that, in addition to you being there around the time of the murder, your fingerprints are on the knife."

"But doesn't debunking Abner's story give us a possible alternative scenario to offer—that he may have done it? He even had motive, his mistress. And the knife was in his house, so he could have grabbed it. The jury is going to want to blame somebody."

"I agree with that. If the blackmail story with your father comes out, as I expect it will, we can attack Abner's credibility and dangle the possibility that he is the murderer in front of the jury."

"Your way, it may come out. My way, it definitely comes out."

"Not necessarily. You tell the ADA, and she'll avoid going anywhere near motive. She does not need it for a conviction."

"You can bring it up in Abner's cross-examination even if he doesn't touch motive, can't you? Especially since he said something to the cops about it? He lied to the police."

"Yes, but if we tell the cops, they'll prepare Abner for that cross-examination. He'll have time to think of a plausible story that is consistent with what you've found to support his original version. We'd lose the element of springing it on him when he had no idea it was coming and had not even thought about it. It will be hard to explain the checks away on the spot, but give him time to think about it, and you're likely to hear another convincing explanation. You yourself say he is an accomplished liar."

"My gut tells me that it's better to scare the DA off from trying to establish motive and then point to its absence to secure an acquittal. I want you to set up a meeting with the ADA where we can reveal the story I put together from old records."

"I don't like this one bit, Tim. You're paying me to defend you. Let me do it my way and show me that you have confidence in me."

"I think you're really good and will continue to defer to you on most things, but I will make the final decisions about my own defense, including whether I will testify at trial."

# 26

I went for a long walk in the morning before our meeting to calm my nerves. I walked to the outskirts of Park Slope, where I had a cup of coffee while I read the paper. There was a brief story in the back section about Lamond suing Abner for paying Burns to beat him. Burns had pled guilty to a misdemeanor for assault and was scheduled to be deposed by Lamond's lawyers about the attack. This must have been the civil suit Burns was alluding to when I last saw him. The newspaper reported that the suit had been settled by Abner for an undisclosed sum and without admitting its allegations.

I took a subway from the station near where I had breakfast to the DA's office, carrying the newspaper with me. The conference room was hot even with the shades drawn. ADAs Brenner and Luzon were there with Hayes and DeCarlo. Ed explained the reason we came in and let me run through a description of what I had found out about Abner supposedly blackmailing my father. As I told the story, I turned over the documents, including the checks, that illuminated what I was saying.

"Now you say Abner Reeves was a part of a pedophile ring and paid your father off to keep that quiet?" Brenner asked.

"Yes, in a nutshell."

"And your father was engaged in blackmail, pure and simple?"

"I believe that's what the checks are for."

"Now, you know about Abner's involvement in the ring how?"

"It's what you guys call circumstantial evidence. The pictures of him and Billy. Abner's story about my father, in which he acknowledges knowing about Billy's actions. Billy raping a teenage boy. The articles about a ring of wealthy men in New York that included Billy. The story that Billy did not actually sodomize the teenager. Billy's suicide. The note to the newspaper reporter. Abner writing checks to my dad. What else was he writing the checks for? And the company Abner kept and still keeps. Abner is at it even today, as you should know from your bust at Fanny's."

I slipped them today's paper and pointed to the story about Lamond.

"Look, he even paid some guy to beat up one of his scouts at Fanny's to prevent the scout from testifying. You know that. The police arrested the assailant, and as the newspaper says, he pled guilty. He's none other than Harvey Burns, whom I warned you about."

"And how do you propose we find proof of this twenty-year-old blackmail scheme?" Brenner asked.

"I'm not saying you should prosecute Reeves for this old stuff. I'm telling you he bears a grudge against me and my family, not the other way around. I didn't have a motive to hurt him or kill his wife. He's got one to go after me, especially now that I've caused the clinic to investigate him. He is lying to make it look like I had a motive so he can frame me."

"And why would he do that?"

"First, to pay me back for what my father did to him. Second, to cover up the fact that he is the murderer and a pedophile. He had motive and opportunity. He was having an affair with a young woman. His wife knew and was ready to dump him."

"We've already charged you, and nothing you say undercuts any of the evidence we have about you sneaking in and killing Mrs. Reeves with the knife," Brenner said.

I turned to Luzon. "Doesn't what I brought you today bolster what I've been saying about Abner and his friends engaging in serious crime?"

"A lot of what you say is conjecture, but we're glad to have it and will evaluate it," Luzon said. "I don't know what it has to do with Micha's case, however. You have not offered us any evidence to support any of your assertions in either case."

Once I had my say, the prosecution team abruptly ended the meeting. Judging from the reception we got, Ed's instincts had probably been correct. We had now laid out our cards for everyone to see and, from all appearances, had not moved the prosecution at all. They were good poker players who would not flinch, so it was hard to tell, but they seemed confident in their answers to the inconvenient questions we were asking.

Gloom set in again. I had naively thought our presentation would make a difference. However they really felt, they were broadcasting a sense of strength in their ability to prevail at trial. I could no longer pretend a miraculous piece of evidence might save me. While we would argue that the government's proof was not substantial enough to establish my guilt, I felt the prison walls starting to close in on me.

I had to calm down before my afternoon session with Philip, who was waiting for me in the reception area of my temporary office when I arrived. Once I got control of myself, I went to get him and walked him back to my office. He sat across from me in his usual spot, rocking back and forth.

"What's wrong?" I asked.

"I think I'm under suspicion for the murder of Mrs. Reeves again," he said, rubbing his cheeks and chin. "The cops called and asked me a bunch of questions I'd already answered. I thought they were trying you for that?"

"As of fifteen minutes ago, they were. What makes you think they suspect you?"

"Is it okay that we talk about this?" he asked.

"It's privileged if it relates to how you're feeling," I said, wanting above all else to hear what the police said.

"I'm feeling anxious and angry. That's why I am raising it, so I guess it's okay. Anyway, they've been asking me questions about what time I left Reeves's office. I've been telling them all along that I left around seven thirty, but they didn't believe me because the appointment was supposed to end at seven fifty and Dr. Reeves said that's when I left. I kept thinking this could be an important detail since it may mean the attack was before eight. I recently talked to a buddy I had forgotten I saw that night, and he reminded me that we met across town a little before eight. He's right. I went to see Reeves a little early that day and was done by seven thirty.

"I told ADA Brenner about my friend, and she immediately started asking why I was still lying about the time I really left. She said they were sure it was seven fifty, as Reeves had said. I told her it takes a good twenty minutes to get from Reeves's office to where my friend was, and I had to have left between seven thirty and seven forty. I suggested she talk to my friend because he specifically remembers me showing up a few minutes before the eight p.m. show we went to.

"So now the ADA is yelling at me," he continued, "saying, 'How do we know you didn't kill her?' She's claiming that, even if I'm right, I still had time to break into their house, kill her, and return to knock out Dr. Reeves. The whole thing is a mess."

I said, "I think they're worried about what impact your timetable has on their case against me. They now have to recalibrate the timing. They're just trying to make you doubt yourself so they don't have to consider that Dr. Reeves may have it wrong."

"Well, as you can see, I'm really stressed over this. My life is coming together in other respects, and I don't need this shit. I'm worried about what I might do under all this stress. They can't arrest me again. They just can't."

"I think they are just bluffing. I had a meeting with them today, and they gave no indication of backing off. They previously told us the murder couldn't have been before seven forty-two because Mrs. Reeves took a call then. So if you and your friend are right, you have an alibi. Have they talked to your friend yet?"

"Two days ago," he said.

"Then they had a chance to absorb it before they played hardball with me today. I'm sure they reviewed the surveillance tape to see if it confirms your story. I'll bet it does."

I telephoned Ed after the session and told him what I had learned from Philip. He got angry at the ADA for not disclosing the story by Philip's friend immediately upon learning it. If Philip was already gone when Mrs. Reeves answered the phone at seven forty-two, there was at least a twenty-minute window when someone other than Philip could have killed her before I arrived. We needed undeniable proof that I didn't come on the scene until around the time the neighbor saw me.

"I'm pretty sure I left from the clinic that evening," I said. "I took a cab. Without much traffic, it would take about eighteen minutes to get there. For an eight o'clock appointment, I would normally leave between seven thirty and seven forty. I know I got there a couple of minutes before eight and went to the house door, meaning I had to have left at around seven forty."

"If you don't have receipts, I can try to subpoena records showing when you arrived and, equally important, when you left."

"I doubt I have anything that shows exactly when I took the cabs there or back. You mean the DA's office can spin this to its advantage?"

"They can say the murder happened earlier and that you lied about your arrival, for sure."

"Doesn't it also mean the third person on the street had more time to kill Julie than we thought?"

"Yes. I've got to go back and see when the neighbor recalls seeing that person. It was sometime between when she saw Philip and you. And what if the murder took place while Philip was in with Abner and the murderer just hung out at Abner's place for a while? The police need to go look at the entire period from seven to nine."

I was not sure how to react to the news that the murder could have taken place earlier than the police originally thought. Ed was right that the DA's office was not apt to rely on my word alone as to my arrival time. The neighbor's testimony that she did not see me pounding on the doorway until after eight would help, but the police might think that was staged and I was in the house before that. The surveillance footage of a car turning the corner at the time I said I arrived buttressed my story, but a time-stamped receipt would dispel any doubts.

After talking to Ed, I picked up my cell and called Liz. I told her I had a bad day and needed to see her. She said she was flattered but had an engagement until about nine, so we agreed to meet at a bar around the corner from her apartment. I made the mistake of heading to the bar at about eight. I was buzzed by the time Liz arrived at nine fifteen. She was in a beautiful silk dress. She had been at a charity event for one of Julie's favorite charities and escaped early to see me. With the booze in me, I showed little inhibition. She was not one for PDA and backed me off, amused at seeing me intoxicated. I slowed my drinking to let her catch up.

"Can I get you a drink?" I asked.

"I had plenty of champagne at the event, so don't worry about me. I saw Abner there. I found it distasteful that he was with a young woman who was clinging to his side. Abner was strutting around like a proud peacock. He introduced me to his new girlfriend, and we chatted for a few minutes about the clinic."

"You almost sound jealous."

She folded her arms across her chest and gave me an icy look. Had I touched a nerve?

"He seemed to know about us. He made some snide remark about you that I can't remember."

"He's the one who sent the photo, so of course he thinks something is going on between us. You don't remember what he said?"

"It made no sense to me. Something about you and liking surprises. Anyway, you told me you've had a really bad day. What happened?"

"I don't have many good days," I said, reaching for her hand. "But this one's not over yet, so who knows?"

She blushed and said, "Aren't we playful tonight?"

"I'm sorry," I said, sitting back. "I'll behave."

"No need," she said, batting her eyes. "I will have one more, but you should be careful not to overdo it."

I did not really want to talk about my cases, so I listened to her talk shop for the next hour. I asked after John, who was now seeing Liz again. She said he was doing well. He told her that the police said his alibi checked out and he was no longer a person of interest in the Stone case. She brought up Nick, and I told her he was struggling, and I was talking to him every other day now.

We went back to her place around ten forty-five and enjoyed a few hours of lovemaking. Unlike last time, I decided to leave and was glad she did not seem to mind. She had had a long day and needed the time to unwind. Exhausted from the beer and the sex, I climbed into an Uber that drove me to my place in Brooklyn. The streets were still alive at one a.m. in the city that never sleeps.

I climbed the stairs to my apartment and went in. I took an ibuprofen and lay down in my clothes. Before I knew it, I was asleep, rib pain and all.

# 27

I was awakened by my cell at eight. It was Briana Simpson. She said that the school was investigating Dr. Levine. Its lawyers were able to dig up his settlement with Lenox Hill and confront him about it. He said that there was no truth to the allegations leveled by the hospital and that he had settled the case without admitting anything so he could move on with his life. He also swore he had not touched any student and threatened to sue the school as he had the hospital if they let him go.

"Since he is denying everything, it would really help if you would give us specifics we could corroborate. Did you talk to the kid's parents about that? For the sake of the other children, you've got to fill us in."

"I'll give you this much: First, he had a similar problem in his private practice. His former partner quit over it. And second, I believe the police are investigating him and the bars he hangs out at. You just have to ask the right questions, though my guess is he'll lie. I'm sorry. I've given you what I can."

"Can you give me the police officer's name?"

I could not give them Hayes or DeCarlo because that would certainly get back to me. I did not know the names of the officers handling Fanny's raid.

"I don't have their names. Look in the paper for a story on a raid a couple of weeks ago at Fanny's Bar and Grill and follow that trail. Just leave me out of this."

Ed called me later in the morning to tell me that ADA Brenner finally let him know about the statement given by Philip's friend. When Ed pointed out that Philip's corroborated story conflicts with Reeves's account, she dismissed it as confusion on Reeves's part due to the head injury. As for my contention that I arrived around eight, she said that the surveillance tapes only proved that a cab turned onto Seventy-Second near eight o'clock, but not who was in it. She asserted that the third person on the tapes, who arrived around seven forty, could have been me.

I thought the prosecution was stretching things. The tapes only showed one car arriving, and that was my cab. I did not walk up Seventy-Second Street from Third and therefore was not on the surveillance tapes at all. All of this was contingent on me proving when I arrived. I was unable to find a taxi receipt for the night of Julie's murder. Ed agreed to subpoena the NYC Taxi Commission. He warned me the ADA would likely subpoena the records too, if it had not already done so.

With fall around the corner, I went out to my sister's house on Sunday to get in one last day at the beach. I had dinner with her and her family that night before taking the train back to the city. Just before I departed, Eve pulled me aside to ask how the criminal cases were going. She assumed the worst because I never talked about them anymore.

I told her that I did not get anywhere with the prosecution over the history between our father and Reeves. The police had disparaged it for involving too much speculation and innuendo. I had yet to convince them that Abner was a liar.

"Ed thinks they might not put Abner on the witness stand at all," I said. "They may just rely on my admission that I was there, the timing of the prior patient's departure, the neighbor seeing me, and the fingerprints on the knife. It's the last one that is my Achilles' heel."

"Is there a chance that you touched it after the barbecue, which might explain how your fingerprints got on it?"

"I wasn't at Abner's house between the day of the barbecue and the evening of the murder, and that's apparently where the knife was, if Beth's story is to be believed. Abner apparently claims they washed the knife after the barbecue, anyway."

"Well, what if the knife wasn't there the whole time? What if you had access to it on another occasion?"

I thought about that on the train all the way back to the city. When I got back to my apartment, I checked the mail and found a few envelopes. One of them contained a birthday card from Eve. I had forgotten that my birthday was coming up later in the week. That's when it hit me—Abner's birthday.

I rushed to my phone and pulled up my calendar. As I thought, Abner's birthday was mid-July, a couple of days before Julie's murder. I distinctly remembered Julie coming to the clinic with a cake for his birthday. We'd all gathered in the kitchen and had the cake. At Abner's urging, I was the one who cut it. I used a knife that Julie handed to me. Was it possible she brought the knife with the cake? We did not have any metal knives at the clinic, because of the patients. We only had plastic ones that would not have been sufficient to cut a big birthday cake. She must have brought a knife, *the* knife.

I dialed Ed's number. He was annoyed that I called him after ten p.m., but when he heard the news, he understood. There would be multiple witnesses to the cake cutting. They could testify that we only had plastic knives in the kitchen. Would any of them remember that I cut the cake? Was there a chance in hell that anyone would remember that Julie had brought the knife and what it looked like?

In an ideal world, we would develop the evidence we needed without tipping the prosecution off. That would be difficult, because everyone at the clinic effectively still worked for Abner, so he would find out if we started interviewing people about the birthday party. I remembered that the party had occurred late in the afternoon, around four p.m., when we usually celebrated birthdays. I looked at my schedule and saw I had had a three-fifteen appointment with my former patient, Dean Jorgenson. I remembered that we ended the session early to join the party. Ed promised to have Ronaldo hunt Jorgenson down.

Jorgenson was not hard to find, and Ronaldo interviewed him at his home the next evening. He remembered the birthday party, but not the date. He told Ronaldo we had broken the session early to attend the "head guy's" party and that I had been asked to cut the cake. On the all-important question, he gave

Ronaldo a surprising answer.

"I remember thinking to myself, as Doctor Shea cut the cake, that was a big-ass knife he was using. It was like the kind you see in a kitchen in a restaurant. It was medium length and shiny with a black stone handle."

On the following Monday, I had another session with Philip. He noted that the video surveillance tape had shown someone leaving the corner of Seventy-Second Street by cab at around seven thirty. As a result, the police now accepted his recollection. He was calmer now that they were on his side again.

I saw Liz that evening for dinner and told her about the knife.

"Gee," she said, rubbing her neck, "I recall the office celebrating Abner's birthday, but I don't remember Julie being there, or a cake. Maybe I was with a patient at the time. But that's good news, isn't it?"

"Really? I could have sworn you were there. Anyway, I think that the DA's office will be surprised when they see our witness list includes clinic staff and a couple of patients."

"Not to burst your bubble, but isn't there a problem with your story? The knife didn't have icing on it when they found it at Julie's side, which means it either wasn't the same one or they washed it. If they washed it, wouldn't it have cleaned your fingerprints off?"

"Depends on how thoroughly it was washed, I suppose. That's for a forensic expert to opine on."

I left her place about midnight by Uber and checked my messages. Since I had turned my phone off while Liz and I were being intimate, I had missed three calls from Ed. I wondered what was so urgent that he called that many times, but it was now too late for me to call him. I left him a message at his office telling him to ring me in the morning. I took a sleeping pill and went to bed.

When the phone rang at eight in the morning as I was sipping coffee in the kitchen, I knew it was Ed.

"Where the hell were you last night? I couldn't get you." He sighed and said, "The DA indicted you for the murder of Brett Stone. You're going to be arrested and arraigned again today. I offered to surrender you, but they said no. They're taking the chance that you won't flee. Don't even think about it."

"Fuck," I said. "What happened? I thought we gave them enough evidence to suspect others."

"They claim they have a confidential witness who maintains you confessed to being at Stone's place. Also, something about seeing the gun."

"Seeing the gun where?"

"I don't know any more details. Tim, I'm sorry to bring this up, but I need you to agree to another retainer, or I can't take this case on. I'm already getting killed on the Reeves case."

"How much?"

"Same deal."

"Shit. Plus another bond? I can't do that without talking to Beth."

I called Beth and explained the situation.

"I wish that I could say I'm surprised, but at this point I'm not," she said flatly.

"We've got to go through another bail hearing, and I'm going to have to pay Ed to defend me. It's basically going to deplete our savings, and we're going to have to tap into the equity we have in the house."

She started to cry. "The house is in your name, so I guess you can do what you need. I'll let you use the savings account to get the bond, but there's a limit to what we can spend on lawyers. The kids and I need to live too. What about your IRAs?"

"I may have to take some money from them too." It was all I could do not to break down on the other end of the phone myself.

"I can't very well deprive you of your ability to defend yourself. But if you're going to spend all our money, you better be convinced you'll prevail."

She did not ask me anything about the merits of the case. She wanted to know whether the cases would be tried together and said that she did not have the strength to come to another arraignment, begging my forgiveness.

I looked out the window of my apartment and saw a crowd, including reporters, on the street and the stoop. A minute later, two police cruisers pulled up, and I saw Hayes and DeCarlo get out of one. I grabbed my wallet, phone, and keys and headed down the stairs to meet them. I could see my landlady standing in the vestibule with a sour expression on her face. I stuck out my wrists as I approached the bottom of the stairs, but DeCarlo turned me around, pulled my wrists behind my back, and cuffed me while reading me my rights.

By happenstance, I had the same judge at the arraignment as last time. Judge Evers was not happy to see me back in her courtroom. After I waived the reading of the indictment and entered my not-guilty plea, Judge Evers turned her attention to bail. Ed argued that the current bail arrangement should apply to this case as well, and ADA Luzon argued for a new and higher bail, stating that, having been charged with two murders, I was a clear risk to the community.

"I don't think I've ever seen a situation quite like this before," Judge Evers said. "Is it the government's intention to keep these two matters separate through trial?"

"Yes, Your Honor. Completely separate murders. Completely separate evidence. Completely different witnesses," Luzon stated.

"All right. I am going to set bail in this second case on the same terms as in the first one."

According to the newspapers, the DA's office had a confidential witness who had seen a Glock in my possession within a few days of the murder. That was a lie. Moreover, it was nonsensical that I would show a gun to a complete stranger. Thus, the informant had to be someone I knew well enough to trust. I did not think anyone I knew would lie about something so consequential, except maybe Abner.

As I was mulling that over on the phone with Ed, I saw another call come through and put Ed on hold. Liz called to say she had heard the news. She asked if we could meet for a drink later, and I said yes. The way she emphasized "drink" made me think we would not be dining together tonight—or for a long time to come.

I went back to conferring with Ed. We now knew that the murder weapon was a black 9mm Glock pistol. This particular one had its serial number rubbed out, but according to Ronaldo, it was standard issue that looked like hundreds, if not thousands, of guns around the streets of New York. It did not seem possible that the witness would be able to testify that the gun he or she saw was used in the murder unless they had been there, and we had no indication that there was an eyewitness to the murder.

The similarities between the two cases struck me. In both, I had been seen at the scene of the crime around the time the murder was committed, which I could not deny. In both, there were ties between me and the murder weapon—fingerprints in one case and a witness in the other. And in both, there were witnesses who were willing to lie to frame me—Abner about motive, and a confidential witness about me possessing a gun. I could not fathom why not one, but apparently two people would be prepared to perjure themselves to get at me. If I was right, there was someone other than Abner who either hated me or had a different reason for testifying against me.

I got to the bar ten minutes late and found Liz sitting at a table in the corner, nursing a martini. I bent down to give her a kiss on the cheek.

"How are you holding up?" she asked with a blank look.

"I am dumbfounded. I am still convinced that Abner is somehow behind the efforts to get me convicted in both cases. I think Julie and Brett were killed for the same reason—they knew too much about Abner's activities."

I watched as she shook her head at the mention of Abner's name.

"The indictment today changes things. My father and friends told me I was crazy to get involved with someone in your situation, and that was before. Now, you've been accused of murdering a second person. While I convinced myself the police made a mistake about Julie, I doubt they'd make two. The newspaper said you had the gun."

"I am innocent," I said. "You've got to believe me."

"I've been an idiot. I could have gotten myself killed. I don't want to take any more chances. I can't even believe I am here with you." She pushed her chair away from mine a tad more.

"Do you honestly think I killed one of my own patients?"

"How can I not when the police have charged you twice?" she asked, frowning. "I can't get the possibility that you are a killer out of my head. Anything I felt for you is dead. I'm trying to be nice about this, but I'm serious as shit. I'm telling you as plainly as I can that I don't want to see you again. Don't try to contact me." She stood suddenly, turned on her heels, and left.

Once she was gone, I pushed back into the chair and ordered a scotch. I telephoned my sister. She also could not understand how I could have been charged in a second case she knew nothing about. Asking for her continued support through my ordeal was asking a lot. Stan would have misgivings about remaining on my side. Like Liz, he would find it hard to swallow that I could be charged with two separate murders and still be innocent. He would not stop Eve from talking to me, but he would keep the family away from me now.

I got home early and moped around my apartment, drinking some more scotch. I intended to get very drunk. I turned on the TV as a distraction but did not look at it. I was going to ignore the ringing phone, too, when I noticed it was a Queens number. It turned out to be Alex Fernandez, the former clinic patient whom I had referred to the police.

"They're fucking with you, man. I know you didn't kill that Stone guy. They are making up stories about that afternoon. Just 'cause the cops are buying them doesn't make them true."

"You lied to the police. I put them in touch with you, and you lied. Why?"

"Because Abner's friends are watching, and they don't screw around. I don't want to get killed too."

"You have any advice for me, or is this just a sympathy call?" I said, betraying my annoyance.

"I'm trying to help you, man. Focus on that Weston dude. He's the key. That's all I can say," he whispered as he hung up.

Major Weston. What about him was I supposed to focus on? Was he going to be a witness against me? Since I'd never met him, I did not see how he could be the person to whom I supposedly showed the gun. Or maybe he would not be a witness at all. Perhaps Fernandez thought that Weston was involved in the murder. I knew he had guns because he'd shown them to a date, and as an Army man, he was probably more comfortable with them than his associates. I knew that I was stereotyping him, but it was easier to picture him as the murderer than Abner or Levine.

Having investigated Abner and his friends, I thought it might be smart to come at the problem from a different angle—from Brett's perspective. I was sure the police had turned his life inside out in search of a possible motive, but

I had access to files they did not. He had spoken of a love interest at several of our sessions. Rereading the files now, I thought in retrospect that I had missed the clues. The relationship with an elderly man. Him falling in love with John.

What if I was wrong about the motive for Brett's murder? It was conceivable that his lover would have been jealous of Brett's relationship with John. Was Weston the ex-lover? I could imagine him growing insanely jealous upon learning of the relationship from Abner and killing Brett in a rage. It was possible Weston also feared Brett would snitch on him as one of the pedophiles.

The one person most likely to know if Weston and Brett had been lovers was John Rankin.

# 28

My relationship with John was virtually nonexistent now. I thought I could use his older brother as an intermediary. I went to visit him late in the afternoon at their shared apartment, using my concerns over John's mental health as an excuse to get into the building. I explained that John was repressing some very traumatic events only I knew about and they were eating him up inside. I told his brother that John needed to confront them for his own good and I wanted to talk to John about it one last time.

"Why would I let him talk to the man who is accused of killing his best friend?" his brother said.

"Is that how he described his relationship with Brett?"

"What do you mean?"

"You should ask John that question. Let me ask you, how has he been since Brett died?"

"He's been miserable. Depressed and extremely volatile."

"He needs help, and you know I helped him in the past. I have a way of breaking the logjam, I think. I can't guarantee it, but I can make him feel useful in catching Brett's real murderer."

He snickered. "I thought that was you?"

"Ask John if he thinks I did it. It was a friend of Dr. Reeves's, the same doctor who abused your brother in ways John won't even talk about. I'm sure you know something about that."

"Yes, I do."

"Then please get him to talk to me. One-on-one. It would be better if you stayed in another room so I could call you if John gets agitated. I only need five minutes of his time."

I stayed with John's brother the remainder of the afternoon. He did not have the details but knew enough about the blackmail to detest Abner. It did not sound like he even knew the truth about John's relationship with Brett. We were sitting on their living room couch when John arrived home. I could see daggers coming out of the narrow slits of his eyes.

"What are you doing here?" he said as he threw his keys onto a table in the entryway. He and I watched his brother rise and leave the room.

"I need to talk to you about something. Please just hear me out. This isn't about you, really. And it's not something I'm going to ask you to share with anyone else. I just need this one favor."

"Why should I help you? You've been charged with Brett's murder."

"Because you know I didn't do that. You told me yourself you think he was killed to protect Abner."

"What do you want?"

"I want to know if Brett had an older lover before you and what his name is. I think there is a chance he's involved, if it's who I think it is."

"I can't give you his name because I don't know it."

"Did you tell the police about Brett's lover?"

"I only told them he had boyfriends before me and that I don't know who they are. That's the truth."

"Do you think this lover had anything to do with Brett's murder?"

"I really don't know. I still think the murder has more to do with Brett's willingness to talk to the lawyers about Abner than a boyfriend. Now, please leave," he said as he approached the front door.

"What if it's both? He was seen with one of Abner's friends a couple of days before the murder. Maybe the guy got jealous of you. Plus, he was told that Brett was going to talk to the lawyers."

"I suppose that's possible, but I don't have anything to add to what I've already told you."

"I saw Brett at ten. He said he was going to talk to the lawyers. Did he?"

"Yes, at around eleven. That's when he decided to talk to them. They made him comfortable, and he made an appointment to see them right after his three o'clock with you."

The lawyers, and therefore the clinic staff who coordinated the interviews, then knew that Brett would talk as early as, say, eleven fifteen. After speaking with John, I went back to my apartment and telephoned Ed.

"Stone, who was bisexual, had an elderly ex-lover. I'm betting it was one of Abner's friends. I don't think the police know about that," I said in a high-pitched voice.

"The cops must know he was bi and must have looked for a boyfriend. That's the first person they'd suspect."

"They weren't together anymore at the time of the murder. My source tells me the relationship was very hush-hush. His latest boyfriend doesn't even know who it was. I'll wager that nobody knew, except maybe Abner, and I'm sure he hasn't said anything."

"You think the lover is mixed up in this?"

"My hypothesis is that the lover found out about Brett's new boyfriend and killed him in a jealous rage. He had a double motive because, if it's who I think it is, he was also afraid Brett would expose his and Abner's criminal activities. My source tells me Brett decided to talk at eleven o'clock on the day of the murder, so the lawyers and the clinic would have known that a few minutes later. That gave the killer ample time to plan something for the afternoon."

"Any idea who the ex might be?"

"My guess is Weston, because he was seen in a bar with Brett shortly before the killing, but I have zero proof."

"We should tell the cops, no?"

"Every time we tell the cops something, it comes back to bite me in the butt. Let's put Ronaldo to work first checking out Brett's life to see if we can prove he was intimate with Weston or Levine."

When Ed called the next day, I ran for the phone, assuming he had an update about Ronaldo's research. I greeted him breathlessly.

"I've got good news and bad news. Which do you want to hear first?" Ed asked.

"The bad news."

"Somehow the ADA found out about the birthday party at the clinic and the knife. I don't know if it was our witness or what, but they know what our explanation for the fingerprints is, and they're not buying it."

"Shit. What does that mean?"

"That Abner will be ready for the questions I ask about the party and probably be prepared to say that he or someone else washed the knife after the party."

My shoulders sagged. "Tell me some good news."

"Well," Ed said, "Ronaldo was able to determine that Brett was dating an older man. The relationship had gone on for many months, according to people who saw them out together. It seemed to cool down more recently. One of the people Ronaldo talked to thought the man looked like the photo we have of Weston, but he could not be sure. Always wore a baseball cap when they were out."

"That is good news," I said. I pumped my fist in the air.

"I don't know that we can count on the witness talking to the police, though. He said his memory fades when he is around cops. And he couldn't positively ID Weston, anyway."

"The man in the photo has a cap on. It has to be Weston."

"You can't tell anything from that photo. Discovery should tell us who took it, and then we can try to question him."

"I told you it was Burns. Can we try to question him now?"

"I think we should wait until we see all the photos he took and then ask him all the questions we have. We may not get another chance with him, if we get one at all."

"I don't know where this is taking us," I admitted. "We don't have enough to suggest that it was Weston because he had it bad for Brett or because he feared Brett was going to tell the truth. But either way, my gut tells me it was Weston."

Feeling brazen, I decided it was time Weston learned that his affair with Brett was no longer under wraps. I hoped that by doing so I would provoke a response from him and unsettle Abner. So I typed and printed out Weston's address at Fort Dix and taped it to an envelope in which I enclosed a copy of a photo I had of Brett.

Two days later, I got a call from Abner. I recorded this one too. He said Weston got my message, but the police had already run that possibility to ground and were satisfied that there was nothing there. I said my own research suggested the contrary and that I was prepared to share it with the police. He accused me of being naive.

"Now that you are forcing my hand, I'm about to deliver my little surprise to the police. You're going to go down for both murders regardless of what games you play in the interim."

"I must be having some impact if you keep calling and threatening me. You wouldn't bother otherwise."

He chortled and said, "You are a minor nuisance. The latest information provided to the police is going to make your defense more difficult than you can imagine. But you brought it on yourself. I warned you."

Irritated by Abner's smugness, I telephoned Hayes. When he realized it was me, he got DeCarlo, and they put me on speaker. They gave me the usual warnings, and I said I wanted to proceed without Ed.

"This is something you need to know. I know you have probably looked into this, but Brett Stone was having a secret affair with Major Weston. Trite as it sounds, I believe Weston blew up when Brett started seeing another man and killed him."

"Wait," said DeCarlo. "You already tried to convince us that Reeves's buddies, including Weston, killed Mr. Stone to prevent him from divulging the existence of some sex ring. Are you saying you were wrong?"

"No, I still think that's true, but the additional reason I think Weston did it is because Brett was in love with John Rankin. I can tell you John said Brett had been seeing an older man because that does not come from a therapy session."

"And how do we know John was referring to Weston?"

"He had to be. Brett told me that he was seeing an older man. They had been seen together by at least two people. Surely, you have better access to witnesses than my investigator does. And Abner Reeves knows the truth. He won't tell you about Weston and Brett, but he essentially admitted it to me today in another threatening phone call, which I recorded."

Hayes spoke next. "You keep throwing these theories our way, and frankly, it makes you sound desperate. Send me the tape if you want. Meanwhile, we will keep developing evidence against you. I was about to have the ADA call your attorney with the newest information we got in the Stone case."

"It's crap, whatever it is. It comes from Reeves."

"No, it comes from a credible witness with firsthand knowledge."

"Reeves put them up to it. It's a lie."

I did not want to talk to Ed and be given more bad news about yet another witness. I left the office for my place in Brooklyn. When I arrived at the building, I fumbled for my keys. Clare came up from behind me on the outdoor stairs and tapped me on the shoulder.

"Got a few minutes to talk?" she asked.

"Sure," I said.

She sat on the stoop and invited me to sit next to her.

"How are you doing?"

"You saw the cops with cuffs and probably read the papers. How do you think I'm doing?"

"Yeah. That's what I wanted to talk to you about. I was at a gay bar the other night with one of my girlfriends and heard two guys talking about some dude they called the major. They were complaining that the major was giving everybody a hard time because he had been dumped by some regular at the bar who wound up getting killed. They said the police had initially thought it was suicide, but it turned out to be murder. That sounded like your case."

"Did they mention Brett Stone?"

"I don't know. I was only half listening but heard snippets here and there. I thought I should mention it to you in the event it had anything to do with your case."

"Would you be willing to tell the police what you just told me?"

"Aw, I don't know, man. I don't like cops."

"This could be important. You could do it over the phone if I give you the number of Detective DeCarlo."

She winced. "Okay. If all I have to do is call him."

"Her, but here, let me write the number down on your grocery bag. Thanks, Clare."

I inserted my key in the front door. After struggling with it for a few seconds, I managed to open the door. I let Clare in ahead of me. I ran up the stairs to my apartment and flopped on my bed. Clare must have been at Fanny's. It was clear that a couple of GIs from Fort Dix were in the city last night and the cops should be able to find out who they were. They might be able to testify to thc kind of link between Brett and Weston that the police could not ignore.

I had enough time to pour myself a scotch before my cell rang. I sat with my feet up on the coffee table.

"How bad is it, Ed?" I asked, picking up the phone.

"Not good. They didn't give me all the details, but they have a witness who said a number of things about you. First, that when you were strolling past Brett's house, you told her his apartment number because you had been there before. Second, that you stayed behind on Thirty-Eighth Street when she returned to her office. Third, that you had a gun around the time of the murder. And finally, that the gun had a nick on the right side of the handle that matches the nick on the gun found at the scene."

"She?"

"Yeah, a woman. They let that slip."

"I've only been on Brett's street the day of the photo, as far as I can remember. Does that mean the witness is Liz?"

"Sure sounds like it."

So that was Abner's big surprise! He got Liz to testify against me—and falsely.

"Holy shit. Why is she lying about this stuff?"

"I don't know. Are you on good terms?"

"She broke up with me when I got indicted this time, but I didn't do anything to make her mad at me."

"You sure?"

"Yeah, I'm sure. Come to think of it, I told her about the birthday party, and I'll bet that she is the source of that leak too. I can't understand what her problem with me is. And why she is suddenly telling tales about me."

"Did you take advantage of her sexually?"

"No way. If anything, she was the aggressor. She invited me up to her place."

"Is there anything we can do to attack her credibility?"

"Well, she initially lied about us being together the day of the murder, same as me. But nothing else that I know about."

"Any chance she and Abner had a fling?"

"I've thought so for some time. I know she had a thing with an older man. Her willingness to testify against me and the leaks about our defense have to make you wonder."

I looked at the photo of me and Liz outside Brett's home. I was not wearing a jacket, given the stifling heat. It did not seem plausible that I would have shown her the gun in broad daylight on a city street long enough for her to notice a nick on the handle. She must be asserting that she saw the gun some other time. But when? I had seen her a dozen or so times outside the office before Brett was murdered, yet nowhere where I would be comfortable flashing a gun.

I caught up with Clare that afternoon, and she said DeCarlo and Hayes had visited her and her boyfriend. They showed her a photo of Brett Stone, and she said she thought she had seen him at Fanny's before. They then showed her a photo of Weston, but she did not recognize him. She told the police the two men in the bar who were talking about the major referred to a doctor at some point in their conversation. All she picked up was that the doctor was mad at the major for something having to do with the man who died.

Clare thought DeCarlo was interested in what she had to say and asked questions about the two men. DeCarlo also asked what Clare knew about me and the charges against me, and Clare said she only knew what she'd read in the newspaper. Then Hayes said it was "a little too convenient" for a neighbor of mine to have overheard a conversation about the major, but Clare pushed back.

The Reeves trial was just a little more than two months away, and Ed was riveted to his computer preparing for it. I did not want the Stone case to become a back-burner matter, so I personally spent time reviewing the discovery the DA's office was turning over in that case, looking for stuff I could share with Ed.

I began with the transcript of Burns's appearance before the grand jury. The first thing I read surprised me. He testified that John Rankin paid him to take the photos outside Brett's apartment house because John suspected Brett was cheating on him with an older man. John knew that Burns performed investigative services for Reeves and contacted Burns on his own. He picked the date and time for the photo, and according to Burns, me showing up was completely random.

Burns took three or four photos of Liz and me and gave a couple to Abner to let him know that two of his staff might be having an affair. Burns claimed that he did not know the person in the windowpane. He spent fifteen minutes across the street from the building from one fifteen to one thirty and left within five minutes of taking the photos. He denied knowing anything about the murder.

Next, I read John's witness statements, which I found equally surprising. He was not asked to delve into his relationship or communications with Abner. He admitted to being in a relationship with Brett and worrying that Brett was still seeing his former paramour, an older gentleman John could not name. John believed the older man planned to visit Brett at around one thirty p.m. on the Tuesday he was killed because he'd seen an appointment marked "rendezvous" on Brett's calendar. He hired Burns to try to get a picture of the man. John said he talked by telephone to Brett the day he was killed but did not see him. He provided the grand jury with an ironclad alibi that he had been at school.

I latched on to the idea that the lover, Weston, had shown up sometime that afternoon and killed Brett. Burns would have seen the man if he came or went between one fifteen and one thirty, but what about if he had come after that? He could have come as late as a few minutes before three and still killed John in the coroner's time frame.

John confirmed that Brett had made the decision the day he was murdered to talk to the clinic's lawyers about Abner. The questioning did not get into the details of the time of day when Brett made up his mind. I found that strange because it could show the killer had advance warning of Brett's scheduled interview and time to kill him beforehand. Why had the ADA not asked about that?

Nothing I had read so far implicated me in the killing. I took a short break and walked around the block, preparing myself to read Liz's lies. Once again, I wondered what I had done to cause her to turn on me so suddenly. Had Abner put her up to it? Did he have something on her that he used to get her to fib to the authorities about me?

She began her testimony by explaining the evolution of our relationship, from colleagues to lovers. She falsely testified that we began sleeping together much earlier than we had, sometime before Brett was killed. I recoiled when I read that, knowing I could not prove it was false.

Most of her testimony focused on the day of Brett's murder. She denied lying to the police about seeing me that day to protect our reputations. She testified that she did not remember we'd met up until I told her of a photograph of the two of us together outside Brett's place. She remembered afterward that I had asked her to take a walk with me to get a cup of coffee because I needed to run an errand.

She claimed I took her to West Thirty-Eighth Street on my way to a place near Penn Station. She said that, when we passed number 418, I stopped and said that apartment 3B was where Brett lived and that I had been there before. She testified that we walked farther and had a cup of coffee in some café on the street. She added that I was anxious about getting where I was going, so she left me there at around one thirty and walked back to the clinic by herself. She did not see me again until I returned to the clinic shortly before three p.m.

The most damning testimony was about a dinner date that had never taken place. She said we had drinks together at Anna's several days before Brett was found dead. She claimed we became amorous over the drinks and passed on dinner to go back to her place. She said that I should have a receipt from the restaurant that would prove we had had several drinks together there that evening.

She testified that I took a shower after we made love, and she straightened up her bedroom. Noticing that my suit jacket was falling off its perch on one of her chairs, she went to drape it over the back of the chair. When she lifted it, she observed that it was heavy. She saw a gun and a small box of ammunition inside the right-hand pocket. The gun, which she recognized as a 9mm, had a small nick on the right side of its handle. She claimed that, after looking at the gun, she hung the jacket over the chair and sat on the bed waiting for me.

She admitted that she started lying to me after seeing the gun, particularly about her feelings toward me. She was suspicious after hearing about Brett's death and no longer trusted me. She was afraid I might do something to her if I thought she suspected me, so she decided to keep up the appearance of an affair.

The police had my credit card receipts and had probably confirmed that I'd charged drinks at Anna's when she said. That did not mean I had gone to her apartment that night, but I figured the authorities believed her. The most confounding part of her testimony was how she knew about the nick on the gun. The only way that would be possible was if she had seen it before or someone had told her about it.

Her testimony about our walk down Thirty-Eighth Street made me remember that I had, in fact, run an errand near Penn Station around that time. I was trading in my father's old watch, which I had found in one of the boxes. While I still did not remember going for coffee with Liz on Thirty-Eighth Street, that must have been the day I ran my errand. I wondered if the Tourneau dealer I sold the watch to would remember; he would certainly have a receipt. I would have given my copy of the receipt to Eve to store with my father's other items.

The thing I could not understand is why there was nothing in the grand jury record about the activities of Abner and his friends. Nothing I saw touched on the subject matter of prostitution or sexual assault on minors. I asked Ed about this, and he said that either they had not brought the matter to the grand jury or, more likely, had convened a separate one to deal with those issues. By summoning a separate grand jury, they would avoid having to give me discovery of the transcripts in the Reeves case unless they planned to call a particular witness in that trial.

Consequently, I had no idea whether, and to what extent, the DA's office was following up on anything we had furnished them or the police. Since I thought the sexual assaults and murders were interrelated, I felt they should be investigated together. I regretted having floated the idea that Brett was killed by a jealous ex-lover because that suggestion may have steered the investigation away from the prostitution angle.

# 29

I instructed Ed to pursue discovery in both cases as aggressively as he could. We filed a discovery motion in the Stone case, demanding that the DA's office and the police turn over all materials related to their investigation of possible prostitution, sexual assault, and child abuse at Fanny's or Emanuel's. Then, we filed for a subpoena to the clinic in both the Reeves and Stone cases for all patient files of Brett Stone and John Rankin, claiming that there were exceptions to the psychologist–patient and psychiatrist–patient privileges to the extent necessary to report and prevent child abuse. We submitted an affidavit from me detailing records and conversations pertaining to the solicitation of underage males.

It was a bold move because we directly challenged the applicability of the privilege in a public forum. We were essentially reversing the position we had taken previously—that we needed firsthand testimony of abuse to pierce the privilege. We argued that John's testimony about what Brett had told him about soliciting underage boys should be sufficient. If we prevailed, the court would order the clinic to release its records and permit therapists, like me, to testify about communications with their patients in the narrow areas covered by the order. Such an order would enable the clinic and the authorities to compel Abner to testify about those communications, subject to his constitutional self-incrimination rights.

The clinic filed an opposition to our subpoena request on the grounds of privilege and under HIPAA. The clinic also moved to seal my affidavit on the same basis. Its brief accusing me of leaking privileged information was vitriolic.

The DA's office took an interesting tack. It took the position that there should be a probable cause hearing to determine if there was any basis to the allegations. If there was, it would enforce the old grand jury subpoena that called for these records. The DA's office suggested that the matter be resolved by having a hearing closed to the public where the court could review the relevant documents and testimony in camera so that confidentiality could be preserved if the allegations were meritless. They brought in a taint team to protect the integrity of the ongoing criminal investigations and prevent what might be privileged materials from falling into the hands of the investigators.

The court asked for a briefing on the privilege issue by all interested parties. The judge agreed to an in-camera review of documents and a closed hearing, denying the media's request to have the hearing open to the public.

We had taken the gloves off. We decided I would testify first and that we would subpoena John and, maybe, Alex Fernandez to testify. John moved to quash our subpoena, but the court ruled that he was required to testify and any privilege issues would be decided at the hearing.

On a cold morning in early November, the court convened the hearing in a cavernous courtroom with bright lights. Only the parties and the judge were allowed to attend, leaving the rows of benches in the back of the courtroom empty. Abner and Sue attended as the clinic's representatives. The judge took her seat on the massive bench at the front of the room. She was a rotund woman in her late fifties with graying hair and a matronly smile.

The lawyers made brief opening presentations, and then it was time for the witnesses. Ed called me to the stand and went through some background questions. I explained my status as a defendant in both pending criminal cases. Through his questioning, Ed elicited the fact that an alternative explanation to the question of who murdered Brett Stone was premised on the notion that he was involved in a ring of persons soliciting sex for hire among underage males.

"And how do you know he was involved in that?" Ed asked.

"Objection. Privileged," said the clinic's lawyer.

"That's the purpose of this hearing," the judge said. "To determine if there is a basis to grant an exception to the privilege. I can't very well rule on that without knowing more about the communications, which is why we are doing this on camera. You may answer."

"Both he and John Rankin told me."

"Let's start with Brett, and I want you to limit yourself to what he said about this issue. Can you do that?"

"Yes. He told me that Abner Reeves had him go to bars and other places to pick up young males who would be willing to engage in sex with him and his friends for money. That it did not matter how old they were."

From the witness stand, I could see Sue straighten her back and look at Abner. He stared straight ahead.

"Did he tell you why he did this?"

"Because if he hadn't, Reeves threatened to tell the police something illegal that Brett had done in the past and had confided in Reeves as a patient."

"Objection."

"Overruled."

"Did you also have a conversation with John Rankin about this?"

"Yes."

"Can you tell us what he told you?"

"Same thing as Brett, only he said that he stayed away from underage boys. He said that he was also working for Abner and some of his friends because he was being blackmailed."

"Did he tell you anything about his conversations with Brett about this subject?"

"Objection. Hearsay."

"Overruled."

"Yes, Brett felt bad about the fact that he had solicited underage boys and was prepared to talk to the clinic's lawyers about it, but didn't get a chance to because he was killed."

"Move to strike the last part of the answer beginning with 'but.'"

"Sustained."

Abner looked down as Sue glanced at him with cold eyes again.

"Did any other patients or former patients of Dr. Reeves make similar allegations?"

"Yes, Alexander Fernandez said that Reeves asked him to do the same thing, but he refused to go along with the request and did not solicit anyone. He just fired Dr. Reeves."

"Did you make contemporaneous notes of any of these conversations?"

"All of them."

I heard a gasp but couldn't tell from where.

"Have you turned them over to anyone other than your lawyers?"

"No, because of patient confidentiality, even though I don't think it applies."

"Do the patient files reflect the things that Dr. Abner allegedly said?"

"It depends on what you mean by patient files. He kept his own private files, and I've never seen those, though I doubt he wrote the threats down. I certainly didn't see any discussion of the issue in the clinic hard copy."

"I pass the witness," Ed said.

The clinic's lawyer rose and stood at the podium, looking at me solemnly.

"You didn't share any of this with the counsel to the clinic's advisory board, did you?"

"I shared the general allegation but not the specifics of the conversations with my patients because of confidentiality concerns."

"But you think there is an exception, so why didn't you tell counsel?"

"My lawyer suggested a path similar to what he called the crime-fraud exception that would allow me to disclose what my clients said, but the clinic instructed me not to breach confidentiality, so I didn't think I had a choice if I wanted to keep my job."

"Which you no longer have?"

"I've been suspended."

"Because you've been indicted now on two separate murders. And you are hoping that by bringing out this fanciful story it may help you suggest that someone else had a motive to kill Mr. Stone, isn't that right?"

"There is nothing fanciful about it. I believe my patients and Mr. Fernandez."

"Please answer the question."

"Yes, I hope it will help if we can get all the facts out."

"But now you've filed a public affidavit about the things said to you in confidence. How do you reconcile that?"

"We did that as part of the process of having a court tell us whether we are right or not. We think there is an exception to the privilege applicable here, so we've asked the court to rule on it in granting us the power to issue a subpoena."

"Now, you don't have any witness to corroborate what Mr. Stone supposedly told you, do you?"

"No, it was just the two of us."

Abner smiled and nodded his head.

"Or Mr. Rankin, for that matter?"

"No."

"You want this court to believe an accused two-time murderer over Dr. Reeves?"

"I am telling the truth. He, on the other hand, has a problem with the truth. And I've got contemporaneous notes to back up what I said."

"How do we know you made the notes at the time of the conversations as opposed to more recently to help with this hearing?"

"Because they are dated, and I am telling the truth," I said, leaning forward in the chair. I could feel myself getting annoyed, so I took a deep breath to restore calmness.

"And have you ever confronted Dr. Reeves with these allegations?"

"Not directly. I brought them to the board. But he's essentially admitted them to me."

"Oh, when?"

"When he threatened that I'd regret it if I continued making the allegations."

"I bet there was no one present for that discussion either?"

"No, but again, I made contemporaneous notes and tapes."

Abner glared at me.

"You hate Dr. Reeves, don't you?"

"No."

"Because you think he blackmailed your father years ago?"

"That's a lie. He did not blackmail my father. I can prove it."

"And that's why you killed his wife?"

"Objection," Ed said, leaping to his feet.

"Sustained," the judge said. "That's clearly outside the scope of direct and irrelevant. No more of that nonsense, counselor."

"You lied about another friend of Dr. Reeves's molesting a grade-school child to get him in trouble with the school he worked at, didn't you?"

"Yes."

"Just like you're lying about what Brett Stone said."

"No, I'm not. John Rankin will corroborate that."

"Nothing further, Your Honor."

Ed then called John to the stand. He was surly and uncooperative in responding to Ed. John gave evasive answers to several open-ended questions. He claimed he did not have much of a recollection of our conversations.

"Did Brett Stone ever tell you that he solicited young men for sex at Dr. Reeves's request?" Ed asked directly.

"Objection. Hearsay."

"Overruled."

John hesitated, looked around the courtroom, and finally settled his gaze on Abner. He took a deep breath. Ed asked him the question again after a few seconds. I tensed. This was the big moment, and John was sweating in the chair.

"Yes. Men under seventeen."

"How about you? Did Dr. Reeves make that request of you?"

"Yes, he asked me to solicit young men for him and a couple of his friends," John said while looking down.

There was an audible groan at the clinic's table. Sue looked at Abner with daggers in her eyes, but he shook his head defiantly.

"And did you solicit men for him?"

"Yes, he made me do it."

"How?"

"By threatening me the way he threatened Brett."

"With revealing something you did in the past?"

"Yes."

"Did you offer the men you solicited money if they had sex with Dr. Reeves or his friends?"

"Yes. I had a price list for different things Reeves and his friends wanted."

Abner bowed his head and rubbed his hands through his thinning hair.

"Did you tell Dr. Shea about what you and Brett did for Dr. Reeves?"

"Yes."

"Did you ever solicit underage males?"

"No, I didn't do that."

"Did Dr. Reeves ever indicate that was to be avoided?"

"No, he did not say anything about age one way or the other. Just that he liked them young."

"Did Brett, to your knowledge, ever solicit underage boys?"

"Hearsay, Your Honor," the clinic's counsel objected.

"There is no jury here for this preliminary hearing. Anyway, even assuming that he is offering the statement for truth, it's admissible under the exception to the hearsay rule regarding statements in furtherance of a conspiracy. I'm going to let it in," the judge ruled.

"Yes, he told me he did on several occasions. I even met one of them."

"Did Reeves refer to you or Brett by any names other than your actual names?"

"Yes, he called us scouts."

"I'm finished with this witness, Your Honor."

Counsel for the clinic stood and immediately started asking questions.

"Didn't you give an interview to the police in connection with its investigation into possible prostitution?"

"I got interviewed a couple of times, but I don't know in what investigation."

"And didn't you deny that Dr. Reeves had asked you to help him meet men?"

"Yeah, I lied to the police because I thought Dr. Reeves would rat me out if I told the truth."

"And when we interviewed you last week, you denied it again, didn't you?"

"Yes, for the same reason."

"You say you never approached any underage males, right?"

"Correct."

"He never asked you to do that, did he?"

"He never specifically asked, but it was understood that there was no age limit."

"Move to strike that last part, Your Honor."

"No," the judge said, "I'll allow it."

"And you were never paid to approach anyone, were you?"

"No, I was not paid."

"You claim Dr. Reeves blackmailed you with something you did in the past. What was it?"

"I'm asserting my Fifth Amendment rights on that one, Your Honor."

"So you committed a crime?"

"I'm relying on the Fifth Amendment again," John said.

"Did it involve fraud or dishonesty?"

"I plead the Fifth Amendment again."

"Nothing further, Your Honor."

Abner sat with his hands crossed at counsel's table for the entire proceeding. I knew he was livid, even if he did not show it. Sue was much more emotive and seemed shocked by John's and my testimonies.

The judge asked the clinic's lawyers if they intended to call any witnesses. I was hoping they would call Abner and that Ed would get a chance to cross-examine him, but after conferring, the clinic's lawyers opted not to call any witnesses. They argued that we had not made an evidentiary showing that an exception was necessary to prevent further child abuse. The court suggested there was an independent basis to report child abuse. The clinic's lawyers said the evidence went to solicitation of adults at best and that there was no evidence that Reeves requested that either John or Brett target underage men. They also attacked my credibility and John's.

An ADA from the taint team rose and said that, after hearing the evidence, the prosecution supported the issuance of the subpoena and, in fact, would be serving one of its own on the clinic and Mr. Rankin. The ADA argued we had established that child abuse had occurred over a period of time that should be reported for purposes of prosecution and prevention and urged the court to enter an order granting a narrow exception to the privilege to allow the witnesses to testify freely about the limited subjects covered at the hearing and nothing else covered by the privilege.

The clinic's lawyer rose to speak again, and the judge motioned for him to sit down. The court ruled in our favor, entering an order along the lines suggested by the ADA. The DA and the police could now examine me, John, and others about Abner's activities, and those interviews would also extend to the roles played by Weston and Levine, among others. And Abner himself would be examined, though it was doubtful he would testify unless he was going to lie about everything under oath. Maybe now the DA, Hayes, and DeCarlo would be open to the idea that Stone's murder was to prevent him from revealing information about Abner's ring.

This was a small victory in a larger war where I still had to defend both murder cases. There were inferences we could ask the jury to draw concerning Abner's sexual activities. The killer in Julie's case, we would argue, was motivated by fear that Julie or Abner himself would disclose the activities of the others. And in Brett's case, the killer sought to mute him so he could not expose the scheme. Even if the court let us broach both theories in front of the juries, the revelation of the erstwhile privileged information would not change the evidence that pointed to me.

As we left the courtroom, I saw Sue arguing with Abner before racing away in tears. She came up to me and pulled me aside.

"I want you to know I lost trust in Abner. He took advantage of my personal feelings for him by lying to me. I became disillusioned as I learned things, like that he had someone steal the files from your house. I was able to get them back from him and send you the missing sheets."

I didn't get a chance to respond before she walked off.

The DA's office subpoena to the clinic for patient records of Stone, Rankin, and Fernandez was not public, nor was the court order on the exception to the privilege. Both made it clear that solicitation of underage males for prostitution was now ripe for investigation. Someone leaked a copy of the order to the press, which wrote stories insinuating that Dr. Reeves himself might be a target of the investigation. They also noted that friends of Dr. Reeves were involved. There was much speculation about who those friends might be, but the press steered clear of naming names.

I heard from Beth for the first time in weeks. She understood the significance of the court ruling and offered her congratulations.

"Thanks. Although the DA's office has not dropped the charges against me, I now think I have a fighting chance in both cases."

"That's good to hear."

"Any chance you'll let me start seeing the kids again?"

"I don't think they are ready for that. I've been taking advice from the school psychologist, who thinks it would be too traumatic for the kids to spend time with you as things stand."

I also talked to Eve, who was pleased with the results of the hearing. I asked her if she could look through our father's things to see if she could find a Tourneau receipt for Dad's watch. She looked in the shoeboxes as we spoke and found a receipt, dated the day of the murder. I asked her to take a picture of it and text it to me and hold on to the original. I forwarded the photo to Ed along with a note, saying that this was where I'd gone when I left Liz on the day of the Stone murder. It might not account for the full two-hour window we were trying to close, but it substantially narrowed the gap.

Ed called and said he was going to advise the DA's office that we intended to rely on an alibi defense. The DA had the burden of proof to show I was there and committed the crime, so evidence of an alibi could be powerful. We estimated it would have taken me ten minutes to walk from where I'd been on West Thirty-Eighth to the shop on Thirty-Fourth Street and ten minutes to get back. Liz said that we'd stopped for coffee, which would have taken at least fifteen minutes if we drank it there.

If the picture was taken at one fifteen or so, as Burns suggested, I would not have gotten to the watch store until one forty at the earliest. Since the receipt was not time-stamped, we estimated it would have taken forty-five minutes to show the salesman the watch and complete the transaction. That would put me back on Thirty-Eighth Street at Brett's place at two thirty-five, and I would have had to leave by two fifty to make it back to the clinic for my three p.m. appointment. Assuming that I was not delayed along the way, that left fifteen minutes to get into Brett's apartment, kill him, and flee.

Ed said the DA would urge the jury to find that fifteen minutes was enough time to kill Brett. The question was whether I could shave off any more time by proving that I had stopped someplace else. I was pretty sure I had not gotten back to the office much before three p.m., so I needed to fill those critical fifteen minutes with something. Liz's testimony was that we had stopped at some café for coffee. Was that before or after the photo was taken?

More critical than finding those lost minutes was finding a basis to undermine Liz's testimony about the gun. The outlines of her story held together. As she had said, my credit card receipts included the one from Anna's, and the date matched her recollection. While I could testify that we did not start sleeping together until much later, I could picture Liz on the stand swearing convincingly that she invited me up for the night and that I had willingly gone. It was my word against hers, and I was betting Ed would be against me testifying. Even so, the thing that would make her story believable above all others was the nick on the gun. We had no way to explain when else she might have seen that.

I needed to find the reason why Liz was lying. Who was she trying to protect? Abner?

# 30

Despite our victory in court, I was glum. While I had several patient sessions a week, I had to invent things to do to prevent me from spending all my time worrying about the upcoming Reeves murder trial. Since the DA's office was, thanks to Liz, plugged into our theory about the birthday party, we still needed to explain how my fingerprints were there on the knife several days later. We hired a forensics expert who would testify that a dishwasher would not necessarily wash away the fingerprints. That attack sounded implausible to me. The science seemed iffy, and it did not account for the possibility that the knife had been washed by hand.

Had I killed Julie, wouldn't I have stopped long enough to wipe my fingerprints off the knife handle or simply taken the knife with me? Notably, there were no fingerprints anywhere in the house but in the downstairs hall, meaning that the murderer either wore gloves or cleaned up after themselves. If I were the murderer, why would I have cleaned up everything except the murder weapon? Or, if I had put gloves on, how would my fingerprints even have gotten on the knife? The real murderer, it seemed, took steps to avoid leaving any trace at all.

Ed got the cab receipts for my rides to and from Abner's house from the Taxi Commission, pursuant to our subpoena. I was relieved that the receipt for the ride there showed I had arrived at seven fifty-seven, and the return receipt showed I left at eight twenty. If the neighbor saw me outside the house at eight ten, I had a mere ten minutes to kill Julie and assault Abner. That was not impossible, but we could argue that it was highly dubious.

I was also still hung up on the prosecution's lack of proof of a motive on my part. People do not generally go around killing others for no reason, and Julie's was not some random killing by a maniac. My hypothesis was that Julie was killed for the same reason as Brett—she had found out about the pedophile ring and was threatening to report it. Her entire life revolved around helping poor, disadvantaged children, even before she met Abner. If she had found out about her husband's depravity, she would have been appalled and forced into action, no matter how much she supposedly loved him. His affair would have made her decision to air her concerns even easier.

Ronaldo dug further into Julie's background to see if we could find any evidence that she knew of Abner's escapades. I met with him to hear his latest report. It suggested that Julie was close friends with Mark Levine's wife, Gail. We assumed that Gail had to know something of her husband's previous antics, like why he was terminated at Lenox Hill. Ronaldo's sources uncovered rumors that Gail knew her husband cheated on her with men, and she only stayed married to him because of the money and the children.

Like Julie, Gail was very active in civic organizations and regularly attended their public fundraising events. Ronaldo interviewed a friend of Julie's who had recently seen Gail at a dinner thrown for a New York educational cause. According to the friend, Gail overdrank that evening and bad-mouthed her husband and her friends. She told Ronaldo's source that Julie had decided to leave Abner over something shocking and sue him for everything he was worth.

Ed believed the prosecutors had not interviewed Gail or, if they did, caught her before she was fed up enough, or drunk enough, to talk. Either way, she was now going to be on our witness list. Though the testimony would be hearsay, Ed explained, it would be admissible to show Julie's knowledge.

Even if we could prove Julie was aware of her husband's debauchery with young men, we still had to establish that she was killed over the knowledge. We had to construct a story suggesting that had been the plan and that it was carried out by Abner or someone else, like the third man the neighbor had seen outside Abner's house. We had to bring the mystery killer to life, to make the jury see him lurking outside Julie's front door, ready to silence her.

Ronaldo and a paralegal picked through the materials the DA's office had produced from Julie's personal effects. The paralegal studied Julie's calendar, not for the day of, or days before, the murder, but the days after. Julie had had a busy couple of weeks planned. The entry that stuck out was an appointment for the Monday after she was killed with Mario Fiorvanti, a reporter for one of the city's big newspapers.

Ronaldo called him, and Fiorvanti was circumspect, saying that he did not wish to talk about Mrs. Reeves. When Ronaldo threatened to subpoena him, Fiorvanti said no court would make him give up a source, thereby admitting she had been providing him with information for a story.

A little additional research revealed that Fiorvanti had written extensively about the results of the privilege hearing and the possibility that Abner Reeves was involved in some sort of sex scandal. But, even with all the attention those allegations had garnered, nothing was written about his possible coconspirators. So as part of our plan, Ronaldo dropped Weston's and Levine's names before hanging up with Fiorvanti.

Fiorvanti was careful. It took him two days to write a piece about Mark Levine. The story asserted that Levine had recently been dismissed from his position at a private school in Manhattan for not disclosing prior allegations of unspecified misconduct. Fiorvanti's article went so far as to point out that Dr. Levine was a long-term friend of Abner Reeves and then rehash the previous story about possible child abuse at the clinic.

Ed, Ronaldo, and I finally found the time to celebrate our court victory over drinks at a bar near Ed's office. Before long, the conversation turned to the murder investigations.

"I'm convinced that both murders are connected," I said. "Maybe it's the beer talking, but I think Liz's readiness to lie in Brett's case suggests she had something to do with Julie's murder. She was one of the few people who had access to Abner's calendar. She could have known that I had an appointment with him at eight on the night of the murder, and Philip before me. She would have known there was at least a ten-minute gap for someone to break in and kill Julie. It turned out there was a forty-minute slot because Philip left early, but she would not have known that *unless* she was there at the time. Who said the third person on the street that night had to be a man?"

"That's interesting," Ronaldo said. "We got Liz's appointment book from our discovery of the clinic's files. I looked at it. Though certainly not conclusive evidence, there were no entries after six p.m. on the day of Julie's murder."

"Liz told me she typically stayed in if she did not have anything specific planned, so she might not have an alibi," I noted.

"But why would she want to kill Julie?" Ed asked, rubbing his chin.

"Maybe she was the one having an affair with Abner," I noted. "She may have done it to help Abner silence Julie and then worked with him to create the illusion that Abner, too, had been attacked. Maybe she had another, stronger motive."

Ed lifted one eyebrow. "You think there is a chance she killed Brett too? She had a lot of time after you left her on Thirty-Eighth Street to visit Brett and kill him. If you left at about one thirty to attend to your errand with the watch, she would have had about ninety minutes after Burns left to kill Brett and still make it back to the clinic by three p.m. Again, the question is why?"

"Liz being the murderer would explain why she made up a story about me and the gun. Maybe she knew it was a Glock with a nick on the handle because the gun was hers. She could have left it there at the scene of the crime, planning to frame me all along."

I was encouraged that neither Ed nor Ronaldo dismissed my theories out of hand. They were natural skeptics, and Ed was right to focus on motive. But I still had time to figure that out. Possible jealousy might explain why Liz wanted Julie dead, but what could her issue with Brett have been?

The next day, Ed called Mrs. Edinger, the neighbor who would testify about seeing people outside Abner's house, to ask if the third person she had seen on the street could have been a woman. She said that she hadn't thought about it, but yes, it could have. They were not particularly large and had a slender build. We rechecked the street surveillance tape and located the person who arrived between Philip and me. The image was too blurry to tell for sure, but it looked like it might indeed have been a woman.

# 31

That evening, I added Liz's name to the top of my whiteboard, next to Abner, Weston, and Levine. I also added the information I had about her. I revised the timetable to add the dates we were together, including the day of Brett's murder. I smiled inwardly after discovering her connection to Weston and Levine.

I went to see Abner the next morning against Ed's advice. I arrived at East Seventy-Second Street, climbed down the stairs, and rapped on Abner's office door. I could hear him approaching from the inside and watched him peer out the reception window to see who was calling. He looked surprised to see me but unlocked the door and crossed his arms, not letting me in.

"You're about the last person I expected to see at my front door. What do you want? Have you come to confess?"

"I want to talk."

"Why would I want to talk to you after what you've done to me? You've already killed my wife and ruined my good name. Are you recording this?"

"No," I said, turning off my phone in front of him. "It's your wife I want to talk about. You know I didn't kill her."

"What do you mean?"

"I know who the real killer is. And so do you."

I looked for a reaction, but there was none. He was a cagey man who did not let on what he was thinking.

"You're crazy. I should throw you out of here," he said, clenching his fists.

I leaned against the doorframe and clasped my hands together. I looked deep into his eyes and saw nothing but darkness there.

"Don't you want to hear my speculation?"

"Not really. You're being tried for the crime and will be convicted. You were seen inside the house at the right time. The knife has your fingerprints on it. Case closed."

"The knife was a nice touch."

"Excuse me?"

"You see, I remember your birthday party and how I cut the cake with a knife Julie brought from your home. Several people remember that. Liz surprised me recently by saying she did not remember the birthday party. I can visualize her standing there next to me while I cut the cake, and she helped serve the slices. I remember she and I cleaned up the cake mess—and that she was the one who washed the knife, which she gave back to you or Julie to take home. I know now that she washed the blade, not the handle. That's why my fingerprints are still on there. Since she planned on using a knife to kill your wife, what better way to camouflage her identity than by using a knife that already had somebody else's prints on it?"

"You're saying Liz killed Julie and then attacked me?"

"She killed Julie all right, using the key you gave her to get into the house. She made it look like a break-in. And then you two staged the attack on you. She hit you with a paper weight or something to make it look good, but you didn't even go out. You just played along."

"You think I arranged to have Julie killed?"

"I think you had no choice. That your 'friends,' including Liz's father, pushed you into it because Julie was about to tell a reporter, a guy named Fiorvanti, about your little sex club. And I think the same is true of Brett Stone. He was going to talk to the clinic's lawyers, and you and your buddies had him eliminated, once again by Liz."

"But she said you had the gun used to kill Stone."

"That's just a lie. She knows guns. Been around them her whole life. She knew what the gun looked like because it was her father's, and she used it for the murder."

"Her father's?"

"Don't give me that horseshit," I said sternly. "Major Trent Weston was the one behind all this. He was a part of your clique and knew he'd be dishonorably discharged and court martialed or tried criminally if word got out that he was a pedophile. So he pushed you to have the two people who threatened to expose your little club murdered. He even let his little girl pull the trigger."

A glint of recognition flickered in Abner's eyes.

"You've known all along that Liz is Weston's daughter," I continued. "He introduced the two of you and overlooked your affair with her. She has always been very close to her father, moving all over the country with him. She would do anything for him, like kill at his request to protect him from criminal exposure for his sexual assaults. She also knew that she'd be helping you, the ex-lover she never got over."

"That's a lot of crap," Abner said. "You can't prove any of it."

"I can prove enough to raise doubt about my own guilt," I said serenely. "You're going to be our first witness."

"And when I deny everything you allege, the jury will think you are grasping at straws."

"Not when we make you out to be a cheat, a liar, and a sexual predator. We will get a ruling that you are a hostile witness and cross-examine you to expose your lies. Like the stuff about you blackmailing my father."

He rose. "I think you are a sick man, Tim. I don't doubt you'll try to prove that anyone who testifies against you is a liar, but you're the one deluding yourself. Now, please leave before I call the police and tell them you are trying to intimidate me as a witness."

Though I had told Abner I knew Liz was the murderer, I was not certain that story would stick. I still did not believe Abner capable of committing the slayings, which left Liz, her father, and Levine as possibilities. She was the most likely candidate for all the reasons I had given Abner, including the fact that she had recognized the murder weapon. But I could not eliminate the others.

We could argue to the jury that, with so many other possibilities, there was substantial doubt that I had committed the murders. Not being a lawyer, I did not know how much leeway we would get from the court to raise those kinds of inferences or to explore hypotheticals. I did not think we would be successful in leaving the jury with a number of alternatives to ponder. Rather, I thought that we needed to target one of the possible murderers and focus on the circumstantial evidence pointing to him or her.

If we chose Liz over the others, it would be because of the gun. She had to have been in contact with it before the murder. We needed evidence that she or her father had a Glock and she had access to it. Ed and I thought it was most likely that Liz had seen the gun in her father's possession. We sent Ronaldo to the shooting clubs and ranges near Fort Dix with photos of Weston. It turned out that he was a regular at a couple of the firing ranges in the area. By all reports, Weston was a fan of Glocks, though no one was able to say definitively that he had a Glock 17.

One gun club had a photo on the wall of an event where a score of patrons posed with their pistols. They were all standing on the porch of the clubhouse on a sunny day. According to Ronaldo, Weston was the third from the left in the first row, and his gun dangled from his right hand. He was smiling broadly at the camera.

After alerting Luzon, we turned the information about the photo over to Hayes and DeCarlo. We told the detectives that the gun Weston was holding in the photo looked like a Glock. DeCarlo's eyes widened when we mentioned the photo, and she asked for the name and address of the gun club.

The DA's office continued to turn over various documents that contained exculpatory information and was being generous in its interpretation of the law. It had recently turned over to us Weston's leave record, showing that he'd been in New York on the dates of both murders. I tried to remember what Liz had said about her father. Given how expensive the Big Apple can be, I wondered if he stayed with Liz when he was in town, at least when he was not in the company of some young man. Maybe they had been together.

I had Ronaldo dust off the surveillance footage from Abner's street the night of Julie's murder. I now looked at the period from six forty-five to eight fifteen. At six fifty-five, I saw a man turn onto Seventy-Second who I assumed was Philip. There were two other individuals who turned the corner in that time frame, as well as three couples, one of whom turned onto Abner's street at seven forty and returned to Third Avenue again at seventy fifty-five. They were each wearing a red baseball cap.

I sent Ed to question Mrs. Edinger whether, in addition to the individuals she'd seen, she remembered seeing any couples loitering around Abner's house between seven thirty and eight p.m. on the night of the murder. Ed called me back after he talked with Mrs. Edinger.

"She said that she remembers seeing a couple outside of the Reeves's house at around seven forty-five, during a commercial on her second-favorite show, *Jeopardy*," Ed reported. "The man was older and the woman was relatively young, maybe in her thirties. They both wore red baseball caps."

"How long were they there?"

"She said she only watched them talking for a minute and then had to get back to her program. They were not on the street when she looked outside during the next commercial."

"I bet it was Liz and her father. Liz and Abner made it look like she took out Abner, and her father took care of Julie. Can they blow up the surveillance tapes?"

"I assume they already did that, but the images may not be clear. The fact that both were wearing caps probably means they were unrecognizable."

"Didn't someone say that Weston always wears a red baseball cap? I've got to go back to my whiteboard and check that out. Any chance the old lady will recognize them?"

"We'll find out later today. I already told her I was going to send Ronaldo up to see her with pictures. I think we heard that Weston wore a cap when he was out with Stone or something."

In the early afternoon, I got a call from Ronaldo. He had visited Mrs. Edinger with both photos of Liz and her father and the surveillance tape showing the couple walking on Seventy-Second Street. She said the two people in the photos looked like the couple she had seen out her window, but she could not be sure. Looking at the tape did not give her any better clarity.

I glanced through the evening newspaper that night. There was a story about the men who'd been arrested for solicitation at Fanny's, including Lamond. All of them pled guilty to misdemeanors. One of them must have given up Weston and Levine, who were reportedly arrested on solicitation charges and freed on bail. None of the charges dealt with more serious offenses involving minors.

A simple prostitution charge probably would not be incentive enough for Weston and Levine to cooperate against Abner. The punishment for soliciting a prostitute, male or female, was often light and might not involve any jail time at all. The fact that the two had repeatedly broken the law might convince a judge to imprison them for a brief period, but avoiding a short sentence probably would not convince them to admit to the far more serious crime of sexual assault of underage males.

On the following day, Ed received an envelope containing a photo of men holding guns outside a clubhouse and gave it to Ronaldo and me. Ronaldo recognized it as an enlargement of the one he had seen at the shooting club. We got a magnifying glass and looked carefully at the portion of the photo picturing Weston holding a Glock.

"Look, over here," Ronaldo said, pointing at the right side of the gun handle. "Do you see anything?"

"Shit," I said, as a smile erupted on my face. "A nick mark."

The envelope was unmarked and had been dropped off by a messenger. Our best guess was that it came from DeCarlo, because she was the one who'd seemed most interested in our revelation about the club. We said nothing since we did not want to get her in trouble for getting ahead of the DA's office. She was sending a clear signal, we thought, that she and probably Hayes did not believe I killed Brett. Would that make her more skeptical about my role in Julie's death?

Several days later, we got the official photo from the DA's office as exculpatory Brady material. The photo did not eliminate the possibility that I'd gotten the gun from Liz and used it to kill Brett, but that would be inconsistent with the story she had told the police about seeing it in my jacket. She would have to say that I stole the gun from her one night, and she lied about it to protect herself from me.

By now, Abner must have told Liz and her father about my theory. That realization rattled me. If Weston was truly a hothead who had killed before to preserve his secret, he would not hesitate to kill again if he knew I was closing in on the truth. The gun club owner had probably given Weston a heads-up that the photo had been subpoenaed by law enforcement. That would mean Liz probably knew too.

I figured I was safe for the time being because the Reeves trial was coming up first and they expected me to be convicted. If I was, I did not know if I could undergo a second trial either emotionally or financially.

# 32

In the middle of the night on Friday, I awoke to a bright light in my bedroom. Someone had turned on my lamps. Half-blinded by sleep, I sat up and, with one hand shielding my eyes, surveyed the room. Liz was sitting in the chair opposite my bed, dressed in all black except for the red baseball cap. She was holding a firearm in her hand, and it was pointed at me.

"Hello, Liz," I said cautiously. I put my pillows behind my back so I could get a good view of her. "How did you get in here?"

"Not too hard. I've learned some Army tricks from my father. Old locks are easy to pick. And your landlady really should install an alarm."

"I'll bet you've learned plenty. Like how to use a gun."

"You think you have it all figured out, do you?" she said in an icy tone.

"Pretty much, I'd say. After you dumped me, I started thinking about why you would go out with someone accused of murder in the first place. I realized you weren't afraid of me because you knew I didn't kill Julie or Brett. I figured you had some ulterior motive in seeing me."

"Men don't use their brains when a woman is involved. You were all too happy to report your little detective adventures, and we needed to know how much you knew. It wasn't hard to seduce you."

"I'm not sure who actually pulled the trigger on Brett. You or your father?"

She shook her head at me. "You're delusional."

"And Julie Reeves? You're no slasher. That was your father, while you and Abner played your little game of giving him a little lump on the head. You wouldn't dream of really hurting your ex-boyfriend."

"Would you believe me if I told you you're wrong?"

"No, especially not with a gun pointed at my head. What do you hope to accomplish?"

"I know about the photo from the gun club. Your MO is to plant doubts in the jury's mind with circumstantial evidence pointing to my father or me. But if you die by your own hand, you'll never get to spin your theories at trial. Everyone will take your suicide as a sign of guilt. They'll have no reason to look further in either case and will close the investigations. And my father and I won't have to worry anymore."

"I wouldn't be so sure of that. They know about you and the Glock 17."

"That's an easy one. I told them I saw it on you the first time we slept together. They didn't ask me where you got it."

"We weren't even sleeping together at the time."

"They don't know that. I swore we were. Why would a woman lie about something like that? All I've got to add is that you stole it from my gun collection that night. They'll understand I wasn't anxious to admit I have guns. And you won't be around to refute my statement."

I tried to remain calm but was feeling a panic attack coming on. I had the idea that I could throw her off if I feigned a more serious attack than I was experiencing. She knew I'd seen Abner about them and would recognize the symptoms.

I started breathing hard. I got out from under the covers and dangled my feet over the side of the bed, with my left side facing her. I stood up in front of my night table and blocked her from seeing me palm my small windup alarm clock made of stone. With my hands behind my back, I staggered a little to create the impression that standing was difficult.

She was too far away to shoot me and have it look like a suicide. She got up and moved closer to me. Her eyes took in the sweat on my face, my trembling muscles. Her arms were straight in front of her, pointing the gun at my head.

"Is that another Glock 17?" I said, panting.

"Shut up." She snorted as she moved even closer to me until she was only about two feet away. "Now turn your body toward the side," she commanded.

She was now an arm's length from me. As I turned sideways, I doubled over, faking a near faint, and came up quickly, swinging at her head with the stone clock in my hand. I hit her in the eye with it and she fell back slightly, covering the left side of her face with her hand. I took her down with a hard tackle. She hit the ground with me on top of her, but held on to the gun. I pinned her arms to the ground to prevent her from hitting me with the butt of the pistol. She was stronger than I imagined and kneed me in the groin. I exhaled with a groan, losing my grip.

She began to raise the arm holding the gun, and I grabbed her wrist, bending it backward. I banged her hand on the floor and felt her losing her grip on the gun. I reared back and smashed her face with my head, throwing my whole body into my forward progress. The gun fell from her hand, and I brushed it away with a swipe of mine.

The motion threw me off balance, and she kneed me in my bad ribs. Then she pushed against my neck, using her forearm as leverage. I fell backward as she tried to reach the gun, but it was too far away. I rocked forward and could see her fist coming toward my throat in an Army move, and I jerked my head back to avoid the blow before coming back down with a crushing left to her jaw.

I slid over to grab the gun, which I barely reached before she pulled on my arm. I swung free, hitting her with the butt of the firearm, then rose on my knees and pointed it at her. She wiped her bloody mouth with her hand and sat up. I stood and, keeping the gun pointed at her, grabbed my phone off the end table and dialed 911.

It only took about six minutes for the police to arrive. During that time, Liz stared at me with fire in her eyes. They were narrow slits of green, especially the one that was swelling from my punch with the clock. Where I had once thought I saw love, I now saw hate.

"Who are you going to say did the actual killings, you or your father?" I asked.

"Fuck you," Liz said as she spat out a mouthful of blood.

"Interesting question," DeCarlo said as she came into the room with Hayes and a small group of police officers to arrest Liz.

Two days later, we met with ADAs Luzon and Brenner and their supervisor, Marty Cochran, at Ed's request. Ed had requested that they drop both cases in light of recent events, and we were there to explain our reasoning.

"Let's start with the Stone case. The only real evidence you have is the testimony of a biased witness and attempted murderer who is lying to save herself and her father. She is your evidence of opportunity, but putting her on the stand to testify as to that will backfire.

"She tried to kill my client because he knows too much. She intended to make it look like a suicide so you'd think he was guilty of both murders. Your theory about the gun in the Stone case doesn't hold water. The photo you turned over shows her father in possession of a Glock 17 with an identical nick mark to the one on the murder weapon. She had access to it through him. She was lying when she told you about seeing it in my client's jacket. Now she says he stole the gun. That's another lie. She had it the whole time. They weren't even sleeping together when Stone was murdered. Without her false testimony, you have nothing to tie Mr. Shea to the gun.

"Beyond Ms. Schreiber having access to the gun, she was there the day of the murder, as your photo shows, and has no alibi for the time of the murder. She had ninety minutes to kill Stone while my client was off running an errand for which we have a receipt."

Cochran interrupted: "He might have run an errand, but your own timeline suggests he also had time for the kill."

"That's your whole case now. That opportunity boils down to fifteen minutes that are not completely accounted for. We're still working on narrowing that down. But you need more than opportunity—which she had. She had a motive to keep Brett from spilling his guts about her father's pedophilia. She'd have done anything to protect him. In contrast, you can't answer the simple question as to why my client would have wanted Stone dead."

"What about being mad at Stone for not giving the interview to the clinic's lawyers?" asked Luzon.

"As John Rankin testified, Stone had decided to give that interview before he was killed. In fact, we think it's the reason *why* he was killed. Remember that the clinic, and therefore Reeves and his friends, learned in the late morning that Stone would blow the whistle on the ring of pedophiles that afternoon. They had to eliminate him so he couldn't talk. You've got at least four people without alibis who were motivated to kill Stone. Count them—Reeves, Weston, Levine, and Liz Schreiber. All with motives, all with opportunity as far as we know, and two having access to a gun identical to the murder weapon. That's four reasons to doubt that my client is guilty."

I looked for a reaction to this, but each member of the prosecution team remained stoic. Were they even listening?

"And why would we dismiss the Reeves case?" Cochran asked.

"We think Schreiber's attack on my client is strong evidence that she is guilty of Julie Reeves's murder, too. But there is more.

"We now know that my client did not arrive at the Reeves's place until seven fifty-seven, as he has always maintained, when the murder could have taken place as early as seven forty-two. We have the cab receipt to prove that. And sweet Mrs. Edinger did not see him until around eight ten, even though she looked out her window earlier. She saw him pounding on the door, from which you can draw the inference that Mrs. Reeves was already dead, because she did not answer the door. In fact, there was no answer to my client's calls a few minutes earlier, suggesting she was dead even before then. Likewise, she was probably dead by the time she would have needed to leave for her own charity event at eight fifteen. But even if that is not the case, my client left at eight twenty, giving him only ten minutes to enter the house, kill Mrs. Reeves, go next door, knock out Dr. Reeves, and get away in a taxi."

"Ten minutes is plenty of time," Cochran said.

"Not really. And you would have to eliminate the possibility that the other people who showed up on the surveillance tape didn't kill Mrs. Reeves before or after my client arrived. The real killer could have been hiding in the house and not killed her until as late as nine, according to the TOD. She could have been held at knifepoint that whole time."

"What about the knife? Are you really relying on the birthday party story?" Cochran taunted.

"There is more to it than you know, and it all points to Liz Schreiber having in her possession the knife used to kill Mrs. Reeves, just as she had the gun used to kill Stone. She had the dirty knife at the birthday party and did not wash it because she wanted those fingerprints on it when she killed Mrs. Reeves."

"Another instance of somebody not washing the dirty knife?" Luzon quipped.

"Let's talk about motive. The same four people had motives to kill Mrs. Reeves. We're going to prove that she was about to divulge her husband's and his friends' depraved activities to a news reporter when she was murdered. She had already made the appointment. It's in her calendar."

I saw Cochran sit up at this. I thought this was news to him.

"We'll prove that Reeves is a liar if he testifies. He was not unconscious for eleven hours and could have committed the murder or worked with the murderer. If Reeves didn't kill his wife himself for planning to leave him over his affair and blow the whistle on his pedophile ring, he had help. We're going to introduce evidence suggesting that a couple resembling Ms. Schreiber and her father was at Reeves's house between seven forty-five and seven fifty-seven that evening. We'll bet they don't have alibis.

"Weston is an interesting candidate for both murders. Thanks to the photo you sent us, we can show that the weapon used to kill Stone belonged to Weston, and we expect to show that he was brokenhearted after Stone broke up with him. We also know that Weston was in town at the time of the murders and that someone wearing his signature red baseball cap was captured on film at Stone's house on the day of the murder and was seen with someone resembling his daughter at the Reeves's house on the day of Julie's murder. Like Weston, Levine had a lot to hide about his sexual assaults on minors, which would explain why he might have resorted to murder. He, too, doesn't seem to have an alibi."

"You think one of these four committed both murders?" Cochran asked.

"We aren't so presumptuous as to tell you whom, if anyone, you should indict. Our intent is only to show you the reasons to doubt my client's guilt. That said, we think all four were involved in a conspiracy to kill both victims,"

Ed said. "Our point is that, in view of all the evidence we discussed, you aren't going to meet your burden of proving my client guilty beyond a reasonable doubt in either case."

The DA herself called Ed two days later and told him they would be holding a press conference that afternoon to announce they were dropping the charges against me in both cases. They were charging Liz Schreiber with murder, conspiracy to commit murder, and as pertains to me, attempted murder. The alleged motive was to prevent the victims from discussing the activities of a pedophile ring in which a close relative participated. The press release would mention that there were three unindicted coconspirators in the conspiracy to commit murder and that the investigation was continuing.

In addition, the DA announced that Reeves, Weston, and Levine had been indicted on charges of sexual assault and conspiracy to commit sexual assault in connection with their involvement in the solicitation of sex with underage males. The indictment described a club comprised of approximately twelve prominent New Yorkers run by Abner Reeves that had scouts find young men who were willing to engage in sex, often for a monetary allowance. Abner was also charged with blackmailing two of his patients, described as John Doe 1 and John Doe 2.

My head stopped hurting for the first time in as long as I could remember. It was like I was alive again. I was sad to learn that the Sommers Clinic would be shuttering its doors in view of Abner's and Liz's legal and ethical problems. What would happen to the innocent staffers and therapists who had worked hard to build the clinic's reputation? I felt a tinge of guilt at having been the one to set the clinic's destruction in motion.

# 33

If you look me up on Google, the first thing you will see is stories about my indictments. You have to scroll down to find the articles making it clear that I had been set up in both cases. Getting my reputation back has proven to be as difficult as proving my innocence. Fortunately, I was able to parlay the positive stories into a new job at a small, private clinic in Brooklyn.

Oddly, even with the criminal cases behind me, my anxiety level increased. I had my first panic attack in a while. They became more frequent, and it got to the point where I decided I needed help. Based on a couple of recommendations, I made an appointment with Gretchen Mankow, a psychiatrist in Brooklyn Heights.

I first met with her the day before Liz was scheduled to go on trial for both murders. I was particularly agitated that day. Early in our session, I started to sweat and feel like I was going to faint. When the attack passed, she asked me what I'd been thinking about when I first felt it come on.

"Julie Reeves's murder," I said.

"What about it?"

"How it never should have happened to that poor woman."

"And that made you go into panic mode?"

"That and the afterthought of Brett Stone's murder. I think they are on my mind because Liz Schreiber is going on trial tomorrow for both of them."

"That's interesting. What about the trial has you upset?"

"She's innocent. And yet I think she'll be convicted."

"How do you know she's innocent?"

"Because I committed the murders."

"What?" She recoiled, and her eyes bulged.

"Julie Reeves and I had been arguing for months. She had learned from her husband a few years ago that my father killed my cousin Billy under a plan hatched with her husband, Abner. My cousin was about to stand trial and testify that both my father and Abner were part of a pedophile ring that had raped a teenage boy. Abner paid my father to kill my cousin and make it look like a suicide. My father strangled Billy and strung him up in our family room to make it appear that he had hanged himself."

I shrugged and continued. "Anyway, Julie extorted a lot of money from me to keep that a secret. I finally told her I was finished paying her. She threatened to make my father's sexual crimes and his role in my cousin's murder public. She even went so far as to make an appointment with a reporter.

"I went to her house one evening under the pretense of a doctor's appointment with her husband. I thought I could convince her not to go public because it would destroy him too. I knocked on the door, but she did not answer it. Knowing Abner was in his office in the basement, I picked the lock to the front door and slipped in. I went upstairs and ran into her in her bedroom.

"We argued for a minute. She said that if I did not pay her, she would tell the story to her friend at the *Times*. She told me that she was leaving her husband and did not care if she hurt him. After a minute or so, she told me to get out.

"I went downstairs into the kitchen and grabbed a knife. I returned to her room, where I found her crying hysterically. She was trying to telephone someone. I took the receiver from her hand and replaced it. I pulled the knife from behind my back and slashed at her, catching her across the throat. She went down in a heap, bleeding profusely. I stabbed her a couple more times in the torso."

Gretchen raked her hands through her hair nervously.

"As I was cleaning up behind me, I realized that I was going to be late for an appointment with her husband and that he might return to the house if I did not show up. I evidently forgot to wipe my fingerprints from the knife handle in my rush. I grabbed Julie's keys from her bureau and went next door to his office. I wanted to make the whole thing look like a robbery gone bad so he would not suspect me.

"I snuck in and found him napping at his desk in his rear office. I hit him hard across the back of his head with a statue from his bookshelf and fled, locking the door behind me. I didn't know if I killed him or not, but it wouldn't have bothered me if I had. I took some money from his desk drawer to make it look authentic, but he must never have reported that because the police did not ask anybody any questions about any missing property."

Gretchen was silent. Clearly, she was stunned and did not know what to do. I looked at her with a devilish smile.

"I think you've told me quite enough," she said.

"That's only part of the story," I said, smiling. "A few weeks later, one of my patients discovered I'd been at the Reeves's residence the night of the murder. He started asking questions and made some remarks suggesting I killed Reeves's wife. He claimed he saw Julie and me out one night and that we were arguing. He became obsessed with the idea that I had killed her. He would not let it go. He heard the police had a knife with my fingerprints on it, and he was going to tell them a lie—that Julie and I had an affair, which she broke off—that would make them think I had a reason to kill her.

"I wanted to stop him. A couple of days before I killed him, I was alone in Liz's office. I opened the top drawer of her credenza and saw a gun buried among her papers. I came back to get the gun the day I killed Brett.

"Anyway, the day of the murder, after swiping the gun, I asked her to have coffee with me and we walked past Brett's house. I knew he was at home. I left her to run an errand and returned to the house and went up to see him. He let me in and we argued over his plans to inform the police about me and Julie. I panicked. I took out Liz's pistol and he came at me, so I shot him in the head at close range. I tried to make it look like a suicide by leaving the gun in his hand. I wiped the gun and the place clean of prints before I left."

I stared into her eyes. She knew I was not finished.

"While being investigated for both murders, I learned about Abner and his friends' sexual escapades and planted the seed with the police that one or more of them was responsible for the murders. I used my defense team to develop evidence that supported my theory and made the people involved in the sex scandal nervous. Liz tried to kill me so people would believe I was guilty of the murders and not look at the members of the sex ring.

"Though I was charged in both cases, we convinced the prosecutor that it was doubtful I had committed the murders and that someone else, like Liz, was the probable murderer. The charges against me were dropped, and she was indicted. I am hoping the circumstantial evidence is enough to convict her. If it is, my worries should be over."

Gretchen rubbed her chin pensively and straightened her eyeglasses. She had not written down a single word. She looked at the clock on the wall, which showed we had another ten minutes to go.

"I don't know why you are telling me this," she said at long last.

"It's cathartic to get it off my chest. Helps to make the tension go away."

"What if the police find out?"

"They won't. I'm not going to tell them, and you can't because of privilege."

"Are you sure of that?"

"Yes, I am. I know the law, and there is no exception for the confession of a past crime that does not involve child abuse or the threat of imminent harm. Besides, I've already killed two people. What's to stop me from doing it again?"

# ABOUT THE AUTHOR

Rich Morvillo is a nationally recognized lawyer who cochairs the white-collar defense and investigations group at a large international firm. He graduated from Fordham University School of Law before beginning his career as a trial attorney with the Securities and Exchange Commission. He is a frequent speaker at professional seminars and has published extensively on white-collar criminal matters, including the Fifth Amendment and ethical considerations for preparing witnesses. He first became interested in the field of psychology when he majored in it at Colgate University. He combines his interest in clinical psychology with his expertise in criminal investigations to create a taut psychological thriller where the search for truth is constrained by ethical rules and evidentiary norms. He resides in Washington, DC, with his wife, two children, and two dogs.